Amreekandesi
MASTERS OF AMERICA

ATULYA MAHAJAN

RANDOM HOUSE INDIA

Published by Random House India in 2013
1

Copyright © Atulya Mahajan 2013

Random House Publishers India Private Limited
Windsor IT Park, 7th Floor
Tower-B, A-1, Sector-125
Noida 201301, UP

Random House Group Limited
20 Vauxhall Bridge Road
London SW1V 2SA
United Kingdom

978 81 8400 395 6

This book is sold subject to the condition that it shall not, by way of trade or otherwise, be lent, resold, hired out, or otherwise circulated without the publisher's prior consent in any form of binding or cover other than that in which it is published and without a similar condition including this condition being imposed on the subsequent purchaser.

Typeset in Palatino Linotype by R. Ajith Kumar

Printed and bound in India by Replika Press Private Limited

*To my family. And aloo paranthas.
You make it all worth it.*

CONTENTS

Prologue	1
A Dilemma	6
On Cloud Nine	15
Tears and Vodka	22
Seven Seas, Three Lives	38
Fresh off the Boat	58
Masters of Science	83
The Buffalo Brothers	96
When in Rome	112
The Janitor's Son	126
Shall We Dance?	143
Hope Floats	156
Condom Balloons	169
Two Festivals	187
India Redux	199
Apples and Oranges	224
Separated	241
Found and Lost	252

Project Kolkata	261
Everything I Do	274
Victorious	288
Masters of America	296
Epilogue	305
Acknowledgements	307
A Note on the Author	309

Prologue

The garage attendant stopped in front of a shiny black car and handed him the car keys. Spinning the keychain on his index finger, he looked at the long, seemingly unending car and gasped, *What have I got myself into?*

He felt like a tsunami of self-doubt was crushing him under its weight. His bushy eyebrows narrowed, beads of sweat began to form on his forehead, and his heart started missing its rhythm like a horribly out-of-tune *American Idol* contestant.

It was an old-fashioned Lincoln Town Car, with its front hood long enough to serve as a cricket pitch. Suddenly he wasn't so sure about the whole plan. So far he had only driven a car in the deserted parking lot of the Presbyterian Church next to their apartment complex, trying to perfect the nuances of straight and parallel parking for his driving license test. Even though he had passed the test a week ago, he wasn't sure if he was ready to take out a car all alone on the streets of America, especially without Dilpreet watching out for mistakes. Besides, he had still not got used to driving on what would be the 'wrong side' of the road back home in India. *Why did Americans have to do everything differently?*

The damn car was far too long, probably the length of two cars, and all the more difficult to handle. He would have felt much more comfortable in a regular-sized one, but the rental company had run out of its regular Chevrolet Impalas and was offering him a free upgrade to the premium segment for his two-week rental. This must have been one of only twenty-seven instances in history where an Indian was getting something for free but was not happy about it.

Nandita, who had been observing Akhil's anxiety from a corner, came forward and gently touched his shoulder.

'It's going to be okay. You will do great. Now let's hurry. We're getting late to the airport. The plane must be about to land.'

Akhil looked at the Titan watch on his sweaty wrist. 1.30 pm. The flight was due to land at 2.

'Okay, let's go.'

Akhil whispered a silent prayer to lord Hanuman and got into the car. He fumbled for the clutch for a bit before realizing that there was none. It was an automatic, as were most cars in America. He sheepishly looked at Nandita who was sitting next to him, trying her best to look positive, when in reality she was as scared as a deer in the path of an oncoming train. She somehow managed to give Akhil an encouraging smile as he moved the automatic transmission into 'Drive' and slowly drove out of the garage. His prayers seemingly went unheard, because a few seconds later, there was a thud as the front bumper grazed the pavement. Akhil's face turned deathly white as he saw the startled look on the face of the garage attendant.

Prologue

As instructed by Dilpreet, he had taken a full insurance cover that whould cover all sorts of damages, or he might well have to sell a body part to pay for the slightest damage to the vehicle.

The garage attendant came by. A shocked Akhil struggled for a minute, but eventually managed to find the right button on the leather-clad controls on his door, and the window rolled down noiselessly.

The Latino man smiled at Akhil with a look that appeared to be conflicted between benevolence and amusement. 'Don't worry, man. You can bring the car back in a box and you still won't have to pay any damages. Now take it easy, and drive safely.'

This was reassuring. Akhil's pulse rate fell back to normal levels. Now all he had to do was avoid killing himself and his precious co-passengers over the next few weeks. He could manage that. Hopefully.

They reached Tallahasseee airport, and it took Akhil all of ten minutes to get the car into a narrow parking spot. One could say he earned the parking with old-fashioned sweat and toil. It was 1.55 pm by the time they entered the terminal. The computerized overhead displays inside the airport terminal showed that the United Airlines flight 23 en route from New York was late by an hour. That meant an extra hour of wait for his dear family—the parents who had raised him to become what he was today, and younger sister Aarti—chirpy, bubbly, and full of life.

Akhil and Nandita took seats in the waiting lounge. There was light brown foam peeking out from tattered plastic seat covers, making him even more nostalgic of the India he had left behind. Akhil ran over the plans for the next two weeks in his mind. There was the graduation ceremony in two days. He had then planned to take his family on a week-long Florida road trip covering the land of theme parks, Orlando, and sun-and-sin-city, Miami. The second week would be a trip up north, covering New York, Washington DC, and Niagara Falls. No self-respecting Indian visits the US and returns home without a smiling picture in front of the rumbling waterfalls on the Canadian border.

Akhil had the entire itinerary detailed down to an hourly schedule, in an elaborate Excel spreadsheet that could put professional accountants to shame. The challenge of finding the cheapest hotels that were also located closest to the prime locations and offered free wi-fi and complimentary breakfasts was not an easy one, and had kept him awake for many nights at a stretch.

He had spent the morning preparing a sumptuous feast of rajma chawal, aloo gobhi, and gulab jamuns for his family. The fridge was stocked with garlic and plain naans, as well as fresh fruits and cans of Coca-Cola. He had liberally sprayed the 'Lavender Fresh' air-spray in the apartment, hoping it would drown out the stench of the burnt utensils Jassi had left in the kitchen sink right before he had to leave to pick up the rental car.

For the evening there were frozen samosas procured from the Indian store.

Samosas.

Akhil's thoughts went back to that evening when they had all been debating whether he should accept the FSU admission offer. A lot of water had flown down the Mississippi since then, and it seemed hard to believe that it was less than two years

Prologue

since that day. America had certainly been a roller-coaster ride.

Akhil looked down at his arms. His abundant hair was standing in attention, like young NCC cadets doing a parade in honour of the dork from Delhi finally growing up.

A Dilemma

'Mrs Arora, these samosas are delicious. Haldiram's?' Goyalji grabbed his third samosa of the evening, and took a sip from his glass of Limca. It was a particularly painfully hot afternoon in May 2004, and thanks to the concerted efforts of movie stars and cricketers, the only legitimate way to beat the heat was to drink aerated soft drinks.

'No, no, Goyalji. I made them myself,' Mrs Arora said wiping the sweat off her face with the pallu of her sari and smiled at the neighbour, who was now submerging the samosa under layers of tomato ketchup and mint chutney. The air conditioner wasn't working, thanks to the scheduled power cut.

'Don't tell me. I think it is time you open up your own restaurant. Haldiram's will go out of business in a week. These are just too good. Too good, I tell you.' Goyalji then proceeded to lick all ten of his fingers into a nice shine.

Goyalji was the retired pot-bellied uncle who lived two houses down the street from the Arora household in Delhi's Punjabi Bagh area. He was feeling full, but the samosas were too tasty to give up. 'I'll just skip tonight's dinner,' he smiled, revealing two golden teeth. Remnants of the samosas peeked from behind one of them.

'Achha Akhil beta, so what university did you say you were going to?' Goyalji took a break from the food and turned to face Mrs Arora's 22-year-old boy fiddling with his phone in a corner of the room, hoping that would spare him the torture of talking to the obnoxious neighbour. Akhil was a lanky young man. He had, to use a term used only in Doordarshan's lost-and-found ads from a bygone era, a wheatish complexion. Akhil was somewhat good looking, provided you looked from the right angles, and he didn't have his usual lost look about him. It didn't help his appearance that he always wore the most atrocious clothes. A particularly callous person new to the neighbourhood had once looked at Akhil in his dirty clothes and asked his mom if he was a new domestic help she had hired.

On that particular evening, he was wearing a T-shirt that his mom had bought on his birthday five years ago. The collar already had a few holes, but he wasn't ready to let go just yet. His mom intervened. 'Goyalji, only you can talk some sense into this boy. He has got a good job in Noida and still keeps saying he wants to go to Amreeka. Akhil, what was the name of your university? Florida University?' (Amreeka is how real Punjabis pronounce 'America'. In fact, it is reportedly recognized as a valid test of Punjabiness by the United Nations.)

Akhil couldn't stay out of the clamour anymore. 'Florida State University, ma. How many times have I told you? It is not the same as the University of Florida.'

Goyalji glared at Akhil but had to wait a few seconds for the food in his mouth to get processed before he could speak. 'Accha Akhil. Where is this University of...what was it...Florida?'

Akhil wanted the earth to open up and swallow him. He knew where the conversation was headed.

'Goyal uncle, take a guess. It is in Florida.' Akhil was beginning to get annoyed. He wanted this conversation to end as quickly as possible.

'Oh okay. Is it near New York? You should call up Priyank. He will be able to help you out.' Goyalji was now attacking the gulab jamuns on his plate. Akhil wondered if there was a second life form inside that massive stomach devouring everything going down his throat.

Akhil suddenly swatted an incoming mosquito onto his clean-shaven face, before replying, 'No uncle. Florida and New York are quite far from each other, just about two thousand kilometres away.'

'Okay, no worries. You can still call him, no? I am sure they would have phones that work long distance in America.' He laughed loudly at his own joke, amused by his sense of humour, before launching into his next question. 'Achha, what is the rank of this university?'

Goyalji's son had a cult status in the neighbourhood. He had gone to the US for his Masters from the University of Texas five years ago, and was now working at an investment bank in New York. Goyalji couldn't stop boasting about the apple of his eye. They had recently started looking for a girl for him and the matrimonial advertisement seeking a 'fair, tall, convent-educated, homely girl' had promptly claimed a salary of 52 lakh rupees per annum for the 'very handsome, foreign-settled' boy.

A Dilemma

'There are different rankings, so a bit hard to say. It is not in the top 100 for sure,' Akhil answered with a sigh and braced himself for the reaction.

Goyalji coughed loudly. Akhil saw small bits of the gulab jamun come flying out of his nostrils. '*WHAT?*'

He kept his plate down and spoke to Akhil's mom now. 'Mrs Arora, your son has gone crazy. There is no use of going to a university that is not in the top 10, and he is going outside the top 100. 100?' His face and tone had a disgusted expression that Indian parents have perfected over the last many centuries. An expression that has been successfully deployed millions of times to flatten the self-confidence of sons and daughters who fail at, what they consider 'trivial' things like winning the Math Olympiad, getting into IIT, and winning *MTV Roadies* (or at least *India's Got Talent*).

Aroraji's tone had now turned to deep sympathy. 'Mrs Arora, you tell your son to take that campus job and enjoy life. He should be thankful for what he has. Later on, you people will only cry and say that I didn't warn you.'

Akhil's mom sighed. 'What can we do, Goyalji? When children grow up, you should let them do what they want to. I am tired of asking him to rethink his decision, but this boy just won't listen. He has gone crazy for Amreeka.'

Akhil couldn't hide his irritation anymore. 'Uncle, I have a full assistantship. I will not have to spend a single paisa. The university will pay my tuition fees, and a monthly stipend that will also take care of my living expenses. Do you remember the hefty loan you had to take for Priyank's Masters? Anyway, rankings are subject to various factors. The computer science programme at FSU is not very old, which is the reason behind the low rank. However, there is a lot of research work taking place now and some great professors have joined the faculty recently, so it is only a matter of time before the ranking improves.' Akhil's voice was a few pitches above where it had started, and his legs were beginning to shake with anxiety.

Goyalji looked at him and then at his mom. 'Just look at this, Mrs Arora. The children have grown up, so they think they have the liberty to shout at us. Just look at their nerve.' He got up from the sofa, his ample body following after his head in gradual installments—first the chest, then the bulging waist, and finally the bottom, which took the most effort to move. He seemed hurt at the apparent show of disrespect. The frantic effort in getting up only made things worse.

'Akhil beta, I know you from when you were *this* little,' he said bringing his hands 6 inches apart. 'You used to run after me to get an ice cream every time Priyank got one. There's no need to get so emotional. We are elders. We will only want what is good for you. I will ask Priyank to give you a call today. Maybe you can discuss it with him. Okay then Mrs Arora, I will leave now. You take care. Say hello to Aroraji.'

Goyalji glared at Akhil for a few seconds, looked with wistful eyes at the remaining half of the gulab jamun he had left uneaten in the rush, and left.

'I don't like Goyal uncle or his stupid son, mom. Why must you keep calling him for advice?' Akhil asked his mother.

She suddenly turned a shade of red. Her eyes were moist. 'You will never understand, Akhil. We are worried for you. We only want what is good for you.'

'Oh great! Now you go Nirupa Roy on me,' Akhil said

referring to the yesteryear Bollywood actress who reportedly holds the world record for the most on-screen time spent crying, over a career spanning more than fifty years. He shook his head in despair and went off to his room.

It had been this way for a week now. Ever since Akhil got his acceptance letter from FSU, the Arora household had been transformed into a scene straight out of a 60's Bollywood epic, with the parents fretting over a stubborn child they were about to lose.

Akhil had spent the last year preparing for the most important exam required for applying to US universities— the Graduate Record Examination, popularly known as the GRE—and sending in his application forms to the universities of his choice. All this, while also completing Electrical Engineering from Delhi University and getting successfully through the most important aspect of college education those days—campus placements. Now finally when he had got through, even if it was to the lowest ranked university he had applied to, there was sorrow all over the place.

Akhil was happy because FSU had met his all-important criterion. In times of recession and uncertainty in the job market, he was sure of one thing. He did not want to take a loan. He was not willing to sell one of his kidneys to pay the hefty fees required for an American degree.

However, to his middle-class parents, this was a big risk. One of his dad's friends had advised them to ask Akhil to not take up the offer and instead accept the job he had in hand with a Noida technology startup. 'That computer company is paying him 4 lakh per annum. He is already in the top salary bracket in his batch. Why does he want to ruin it?'

Goyalji had just reinforced all of that though Akhil had already made up his mind.

Akhil Arora had always been an underachiever. His teachers expected him to crack IIT, but he didn't get a rank good enough for a decent programme. Getting Computer Science was out of question. Civil engineering at IT-BHU (Institute of Technology, Banaras Hindu University) didn't really work out. Akhil had reached early in the morning with his parents after an overnight train journey, paid the registration fees, and checked into the hostel. Five minutes later, there was a knock on the door and Akhil had been summoned by seniors who looked more like unbathed hired assassins, with orders to present himself in room 43. They made him shave off all fifteen hair of his still-budding moustache. What happened in that room for the next three hours was a painful memory that Akhil had never shared with anyone. He had returned to the room, picked up his bags, and told his parents he didn't want to stay there. The Delhi University counselling was due shortly and he decided to try his luck there.

In the end, all Akhil got from Banaras was a face devoid of hair and a month of recurring nightmares. *So much for my IIT dream*, he had thought.

He ended up doing Electrical Engineering from Delhi University. It was good, but it was not IIT. If only he had scored ten marks more in the IIT-JEE, he would have been treated for the rest of his life with reverence by the 99.99999 percent Indians whose inferiority to him would have been established for eternity. He had spent many restless nights thinking that if only he had studied a little harder, things could have been different.

A Dilemma

His college years had been uneventful, and he had spent more energy running behind DTC buses than on his lectures, which bored him. Halfway through his engineering, he was convinced that he had no interest in stepper motors or the concepts of air conditioning. It was during one particularly boring High Voltage AC Transmission class that the epiphany struck him that a Masters degree in Computer Science from the US would perhaps be the one redeeming factor that could help him get over the IIT disappointment. That very evening Akhil had taken the bus to Chandni Chowk to procure that Bible of every American post-graduate education aspirant, the book filled with impossible lists of arcane words and equally easy math formulas—the *Barron's GRE Guide*.

Over the next few months, Akhil burned tankers worth of midnight oil preparing for his GRE, and managed reasonable scores of 2200 out of 2400. His letters of recommendation from professors proudly proclaimed him as one of the top 2 percent students in his class of eighty, just like the forty others who were also applying. He applied to ten universities, most of which rejected him due to his lack of formal Computer Science education. FSU on the other hand was offering him a fully 'funded' education. From where he saw it, Akhil had nothing to lose. He would get to experience what America was all about, while getting a formal degree in Computer Science. It was going to be a once-in-a-lifetime experience.

Akhil had always lived a sheltered life, with his parents making all decisions for him. Figuratively speaking, he had never stepped out of his house. He had never even gone on one of those annual school treks to Kullu Manali. From what he saw, FSU could change all of that. This was his chance to finally grow up and live independently.

This was May 14, 2004. The session started on August 30. In less than three months, Akhil would leave for the hallowed land, if only he could convince his parents.

A week later, the decision was made.

It had taken a lot of intense deliberations, plenty of heartache for all parties involved, bucketfuls of tears, and melodrama worthy of those TV serials his mom loved watching, but Akhil was finally going to go to FSU.

There was only one caveat. His dad would go with him.

Mom's ultimatum had been strict. 'If you go to Amreeka, your dad goes with you to help you get settled. Otherwise you don't go. I can't let you go to a foreign land so far away alone. We don't even have any relative to help you if you get into any trouble. He will help you get settled and return in a week or so.'

Akhil had seen his mother's Hitler avatar earlier, and knew better than to mess with it. She even had a hint of a small moustache if you looked closely. Akhil didn't have any option. His father was going to accompany him—whether he liked it or not.

On Cloud Nine

Jassi's mom stood at the door and saw him slowly get out of bed and stumble into the bathroom, carrying with him a round roll of paper. He had been doing this for a month now, ever since he got *that* letter. She wondered what he was writing on that thin paper in the toilet every morning. She thought maybe her son had started writing poetry, though she wondered how he could do it half asleep.

'God only knows what this boy keeps doing! He has become completely crazy,' she muttered to herself in disdain.

With Jassi, nothing surprised her anymore. She had seen the quizzical look on his father's face when Jassi addressed him as what sounded like 'doodh' last week. Milk! Of late, he had started answering every question with a 'Yo'.

'You want a parantha?' 'Yo.'
'Did you take a bath?' 'Yo.'
'Have you become crazy?' 'Yo. Oye!'
The boy was crazy, all right.

Jaspreet Singh aka Jassi was a 23-year-old Sikh boy who lived in a small town just north of Ludhiana, the hallowed city of Mercedes and BMWs. He was the latest celebrity in his sleepy town of farmers. He was going to America, after all.

Fame comes at a price though, as Jassi was finding out. His days were being spent trying to get rid of the pesky kids from the neighbourhood who kept following him all starry-eyed, ever since his mother had announced that her son was going abroad. Just yesterday, Vicky, the neighbour's teenage son, had been on his tail. He wanted Jassi to take him along to America. Jassi felt like he was the Shahrukh Khan of the village. No, make that Tom Cruise.

Jassi had got him off with a quick, 'I have gotta rush. Talk to you later.' He had run inside the house, his chest swelling with pride at his ability to use American slang in daily language, even if it wasn't done quite right.

Growing up, Jassi had only one dream. He had to go to America. The land of *Baywatch*, red swimsuits, and Coca-Cola. It didn't matter that Coca-Cola was available in India too. In his head, the American one surely tasted better and quite definitely didn't lead to diabetes or obesity. India had poverty, disease, and corruption. America had dollars, girls, and overall awesomeness. Jassi idolized America. For him, there was nothing that America or Americans could do wrong. India was pathetic in comparison.

Jassi's dad was a bank manager and his mom a housewife. He had a younger brother Sukhvinder, better known as 'baby' around the house. Baby had just started his engineering classes. Jassi was no baby though, even though his friends called him Guttu for his 5 feet 6 inch frame. What he lacked in height, he made up for in girth. He had recently upgraded to a 36-inch waist, which made him borderline fat. His mom's butter-laden paranthas didn't help the situation. In the eyes of Punjabi mothers, there are only two weight categories for their children—thin, and very thin. Jassi fell in the first category.

For Jassi, an average day started with spending about half an hour getting his spiked hair right. He compensated for the extra time spent on the activity by shaving once every few weeks. He had read on a website that American girls loved guys with spikes and a stubble, the perfect mix of style and ruggedness.

A year ago, he had heard the term 'metrosexual' and had decided to try to become one himself. Jassi could have well become the first man in Punjab's history to get a pedicure, if only the ladies at Sweety Beauty Parlour hadn't shooed him away. Besides, walking around the neighbourhood in shorts after shaving his legs had proven too awkward even for him. Being metrosexual wasn't for Jassi. Spikes and stubble were much more convenient.

He was a Sikh, but had got his hair cut off five years ago. After the last 12th class board exam, he and his friends had gone off to Ludhiana to celebrate, and he came back without his turban. He could still feel the sting on his face from his dad's slap, and his mother crying for a week. That month he had come to understand what the Emergency of 1978 must have been like, as he had lived a terrified life devoid of the usual liberties, and had got used to random slaps hurled at him when he least expected, like while watching an episode of *Friends* on the laptop. His parents eventually got over it. On his part, Jassi had no regrets. He did not want his religious identity to create problems assimilating in America.

Jassi had completed his engineering from Patiala last year, sat for the GRE, and subsequently applied for MS programmes for the 2003 session. The only problem was he got too ambitious, far beyond his 2030/2400 score, only applying to top ranked universities. No acceptances. The dream had to wait.

He then spent a year working for one of the big Indian technology services companies in Chandigarh. He got to work on a project for an American client, in an office set to American aesthetics and specifications. He even had an American manager and an 'onsite' team with whom they had daily conference calls. It was his own little piece of America, all from the comfort of Punjab. He ate from McDonald's and Pizza Hut almost every day. The inches piled on his stomach, but if that brought him closer to America, he didn't mind paying the price.

Life was great. Well, close enough. He felt like a frustrated Sachin Tendulkar stuck at the non-striker's end of the pitch while the tail-enders failed to rotate strike in the slog overs of a nail-biting cricket match. It didn't help that he kept hearing stories of seniors from his college who were already in the US, and wouldn't stop going on and on about the number of hot girls who wouldn't take no for an answer, especially from 'gabru' Punjabi hunks. Then there was the legend of Honey Malhotra from their town. He used to be good-for-nothing before he went to Canada for a hockey tournament back in the 90s, and didn't come back. Honey was now running a multi-million transport business in Toronto, and had helped his parents build the biggest house in the area.

Over the years, Jassi had seen far too many movies to know that America was the land of dreams. India was nothing in comparison. There was only one country where he wanted to be, and it wasn't India.

The year spent working in Chandigarh wasn't a complete waste though. Jassi worked hard at picking up the American accent, practicing his speech in all conference calls like they did in that wonderful documentary of everything American life is all about, *Friends*. It didn't quite work on his thick Punjabi tongue, but he kept trying. Jennifer Aniston was turning out to be a great English tutor, besides being a shapely one.

In the year 2003, he applied again to universities that were more realistic. His criterion was simple this time. He wanted somewhere close to the beach. He had seen too much *Baywatch* to be anywhere that wasn't within driving distance from a beach towel.

Last month, the letter came.

Dear Jaspreet Singh,

We are pleased to invite you to join our Masters of Science program in Computer Science.

With your academic background, you will be a strong addition to our graduate program, and we look forward to having you join the department.

At this time, we are unable to offer you an assistantship position. However, please be advised that there are several teaching assistant positions that are available for graduate students and are finalized in the week before the semester starts. You can apply for a position after arriving at Tallahasseee.

Please confirm your acceptance by 25 May.

Regards,

David Apostolov
Director, Admissions

Department of Computer Science
Florida State University
May 1, 2004

Jassi read the letter twice over. 'Ha. Strong addition!' He had never been a strong addition to anything. Thanks to his average looks, Jassi had never had to face the problem of being chased by too many girls. He didn't care about it though, for he wasn't attracted to any of them either. Every morning he woke up to the strategically sized 36 by 24 poster of Baywatch girl Pamela Anderson on the door of his room, and nothing less would do for him. He had loved Pamelaji, as he fondly called her, ever since he first saw a *Baywatch* episode on TV as a pimpled teenager in the neighbour Bholu's room while their parents thought they were practicing Trigonometry.

For now, his stardom had reached unprecedented heights. He was going to America. Jassi wasn't the first from his town to go to the US, but he was certainly among the few to travel abroad for higher education, instead of working at restaurants or driving taxis.

The news had spread like wildfire. The letter had passed a hundred hands in a week, and people were still trickling in to bless the young lad. The last time the town had seen so much excitement was ten years ago when somebody had noticed a pattern that looked like a trishul on the head of a stray bull, and people had come in from all over Punjab to get the blessings of the divine creature—a vehicle of lord Shiva, no less.

The comments he was getting these days were a mixed bundle.

'Make us proud, puttar. Do well, and don't keep chasing girls all the time. Do some study also.'

'Bhai, ek pack Marlboro ka bhej diyo wahan se.'

'My chacha's son Gurpreet is in Canada, which is close to Amreeka. You must go meet him.'

Jassi took to his stardom like a fish to water. He had already abbreviated his name further to a single syllable 'Jazz', in keeping with the American spirit. He didn't even respond to Jassi anymore, let alone Jaspreet. Only his mom still insisted on calling him by his full name.

Meanwhile the young kids from the neighbourhood were eyeing him with great reverence. Not just because he was going for an advanced degree, but because in their eyes he was going to get off the flight and land straight in Pamelaji's waiting arms.

Aunts, uncles, cousins, boys, girls, everybody suddenly loved him. Even the neighbour's dog Monty no longer snapped at him. HE loved himself. He was going to America. He had already started getting his '01' Santro filled with 'gas', often confusing the petrol pump attendants. One idiot had actually tried to dump CNG into his car. *Retards.*

Jassi was gonna live the American dream. He was gonna make a lot of money. He was gonna get away from the misery called India.

Jazz was gonna go to America. He was gonna be big. Huge.

Tears and Vodka

If there is one word that can cause instant palpitations in the hearts of young, physically-able Indian kids, it is the dreaded American visa. Those who think the Indian cricket team is unreliable should try getting a US student visa. The experience is sure to break all records of inconsistency.

The vagaries of the American student visa interview have been well-documented on the Internet in innumerable personal experiences on myriad chat forums frequented by frustrated, desperate students with dreams in their eyes but no sleep.

'I walked in. They said you would get your stamped passport in three days. I walked out. Breezy. I wasn't even carrying the bank statements. Forgot them at home. LOL.'

'I went with a nicely compiled folder comprising 268 documents, including the birth certificates of my entire extended family. I had bank statements showing full funds (wink wink) to cover my tuition fees, living expenses, cable, Internet, utilities, and then some left over to buy a second-hand Toyota. I had all the marksheets I have ever got. I had my 19,000 rank certificate from IIT-JEE. I had the consolation certificate I won at that art competition in the 6th standard. I even took my dog's vaccination records along. It was so heavy that I sprained my wrist from holding the folder. THEY STILL DENIED MY VISA. BLOODY BASTARDS. I WILL KILL THEM!'

Experiences posted on said forums tended to vary between these two extremes.

One was expected to go for the visa interview with a whole bunch of documents to validate one's educational background, university acceptance, and most importantly, proof that you were able to take care of your finances and would not end up becoming a homeless liability on the already debt-ridden American government. One was also expected to be smart, confident, and wear a nice deo to the visa appointment. The cautious ones would pray to all of the two million Hindu Gods, Jesus, the Prophet, and their favourite member of the Gandhi family, asking for their blessings for the license to study in the United States of Amreeka.

Jassi and Akhil just had a little piece of paper remaining between them and their American dream. It was soon time to start preparing for the visa.

Akhil had a visa appointment scheduled at the Delhi consulate for June 30. A week before the interview, he meticulously put together that precious folder and stowed it away in the family locker. Everything was in there, from his 10th standard marksheet to detailed bank statements from the last ten years.

His dad would travel on a tourist visa, and his appointment was set for the next day. Akhil secretly hoped they would deny him visa. Who travelled with their dads anyway? He wasn't six anymore, for dad to drop him off to school with instructions to the teachers to treat his boy nicely, because 'he's a bit sensitive and wets himself if you get angry at him'. There were painful memories down that road.

Akhil had planned the driving route to the consulate, the shirt he would wear, and practiced some voice modulation for that extra edge. He had brushed up on his math, and was now confident of finding the inverse of a matrix in less than 30 seconds (You could never be sure what they'll ask you). A day before the appointment, he conducted a full dress rehearsal of the visa interview, upto the point of entering the consulate whereupon he was chased away by a rifle-toting guard.

D-Day was soon upon him. He went. He stood in a long line. He gave a short interview. He got photographed. Finger printed. They told him the stamped passport would be home in three days.

The lady at the interview counter asked just one question. 'Why did you choose FSU?'

Akhil didn't bat an eyelid before coming up with the response, carefully practised twenty nine times. With voice modulation. He remembered Khurana Ma'am, his English teacher from high school, who would have been so proud of his performance that day.

'FSU is a world leader in the field of research in computer networks. The department is young and has been involved in some great work in this area in the last few years. My research interest lies in the area of wireless networking, which is why FSU would be ideal for me.'

Nowhere was it required to add that finances overruled every other criterion. Honesty was for Mahatma Gandhi. Not US visa officers.

On July 2, 2004, Jassi went for his visa appointment, also at the Delhi consulate. He had travelled to Delhi with his dad the previous evening, and they had stayed the night at one of his uncle's place. He reached the consulate thirty minutes late, and had to beg at the feet of a guard before he relented and let him inside, thanks to the five hundred rupee note that he slipped into the guard's hand.

Once inside, he realized that he had brought his dad's folder of loan applications with him. NOT HIS VISA APPLICATION FOLDER. Jassi felt his legs go weak. The ground began to shake. He didn't have any of the supporting documents he needed to show if asked for. Beads of perspiration started forming faster than Al Gore could say 'Global Warming'.

He could feel his entire life revolving around him. The dream was about to crash. Mom would get him married next year. A year later, the first baby would pop. Another one. Bam. Life over.

Jassi's turn came and they called him to the window.

The frowning American visa officer asked him. 'What's your name?'

'Jassi. Jaspreet Singh,' Jassi replied.

'Where are you going?'
'Florida State University, Tallahasseee.'
'What programme?'
'Computer Science.'
'Okay. Get your finger printing done. You will get your passport in three days.'

Jassi ran before the visa officer could change his mind. He knew well enough that he had been saved from crucifixion by a whisker. Visa done. Nothing could stop him from going to America now.

Pamelaji was only a few months away.

Four days after his interview, Akhil went to the Blue Dart office to pick up his passport. Passport collected. Visa checked. It was all coming together, like the climax of a Rocky Balboa movie. Akhil was all set.

Unfortunately, his dad got the tourist visa he had applied for and would be accompanying him to America. He would return within a week after Akhil settled in his apartment.

A few of his college classmates were also heading to the US for their Masters. None to his university though. Well, most others had anyway targeted higher ranked universities. Of the bunch, he was the only one with a confirmed funding offer. The others would fight it out once they got there, and had already taken hefty loans. One of his friends had seemed positively weaker the last time they met, and Akhil wondered if the stories about people mortgaging their kidneys for education loans were in fact true.

Tears and Vodka

The final month was spent in preparing for the 'next life'. There was shopping to be done, room arrangements to be finalized, health insurance and foreign exchange procured, and all the important paperwork to be compiled.

However, all that was nothing compared with the hard time his mom was giving him. She would spend her entire day sobbing. She would sob while brushing her teeth in the morning. She would sob while making Akhil's breakfast. She would sob at lunch. She would sob while watching *Kahani Ghar Ghar Ki* during dinner, though he suspected that was because everybody was fighting everybody else on that show. She would sob every time she saw Akhil. She had turned into an unstoppable sobbing machine.

Every day she would find something new to worry about. One day she said, 'Akhil, you have never even washed your underwear. How will you survive in Amreeka, I cannot understand.'

'Don't worry ma, maybe they have a course on it in the department. I'll learn the secret art of washing somehow.' Akhil could never have enough of pulling his mother's leg. He looked closely at her face and noticed the additional wrinkles on her forehead and bags under her eyes. The stress of his departure was getting to her.

He had procured shopping lists from the Internet and his mom had packed everything in two large suitcases.

His dad brought a permanent marker to scribble 'AKHIL ARORA' in large letters on top of both bags. 'You'll realize the importance of identification when there are 400 other desis ready to run away with your luggage at the Atlanta airport. Besides, if you don't like your college, you could open a store with all the stuff your mom has packed for you. If you want, I could stay there permanently and become your cashier at the shop.'

'Thanks for the offer, dad, but I think I'll pass,' said Akhil, as his sister Aarti giggled from across the room.

He had already planned his courses for the first few semesters, looked up their websites, and bought as many textbooks as he could. Seniors had warned him about the high prices of textbooks in the US. Indian editions worked out much cheaper. There was great scope for arbitrage in selling books as another alternative career option.

They were going to fly on August 10, on board an Air France flight via Paris and Atlanta.

He had got in touch with the FSU Indian Student Association on the Internet and they had helped with his arrival plans. Abhijit, the president of the student body, would meet him at the Tallahasseee airport and take him to his initial accommodation. Akhil would stay at somebody's apartment for the first few days while he finalized his own place to live. They had already put him in touch with another new student, Jassi, and both had agreed to share an apartment.

Akhil was ready to make that long cross-continental journey to the land of his destiny. His voyage of dreams would happen soon. With his 50 year old babysitter father in tow.

Jassi received his passport via courier on July 3, 2004. He had taken leave from work to be home when it arrived. The visa was right there, on page 24. His heart skipped a beat. He could smell American soil on that piece of shiny, colourful paper. He could almost see Pamelaji smiling at him from inside that visa. Jassi winked at her, and kissed the visa. Thankfully nobody was around to watch the show.

Next day, he served his letter of resignation. In two weeks' time, he would be back home, where he would spend the next three weeks and fly out to Tallahasseee in early August.

The ten days of notice period passed by in a blur, in part due to the copious amounts of alcohol consumed during latenight celebrations. Jassi was home. A new river had sprung up overnight in Punjab. Never before had a single person produced such volumes of tears as his mom was managing these days. This day wasn't much different. She was sobbing while cooking breakfast. 'Here, take this parantha. Get the butter from the fridge.'

As Jassi watched the next drop of tear land on top of his gobhi parantha, his mom continued, 'Finish fast and then we need to go shopping for you. Do you have your list ready?'

'Yo. All sorted out. Spent the last three nights searching on the Internet for things Indian students take with them to the US. People take pressure cookers, soap, toothpaste, tawa, spices, dals, and books. Some idiots even take whole grain wheat flour.'

'Yes, you will too.' Her tone left no room for argument.

A few days later, a room full of stuff was waiting to be packed in two large suitcases. There was a large pressure cooker, a small one, a dozen boxes of assorted MDH masalas, a kilo of Tata tea, salt, bedsheets, a nailcutter, bhujia from Haldiram's, Parle-G biscuits, Maggi noodles…the items were endless.

Jassi picked up the packet of salt and exclaimed, 'Just where am I going? Antarctica? Pretty sure they sell salt in the world's greatest country!'

'Shut up. Let me pack. You go play games on your computer.'

Jassi's life was a party those last few days in India. There was that memorable booze party with his college buddies. That night liquor had flowed like, well, his mom's tears over the past few weeks. Rivers upon rivers of Smirnoff and Kingfisher. He was beginning to wonder if beer had replaced the blood in his body.

He gave away all of Pamelaji's posters to his buddies. He felt since he was going to be so physically close to her, there was no need for the posters. 'Gave away' was an understatement though. There had been a mad scramble for the big one on his door. At least two shirts parted with their pockets in the melee, which ended up looking like people from a remote Indian village fighting for their daily water supply from a Jal Board tanker delayed by two days.

Jassi was all set for America. He had already converted to the pound system. He had gone to the neighbourhood Aggarwal Sweet Store a few days prior to his US trip and asked for two pounds of kaju barfi. When they insisted on weighing in kilos, he called them ignorant and created a ruckus, forcing the owners to chase him away. *Their loss*, he thought. *I am going to America, kaju barfi or not.*

He had practiced that American accent at all the local bookshops and government offices. He even called up the BSNL telephone helpline and talked to them in his new accent. But the lady at the other end just laughed at him and hung up. He had switched from *AajTak* to *CNN*. He was no longer interested in Cricket. Move over Sachin, Basketball star Shaquille O'Neal was his new God. He even swore only in English. He decided against using crude Punjabi or Hindi words anymore.

Jassi was ready to be the next big-shot Indian import in the US.

Jassi's family would drive down to Delhi to drop him off for his flight on August 10. British Airways, Delhi-London-New York-Tallahasseee.

The FSU Indian student association had put him in touch with one Akhil Arora from Delhi. They had talked over the phone a couple of weeks ago and agreed to be roommates. Dorky guy, but seemed okay. In fact, he also mentioned that he was flying out the same day, though on an Air France flight.

He had been told that someone from the local Indian Student Association would pick him up at Tallahasseee airport.

It was August 10, 2004. Akhil's flight was due to leave at 11 pm. Mr Arora had taken extra care with his attire before leaving for the airport. He was wearing his 20-year-old navy blue Raymond's suit with a red shirt, topped off with a blue tie that had the American flag printed on it. An embarrassed Akhil had begged him to wear a different tie, but his pleas had fallen on deaf ears. His dad had spent all of yesterday afternoon searching for the right tie in Palika Bazar, and just wouldn't let go until he found one. 'Akhil, we need to be dressed appropriately for the occasion,' he had said.

Mr Arora had a leather pouch around his waist. It contained 500 dollars in cash, both passports, printouts of their tickets, and thanks to a brilliant idea of his, a letter addressed to prospective thieves. Akhil was confused whether to marvel at his dad's creativity or to worry about what he would think of next.

The letter read,'*This pouch belongs to a relative of the Delhi Police Commissioner. If you have been brave enough to steal it, please return the contents to the undersigned address within seven days, or be prepared to face the consequences.*' The Arora household address was prominently written below the traditional sign of a skull crossed by two bones.

He had evenly distributed the rest of the cash across the hand baggage, wallets, and the pocket in his underwear. 'You just can't take any chance, Akhil. The world is full of cheats.'

It was decided that Aarti and mom would drop them off at the airport. 'We just want to make sure you get on that plane all right and don't run away scared at the last minute,' Aarti joked. Akhil smiled, but a tight knot was forming in his stomach. It just dawned on him that he didn't know when he would see them next. It was all sinking in now. Suddenly his dad's presence on the flight felt reassuring.

A week ago, Goyalji had come back for some more tea and samosas, and like the well-informed Delhiite, he had recited stories of at least a dozen kids who went to the US, never to look back.

'Aroraji, I am telling you they all just change once they land in that country. Say goodbye to your son. He is gone for good. It is our good fortune that our Priyank turned out to be an exception, but they all change. It is inevitable, like a car getting stolen in Delhi if you don't get a gear-lock installed the day you buy it.' He had laughed loudly—being the lone person who found his own joke funny—making his large belly vibrate violently, and in the process, spilling tea on the brand new sofa.

Akhil had looked at his mom as she rushed to attend to the stain on the sofa using tissue paper and the dishwashing soap from the kitchen, and shuddered at the thought of deserting his parents. His family was the world to him, and in his heart he knew that he would never turn his back on them. *I'll get my degree, work a few years, and then come back.*

Goyalji had left with a last grim look at Akhil when he touched his feet, as instructed by a still-distracted mom. 'Goyalji, please bless Akhil to be as sensible and hardworking as Priyank, who has made us all proud with his achievements.'

'Chalo chalo, let's go,' said Mr Arora, looking visibly excited. For him, logistics were everything. 'We must leave for the airport at least four hours in advance. What if we get stuck in traffic? What if we have a flat tyre? We should leave early, and then you people can talk as much as you want at the airport.'

Akhil lugged the two heavy suitcases into the Santro. One in the back, and the other on the backseat.

The airport trip was morose. While his mom was subdued and trying hard not to cry, his dad was giving away instructions on what not to do in the US, even though he was going to be with Akhil. Eighteen-year-old Aarti sat balanced precariously on her mom's lap, thanks to the suitcase occupying her half of the backseat.

'Always be careful going out alone. Don't mess with "those" people. Stick around with your Indian friends. Be careful of black people, I hear they get very violent when provoked. Don't let their girls trap you. Goyalji was saying they are very sneaky, and go after handsome Indian boys. Concentrate on your studies. You have your entire life left for those things.'

'Don't worry, dad. I'll be fine. You will see for yourself.'

An hour later, they were at the departure gate of Delhi's Indira Gandhi International airport—an international airport that looked more like a crowded railway station. (Remember, this was still 2004. The swanky Delhi T3 terminal was yet to be constructed.) Some people were carrying gunnysacks rather than suitcases while others were sprawled on the ground awaiting the arrival of their near and dear ones. The air was thick with dust and a cacophony of voices rendered hearing your own voice impossible.

Akhil noticed a Punjabi family nearby. They had just got off a Toyota Qualis and seemed rather rushed. A short, slightly plump young man with spiked hair piled up his bags on a trolley. He was wearing a red Benetton T-shirt layered with a green jacket and Ray-Ban shades in the night. His two large suitcases were bursting at the seams just like the ones in the back of the Arora Santro.

Akhil thought, *Could this be…?*

'Jassi, jaldi kar, it is getting late'. A powerful voice, much like a subwoofer, ran out over the din. *That must be his mom, and indeed, this should be Jassi, my to-be-roommate in Tallahasseee,* Akhil told himself.

The line at the entrance was getting longer. Akhil quickly touched his mom's feet, hugged Aarti, and rushed with his trolley. Mom hid her face in the sari pallu so no one could witness her outpouring of tears, much like the gates of a dam trying to hold back an overflowing river. In a happier moment, Akhil would have cracked a Bhakra-Nangal joke, but he let it slip this time.

Mr Arora took the trolley while Akhil bid goodbye with one final wave of the hand to the now openly sobbing mom, and they were gone.

Jassi's flight was at 10, but they got lost in Delhi traffic and ended up being late at the airport. He bade a hurried goodbye to mom, dad, brother 'baby', elder mama, elder mami, and the three other cousins who had squeezed into the cramped Toyota Qualis at the last minute. Large family send-offs at the airport are as much a part of the Punjabi tradition as are aloo paranthas.

Akhil must be around. His flight was at 11 pm, Jassi recalled. However, for now he was more worried about checking-in for the flight. He couldn't afford missing the most important flight of his life. *Will try finding Akhil at the departure gate for the Air France flight,* he thought.

He rushed into the terminal, got his bags scanned, and ran to the check-in counter. As per the rules, one needed to check-in three hours before international flights. Jassi was now one hour late, and in serious danger of missing the flight. He almost knocked over a security official as he ran to the check-in counter. Luckily, they let him off with a mere stern look. More importantly, they allowed him to check-in without any further excitement.

An hour later, Jassi was done with his security check, and was standing in line at the departure gate. Boarding would start in ten minutes' time. *There's no time left to go find Akhil; will just meet him in Tallahasseee,* he told himself.

Soon he was on board the plane and tucked into his seat. Jaspreet Singh from Ludhiana was now Jazz from Florida. The jet engines roared and Jazz was off on his way to the land of his dreams where a new life awaited him. As did all the pretty girls, the never-ending supply of beer, his American dream, and that one person he had dreamt of all these years.

Pamelaji, this is it. Here I come.

From a distance, Akhil saw Jassi hurry into the terminal, obviously running late. He chuckled as he saw him ram into a police official enjoying a cup of coffee next to the Nirula's snack counter.

'Saala sardar. Lucky to not get shot there.' Post 9/11, you couldn't mess with airport security anymore.

At the check-in counter, it turned out Akhil had 2 kilos of excessive luggage. They made him pay a penalty for the additional weight over the permissible limit of 32 kilos per bag. (Yes, back in 2004 people could check-in two bags weighing 32 kilos each, a princely sum compared to the single 23 kilo bags allowed by airlines today. The smuggling business has been in the doldrums ever since.) *Bloody merceneries*, he thought, while Mr Arora let loose a barrage of muted expletives. The required forms were duly filled and the passport stamped. The first stamp on his virgin passport. The security check that followed was extensive, and the kilometre-long line reminded Akhil of tortorous telephone-bill payments at the post office back in the days. He saw Jassi going through the various lines ahead of him, but couldn't catch up with him.

Anyway, there's going to be plenty of time to talk eventually.

The father-son duo found seats at the departure gate. Akhil got cups of Nescafe to kill time, though Mr Arora was already busy trying to read the document the man on the adjacent seat was typing out on his laptop. Soon, the boarding call was made. Another line formed in no time. Akhil smiled. *They should make lining up an Olympic sport. We Indians will definitely win something there. Add an event for jumping lines, and there's two sure-shot medals right there for India.*

A few latecomers tried to squeeze their way into the front of the line, and were promptly and loudly reprimanded and made to return by Akhil's dad who beamed at him, clearly proud of this achievement. Twenty minutes later, they were on board the huge Boeing 747 that would fly them to Atlanta, with a four-hour stopover at Paris. Akhil muttered a silent prayer to the Gods as he settled into his seat. The plane was due to take off in a few minutes.

A new life beckoned him.

Seven Seas, Three Lives

Akhil kept his backpack in the overhead compartment and settled into the aisle seat. The lady at the check-in counter had shrugged her shoulders saying they were among the last to check-in, and as a result, there were no two seats available in the same row. Mr Arora ended up getting a seat all the way back towards the rear of the plane. He decided that once the person seated next to Akhil arrived, he would request him (or her) to *adjust* so he could exchange places and sit next to his dear son.

People were still boarding the plane. Akhil looked at the variety around him. There was a Punjabi couple seated on his right who, he adjudged, were probably going to America for their honeymoon, for the bashful wife's arms were laden with shiny red bangles—the sign of a newly-married woman. Two rows ahead of him was, what seemed like, an NRI family comprising of a balding middle-aged dad, mom dressed from head to toe in fancy brands, and two young boys quarrelling over a video game in their American accents. A thin, seemingly young girl clad in pale blue denims and a T-shirt bearing a

Reebok logo was sitting across the aisle from Akhil, trying to comfort the baby howling in her arms. The child's parents suddenly appeared on the scene, the mother giving instructions to the girl to feed the child some milk as soon as the plane takes off, after which both husband and wife disappeared behind the curtains to their business class seats. *She must be the maid*, Akhil guessed.

'Hi, mind if I get into my seat?' questioned a jittery female voice interrupting his social observations.

Akhil looked up to see a young woman who, he figured, was his co-passenger. She seemed to be of a similar age, and was mumbling something in what Akhil knew to be Bengali from the maid at home who would mutter similar words every time she had a fight with mom. She was petite, pretty, and her long hair reached almost all the way to her waist. She appeared to be by herself. Quite likely a student. Or how young boys from engineering colleges would term it—Jackpot.

As Akhil got up to let her get into her seat, she seemed to be struggling with her bag, which was too heavy for her to heave up to the overhead shelf. Ever the gentleman, Akhil took her bag and helped it to a spot in the overhead compartment The bag was heavy and Akhil nearly pulled a muscle while lifting it up, but of course, he couldn't let it show. Not in front of a pretty girl. Real men feel no pain. Or, as a wise man once said, *Mard ko dard nahi hota*.

She smiled at him. 'Thanks.'

'No worries. I'm Akhil. Nice to meet you,' he replied.

'Hi. I am Nandita.'

The two got talking. Akhil was pleasantly surprised to find that Nandita was also travelling to Tallahasseee, especially because he hadn't heard about her on the Indian Association (INSAT) forums setup for coordinating among the freshers. Apparently, she had directly talked to some of her friends at FSU and bypassed the INSAT route, which was why no one knew about her. Akhil didn't mind the serendipitous meeting one bit. Such chance meetings are the stuff young engineering graduates dream of. In the last few years, the only time Akhil had sat next to a girl that wasn't his sister was on the ladies seat of DTC buses, before a 'ladies' came along and asked him to vacate the seat.

Nandita disclosed the reason for her angry mumblings, saying she was upset with her taxi driver who had taken her and her parents on an extended trip through Delhi roads that nearly made her miss her flight, and then asked for double the regular fare. Her dad had left her at the airport entrance still in a sullen mood thanks to the driver, who in his words was a 'typical Punjabi Delhiite—stupid, uneducated, and an overall scoundrel.'

Nandita was going to join the Geology PhD programme at FSU. She was Bengali, but had spent enough time in Chandigarh over the course of her Bachelor's from Punjab University to be deemed an honorary Punjabi. She was from Kolkata, but there were no flights originating from the city, which was why she was boarding from Delhi.

The next few hours would go by quickly, Akhil thought. He was glad to have made a friend early in his journey. 'Is this my *Hum Tum* moment?' he murmured to himself thinking of the recent Bollywood blockbuster in which the lead characters meet each other on board an international flight, and end up falling in love.

As the doors of the plane were being closed, Mr Arora came by his seat to check if his co-passenger had come. Akhil told him Nandita was a friend, and asked that if he didn't mind, could she stay put in the seat. He reasoned it out saying they could compare notes and prepare for the life ahead at FSU. Mr Arora seemed confused at first, but eventually agreed. His 'Star Spangled' tie fluttered in a sudden gust of air as someone went past him. Akhil closed his eyes in dismay, as Nandita looked on with an amazed expression in her eyes. 'Nice tie,' she remarked to Akhil as Mr Arora returned to his seat.

Delhi to Paris took about nine hours. The French airhostesses were friendly, and *Real* fruit juices and *Lay's* chips were readily available for snacking. Akhil watched bits and pieces of some movies on his personal LCD screen, and chatted up Nandita through the rest of the time, while his dad slept in his seat for the entire duration of the flight, somehow never failing to wake up at the exact times when meals were being served.

Nandita was loud, extremely talkative, and had a funny high-pitched laugh that reminded Akhil of the screeching tyres of a hurriedly braking DTC bus. Like Akhil, she hadn't done much in her life other than studying and getting good grades through school and college.

The plane landed at the famous Charles De Gaulle airport in Paris. To Akhil, it didn't feel like nine hours had passed. Female company makes for a great time machine for boys.

There were four hours to kill before they got on board the next leg to Atlanta. Mr Arora was, in his own words, sleepy — like a bored MP in the Parliament — and was going to rest some more in the waiting area. Akhil located Nandita sitting in the next row of seats, tired but radiant, her legs propped up on her seat, flipping through a *Reader's Digest* magazine.

'Let's get some coffee, shall we?' he asked her.

'Sure,' she said, for she was famished as well.

His dad was too sleepy to even register their suggestion. He waved to the two to carry on and dozed off.

Jassi's heart was aflutter. *This is it. This is it. This IS IT.*

He was finally going to America. This was huge. No more American diction practice in front of the mirror; this time it was for real. His American dream was going to be fulfilled. He could already visualise himself a few years in the future, rolling in cash while bikini clad models vied for his attention as he nibbled at a bunch of grapes like they showed in those MTV music videos.

A high-pitched voice that sounded like the lady from the automated voice response at the telephone exchange broke his chain of thoughts. 'Sir, please fasten your seatbelt. We are about to takeoff.'

He sized up the pretty airhostess in the snug blue dress. She was either just too thin, or the airline was not paying her enough to eat sufficient meals. Jassi fastened his seatbelt, admired her hourglass figure as she went down the aisle inspecting everybody's seatbelts, and picked up the inflight magazine hoping to find some more content on America and Americans. He wanted to know everything about the country. He wanted to imbibe everything American. Jassi wanted to become American, if he could.

In the last month, he had read at least a dozen books trying to research the American way of life. He had gone through the *Friends* series thirteen times and felt quite confident of being able to quote dialogues at will. *Seinfeld* had been a tad boring for his taste, but Jassi had gone through it about half a dozen times nevertheless. Then there was *American Pie*, that wonderful epic of American college life. He had seen all three movies released so far, and hoped in his mind that his university would be like the one in the movie, where the parties would be wild and the girls easy enough to take off their clothes at the first available opportunity to get it on with a 'hot guy' like him. In fact, Jassi was worried about how he would manage the invariable problem of plenty.

At FSU, he was going to be Jazz, a name he thought would be just perfect. It was inherently American, and easy to say. Would help brush aside the 'painful' issue of his Indian identity.

The plane was in the air. Eight hours to go to Heathrow.

Jassi was disappointed with his company. A pot-bellied middle-aged uncle wearing a safari suit was to his left and a teenaged boy with spiked hair on the right. The uncle had definitely let off some poisonous gas ten minutes into the flight, and Jassi got disgusted looks from the kid.

In the movies, they always had a pretty woman sitting next to the hunk in flights. Bloody liars, he thought cursing his luck. As his neighbour switched from emitting hydrogen sulphide to snoring loudly, Jassi discovered that the in-flight personal entertainment system had the *American Pie* movies in their video library. So he spent the next six hours going through them, taking pauses only to call the air-hostess for Coca-Cola and peanut snacks every thirty minutes.

As Jassi was ambling up the aisle after returning from a bathroom break, he noticed a young couple a few seats behind where he was sitting, and stopped short in his tracks. The guy was probably from Andhra. He was dark, geeky looking, with a face covered deep in craters that reminded Jassi of the surface of the moon. The woman with him, on the other hand, was a stunner. Luscious light golden hair, blue eyes, and killer looks of a model from a Pirelli calendar, minus the anorexia. Jassi was amazed. *How did a man as ugly as him land up with such a beautiful white woman despite being quite ugly himself?* He was deep in slumber, and she was sleeping with her head on his shoulder. Jassi wanted to shake his hand, hug him, and if possible, get some tips from him. He was ecstatic. *If HE could do this, surely Jassi would have to manage a long waiting list of desperate American women. This was inspirational stuff.*

Just as Jassi was planning his next move, the man woke up and looked at him staring at him and his girlfriend. Jassi pretended to search for something in his pocket and moved on.

The flight landed in London after nine hours. For some reason, the airhostess at the gate, *his* airhostess, the one who had got him fifteen glasses of Coca-Cola during the flight, didn't respond to Jassi's attempts to shake her hand as he exited the plane. He thought he heard her mumble something as he left.

Poor girl, he thought and got off the plane feeling sad for the malnourished airhostess and wondering if he should write a letter to the airline asking them to increase her salary.

✈

Akhil and Nandita had managed to locate a coffee shop at the terminal. Akhil went into shock looking at the prices listed on the board hanging on the wall, as the tall French woman at the counter stared at the excited kids.

'A small cup of coffee for 4 euros? Almost 280 rupees? That teeny muffin for another 320? This is ridiculous. The Nescafe I had at Delhi airport cost me only 20 rupees. What's with the prices here?'

Nandita nodded in amused disbelief. Though the high prices had shocked her as well, she was enjoying watching Akhil's reaction more.

Eventually, hunger trumped economics. The youngsters decided to buy a single cappuccino and get an extra cup to split the drink. An already small muffin got carefully divided into two. Four euros of hard earned money was spent by each towards the most unsatisfactory meal of their lives. It was over in a minute. The quickest possible meal had just cost Akhil some 300 rupees worth.

Akhil felt an urge to call up home, and not because mom's paranthas came free. He was suddenly conscious of being in a foreign land, and the homesickness was kicking in. They found a pay phone, which was another mercenary that charged a couple of euros for a minute.

Akhil called up home. 'Hello ma. I have reached Paris. How are you?'

'Arre Akhil. Aarti and I were just talking about you guys and wondering if you had reached safely. God bless you. What is your dad doing?'

'Dad is fine. He is busy catching up on the lack of sleep from the last few weeks.' He glanced at the display meter and panicked. 'I'll have to hang up now. This bloody machine is going so fast I am already having palpitations. I'll call you once I reach Tallahasseee.' And with that he hung up.

Akhil and Nandita roamed around the passages of De Gaulle. There was no water in some of the taps in the men's washrooms. Akhil smirked. *And they call India a poor, hungry nation!*

The four hours went by in a flash. For Akhil, the biggest discovery at the airport was how high the prices were. Little trinkets at a gift shop for 20 euros. They went to a bookshop and magazines were a minimum of 5 euros, while novels were all priced upwards of 15 euros. This was crazy. Akhil wondered how he would survive America if things there were equally expensive.

The flight to Atlanta turned out to be fun for Akhil, all thanks to Nandita's company. The two had known each other for less than twenty-four hours, but a bond had been formed between them. They discussed their dreams, their apprehensions, tried to calm each other down, watched movies together, realized the enormity of what they were getting into, cried a little, laughed a lot, and went through a whole range of emotions in each other's company. Mr Arora was up now, but had discovered that he could watch movies of his choice on the entertainment system and was going through the collection of Amitabh Bachchan movies on offer. His target was to watch three movies in the 9-hour flight. It seemed like he had found his mission for the day, and was going to do all it took to extract full value for the expensive tickets, even if it meant depriving himself of any sleep. Akhil didn't mind if this meant spending all the time talking to Nandita undisturbed.

An hour before landing, the flight crew handed out the

customs declaration forms. Pens were drawn and the forms promptly filled up, with all sorts of personal declarations.

'Have you ever been arrested?'

'Have you ever been deported?'

Akhil confidently filled out 'no' to all the awkward questions, though he marvelled at the inherent trust in this form. *What if I have served a jail sentence and don't say yes? Will they just accept it like that? What's the point? No wonder they say Americans are funny.*

✈

They finally landed at the London Airport. Jassi's first steps on foreign soil. He walked around the terminal like a dizzy toddler at a cartoon convention. He had done a lot of preparation, but the reality of being in a foreign land was nerve wracking. *So many people. Black. White. Other colours. Such a variety of tongues I can barely understand. How wonderful,* he thought gleefully.

Three hours passed by in a jiffy. Just one more flight and he would be in the land of Jim, Oz, Kevin, Finch, and Stifler, the dudes from *American Pie*, the boys who had finally managed to lose their virginity by the end of the first movie. Jassi was still to get there, but all that was going to change soon. It was just a matter of time, he had no doubt in his mind about that.

He saw that the ugly Indian guy and his white girlfriend were also continuing on to New York. Jassi tried following them for a little while, but they soon got suspicious and disappeared inside a lounge where Jassi was not allowed to enter. 'The lounge is only for premium customers, sir,' said the man guarding the entry door.

Jassi went back to the gate and spent his time watching

people go by. By the time the boarding call was made, he had counted about two dozen women he was willing to consider for marriage.

The plane took off for New York, and with every passing minute, the visions in Jassi's head grew bigger. In his mind, he was already on South Beach, partying with a bunch of Latino women in teeny swimsuits with floral patterns, a glass of Martini in his hand.

The flight stewardess came down the aisle with the dinner trolley and asked if he preferred an Indian meal. 'Oh no, thanks. I'll have the continental option.' India was passé. Jazz did not want anything to do with India.

He struggled for the next half hour with the bland salad on his tray. The stomach grumbled, but his pride was salvaged.

The captain came on the speakers and announced, 'Ladies and gentlemen, we are beginning our descent into New York's John F. Kennedy airport. Please fasten your seatbelts. We expect to land in about fifteen minutes.'

Jazz's heart was going like a rocket. He felt dizzy. This was it—the culmination of many years of longing for the American dream.

✈

The flight landed at Atlanta, and Akhil, his dad, and Nandita followed the rest of the flight's desi crowd in a mad scramble to be first in the immigration line. Akhil was surprised at the length of the long, serpentine line. He had thought long lines happened only in India, not in the great United States of America.

After an hour-long wait in the winding line, Akhil was up next. Mr Arora and Nandita were right behind.

As the person in front of him left the immigration counter, Akhil waited for the officer to call him. A few seconds passed, and Mr Arora started getting impatient.

'Go Akhil. Why are you wasting time?'

'Wait dad.'

'Go,' he pushed him. Akhil walked up to the counter nervously.

The officer looked at him and frowned. 'Sir, I have to ask you to step back into the line. I'll call you when I am ready.'

Akhil walked back. His dad was busy picking his nose, and stared at Akhil like he was a soldier who had run away from battle.

A minute later, the young officer shouted 'Next' and Akhil marched to him for the second time in eighty seconds. Mr Arora seemed annoyed as he wiped his hands on his trousers.

'Good morning, sir.'

'Passport please.' The response was business-like and the tone gruff.

Akhil handed over the passport and immigration forms.

'Where are you travelling to?'

'Tallahasseee, Florida.'

The immigration officer looked at the US student visa stamp, checked the photograph, looked at Akhil, checked the photograph again, fiddled about on his computer, and took Akhil's fingerprints, a photo, and a retina scan. He finally stamped the passport and handed it back to Akhil.

'Welcome to America.'

'Thank you, sir.'

The welcome felt awkward, like he was entering a prison, but Akhil was now in the United States of America. Nandita and Mr Arora were next, and completed their immigration formalities without any hiccups. Now fully awake, Mr Arora was eyeing Nandita suspiciously, wondering if his son was showing undue interest in this loud Bengali girl.

Now it was on to the final connecting flight to Tallahasseee. Akhil, Mr Arora, and Nandita found the terminal for the onward flight from an overhead display and took the inter-terminal train, marvelling at the size of the massive Atlanta airport. There was still an hour for boarding the Tallahasseee flight, and Akhil chanced upon a TV terminal near their departure gate. CNN was on.

BREAKING NEWS: Hurricane Charley expected to strike Florida tonight.

There were visuals of heavy rains and violent winds blowing away parts of houses. Flooding was expected in parts of Florida.

Excellent. What a welcome! There's a massive hurricane hitting Florida on the very day we fly in. The three panicked. *Was there any risk to their flight? What if the plane crashed?*

Hearing the final boarding call, the three hesitatingly moved into the line to get on the plane. Onboard, the captain came on the speakers.

'Good morning ladies and gentlemen, we are now ready for departure to Tallahasseee. The flying time is one hour. As you may already know, hurricane Charley is expected to hit Florida today, so there might be some turbulence expected over Tallahasseee. However, there isn't much cause to worry.

We expect a safe flight into Tallahasseee. Please watch for the seatbelt sign during the flight.'

Good luck Akhil, now that you've landed into this mess, just pray to God that you get out of this safely. Akhil's palms were sweating like a leaky water pipe. Nandita was silently muttering prayers in Bengali. Mr Arora looked on anxiously. A few seconds later, Akhil heard him mouth a Punjabi expletive.

The plane landed at Tallahasseee airport in an hour. Apart from two minutes when the plane shook violently, nothing unpleasant happened.

The airport at Tallahasseee was a small one, much like the ones at small Indian towns, and a drastic change from the massiveness that Atlanta airport was. Akhil, Mr Arora, and Nandita reached the creaky baggage belt to collect their luggage. Mr Arora's face broke into a smile as he was able to locate their bags from a distance, thanks to the identification marks he had made on them.

'See. I told you,' he told Akhil, who nodded in agreement. While Mr Arora was fresh after a long sleep, Akhil hadn't been able to catch a wink of sleep, and didn't have any energy left in him.

Akhil noticed a group of Indian students enter the terminal. One of them had a placard with 'Akhil' scribbled on it. Akhil waved at them, and walked up to the group, his dad in tow. Nandita had spotted the seniors who had come to receive her, and had gone off in their direction.

'Abhijit?' he asked.

'Yes. Akhil?'

"Yes. Good to meet you, Abhijit.' Akhil beamed at Abhijit like he was a long-lost friend, though in reality they had never met before. In a foreign land, he was the only person Akhil knew so far.

Abhijit shook his hand. 'Welcome to Tallahasseee, man. How was your flight?'

'Thanks. It was good, except for the part where I feared my plane wouldn't ever reach Tallahasseee,' Akhil replied with a wry smile.

Abhijit grinned. 'So you found out about the hurricane? Don't worry buddy. We're a bit inland, so hurricanes fizzle out by the time they reach here.'

'Ah, that's good to know. Anyway, my heart regained normalcy as soon as the plane hit the Tallahasseee runway successfully,' said Akhil smiling after what seemed like an eternity.

Abhijit looked at Akhil's dad with curiosity. He had not expected Akhil to come with *this* much baggage.

Akhil introduced him. 'Abhijit, this is my dad. He'll stay here for a week with me.'

Abhijit said hi, but he was clearly befuddled. He had no idea Akhil wasn't travelling alone. Besides, nobody had come with their dads to accompany them in the last two years he had been in Tallahasseee. It intrigued him, but for now, they had to get back. It was getting late.

'Cool. Let's get you home now.'

'Sure, let's go.'

Nandita and the two girls who had come to receive her joined the group and there was a quick round of handshakes, after which everybody was ready to head back.

Abhijit and the others got Akhil and Nandita's bags, bundled them in the two cars, and both parties were off to their respective destinations. It was dark outside, so Akhil couldn't make much of the surroundings. Thirty minutes later, Abhijit stopped in front of an apartment block. 'Home,' he said and got out of the car.

Abhijit walked up to an apartment and rang the bell. Akhil and his dad followed him.

The bell was answered by a tall, dark, moustached guy. He was South Indian, and Akhil thought he resembled the movie star Chiranjeevi, except for a perfectly oval shaped head with a mildly receding hairline.

'Hi Sundar, meet Akhil and his dad,' introduced Abhijit.

'Hi Akhil. Welcome man. Venkat and I have been waiting for you.' He then turned to Mr Arora and welcomed him with the same pleasant expression. 'Welcome uncle.'

'Hi Sundar,' Akhil said to the now beaming Sundar. Mr Arora had already entered by then and was curiously looking around the sparse living room, occupied by just a single couch and a centre table. Akhil noticed it was all carpeted though. *You could probably just sit on the ground,* he thought.

'Akhil, you'll stay with Sundar for the next week while you look for your own apartment,' explained Abhijit. 'Your new roomie Jassi is also expected tonight. Once he is here, you two can finalize your apartment lease, but until then, we'll accommodate you with others living here. I'll let you get some sleep now, you must be tired. Talk to you guys tomorrow,' he said as he left the apartment.

Sundar turned to his two guests. 'Make yourself comfortable guys. Why don't you freshen up while I set up dinner?'

Akhil smiled at his generous host. 'Thanks a lot, Sundar. I hope we are not causing too much trouble for you guys.'

'Oh no, not at all. Even I came here two weeks ago and went through the same process.'

Akhil found some night clothes in his luggage and asked Sundar to guide him to the loo. When he returned five minutes later, Sundar had already laid out the dinner. By then, his dad had also changed into his kurta-pyjama and had taken his seat at the dinner table. Akhil took a bite of the parantha with the saag paneer and was amazed at how delicious the food was. He had been away from home for just over twenty-four hours now, but it felt like he hadn't eaten decent food in a long time. He looked at his dad who also seemed to be enjoying the meal, and turned to Sundar.

'Whoa. This is yummy. Sundar, you are a great cook man.'

Sundar laughed. 'This is ready-to-eat frozen stuff. I didn't make any of it.'

Akhil couldn't believe it. 'You mean you get all this Indian food readymade?' Suddenly life seemed good to him. The Punjabi DNA responds to good food like Popeye to spinach.

A scrubby, short, unshaven man walked into the apartment with a carton of beer in one hand and a pack of cigarettes in the other. Sundar introduced them. 'Hi Venkat, see Akhil and his dad are here.'

Venkat mumbled a meek 'hi' and went to his room. Mr Arora took a break from his dinner, and his eyes followed Venkat all the way to the door. He was already getting nervous imagining his precious son turning into a drug addict dancing to *dum maaro dum* on the streets of America, while wearing yellow coloured bell-bottom pants and shirts with red and orange floral patterns. Akhil was too tired to notice his dad lost in thoughts. After a quick dinner, both retired to bed early.

Thanks to the jet lag, Akhil woke up the next morning at 5 am with a splitting headache. Mr Arora was up already. He had gone through the fridge and kitchen cabinets, found required supplies to make a cup of his morning tea and had two cups ready by the time Akhil brushed his teeth. He was determined to stop his son from getting into bad habits. Caffeine was certainly preferable to cocaine.

Father and son drank their first American cup of tea in silence. Akhil was overcome with emotion. He wanted to talk to his mother, who he realized must be feeling even lonelier with his dad being here. Mr Arora's return flight was still a week away. While he had earlier felt awkward about his dad coming to drop him off, he now felt thankful for it, though he wondered if it would hurt even more now when his dad returned home.

Sundar was up a couple of hours later, and surprised to see the father-son duo done with their breakfast. He shared his calling card details with Akhil to call up home. Akhil called up on his mom's mobile and spoke to her for the first time from American soil. She sounded calm and composed, not jittery and morose like he thought she might have been. This was reassuring. Akhil felt slightly better. He could manage missing home, but couldn't take his mother being unhappy in his absence.

✈

Jassi's flight landed at Tallahasseee airport. The plane taxied for a few minutes before stopping a short distance from the terminal building. There was no aero-bridge. They were going to have to walk to the terminal. Jassi was shocked. *This is odd. Isn't America supposed to be all about technology?* Jassi had expected third-world countries to make people walk from planes to airport terminals, not the world's biggest superpower.

The doors of the jet opened, and people started climbing down the steps.

Jassi reached the door and took a deep breath of his first whiff of American air. This was momentous. His childhood dream had finally come true. All those years of pining for America, those plans, the hours spent memorizing the stupid word lists for his GRE when he could have been playing cricket instead, it had all come to fruition. The American air felt different to him. It was cleaner. Jassi was in a trance. He stood at the gate for a few minutes savouring the moment as a line built up behind him. An impatient tap on the shoulder from a cranky old lady behind him brought him back to his senses. He got off the steps and onto the tarmac, as the grumpy woman rolled her eyes and smirked. 'These Mexicans will ruin the country one day!' Jassi didn't hear her. He was already singing that epic James Brown song he had heard in *Rocky 4*—'Living in America'. He had memorized the lyrics just for this day.

The last twenty-four hours had been rough. His flight landed at New York a few hours behind schedule and he had been forced to spend a sleepless night at the airport terminal awaiting his final connection to Tallahasseee. The airline didn't even offer him a place to stay. A black woman at the counter simply said, 'I am sorry, sir. You are late for your connection to Tallahasseee. You'll need to wait for the next one.' She then checked the computer screen in front of her, raised her eyebrows, and coughed ever so slightly before continuing, 'In twelve hours.'

As Jassi stared at her face, she asked him to move away from the counter. 'Sir, can you please step aside for the next customer?'

He found an empty row of chairs in the waiting area to sleep. It turned cold soon, and Jassi covered himself with his jacket to keep warm. The jacket hardly provided any respite from the cold, but he had little option besides waiting for the morning.

The flight to Tallahasseee finally left from New York at noon. Jassi had managed to brush his teeth in the men's room in the terminal, and enjoyed a breakfast of a Burger and Coca-Cola at McDonald's. As he had expected, the Coca-Cola here indeed tasted better than the one in India. The night's travails were all forgotten.

He had finally reached Tallahasseee airport a full fourteen hours behind schedule. He took his first steps on American soil and thought, *A few small steps for man; a giant leap for the Jazzminator.*

The airport terminal was small, but it was squeaky clean. Jassi sniggered. *In India, you couldn't imagine the best airports being this well maintained, but of course, this was America. The land where the air was pure, the people disciplined, and the walls without any paan stains.*

He located a pay phone near the baggage area and called up Murari from the Indian Student Association of Tallahasseee, who promised to be there in ten minutes. He arrived two hours later, still operating on Indian Stretchable Time, even in the US.

Jassi was accommodated in the apartment of two Telugu boys, Vijay and Suresh, who were both Math majors doing their PhDs, in addition to being lovers of Grey Goose and Marlboro. Not that Jassi would complain about that.

The Jazzminator had landed.

Fresh off the Boat

Akhil felt some relief after talking to his mom. It was 6 am. Sundar had gone back to bed, and Venkat was still shaking up the foundations of the building with his loud snores. Having nothing better to do, he got up to look around.

The apartment was spacious. Two big bedrooms and a living hall, with the entire floor covered from wall to wall with a lush light brown carpet that was so soft, it probably admonished you if you walked on it with dirty shoes. The place smelled of fresh paint, varnish, and the dirty dishes in the kitchen sink from last night. Not wanting to wake up the others, Akhil decided to step out for a little walk. He noticed his dad busy going through the stack of recently arrived mail on the fridge. He had already gone around knocking on the walls of the living room to check the material they were made of.

'This is very flimsy construction, Akhil. Some of the walls seem so thin, your mother could break them with a sneeze,' was the disappointed verdict. 'You know how thick the walls in our home are? Twelve inches. Unbreakable.'

Akhil stepped out of the door, requesting his dad not to touch the personal belongings of their hosts. The apartment block was called University Club. It had around 200 apartments in the three-storey building. The whole area had plenty of greenery, and a swimming pool in the middle of it all. The parking lot was full of unfamiliar cars. None quite like the trusty old Marutis and Santros he was familiar with in India. He noticed that the cars here were longer, smarter looking, with a lot of them having open backs. Akhil was to find out that they were called 'pickup trucks', though he wondered why college students would need one. He could imagine the doodhwallah back home requiring one of these to ferry their big metallic jars of milk every morning, but students?

America was intriguing. There were hardly any people on the road at this time of the day. There were no stray dogs barking in a synchronized early-morning show. The setting was very serene and peaceful. It all seemed so different to him from how things were back in India, with its shrinking spaces, polluted air, and harried people struggling to get through the day.

That feeling was back. Akhil was where no one in his last many generations had ever been. Thousands of kilometres away from the safety of his home, which was no longer a train ride away. There was tremendous distance involved, besides tough US visa regulations and stern immigration officers capable of decapitating with a stare.

No more parents taking decisions on his behalf anymore. No more mom to wash his underwear, all fifteen sets of them, as advised by the online shopping lists. Apparently, you washed your clothes only once in two weeks. He would have to fend for himself from now onwards.

After sleeping the entire evening, Jassi woke up to the loud whistle of the pressure cooker and found his hosts Suresh and Vijay in the kitchen preparing dinner. There were a few empty beer bottles on the counter, and one each in their hands. The smell of sambhar filled the entire apartment, and smoke levels were rising at an alarming pace.

All Jassi saw were those beer bottles, whose sight filled his heart with joy. He tried talking to the two, but was too tired for any conversation and went back to sleep, dreaming of pretty American girls lining up to be with him, while he kept rejecting them one by one, until Pamelaji finally appeared and said, 'I'm all yours, my Jazzminator.'

He was already fast asleep a few minutes later when the fire alarm went off and Suresh stood for ten minues on a tall stool below the roof-mounted smoke detector, a soaking wet towel in his hand, to calm the shrieking contraption down.

The next day Akhil and Jassi met for lunch at Suresh's place. After months of telephone calls and anxious emails, mostly from Akhil's end, they were finally meeting face-to-face.

'Abbe Jassi, I saw you nearly take down that police officer at Delhi airport. You got lucky beta, it could've gotten ugly,' Akhil grinned at his to-be-roommate as Mr Arora carefully studied the roommate-designate like a prospective father-in-law observing a nervous 25-year-old groom being considered for marriage with his precious daughter.

'Dude, you saw me at the airport? Why didn't you talk to me there? As for me, I got so late, I had no time to look around. It was chaos.' Jassi replied.

Akhil laughed remembering the sequence of events that night. 'Sorry man. I just couldn't get the chance. Plus you were going too fast. Anyway, it is good that you were able to make it to the flight. So how have you been?'

'I am in heaven, dude. I've been dreaming of this for years and that dream has finally come true. What more could I want?'

As his dad stared on, Akhil smiled nervously. 'I am already getting jittery about coursework.'

Jassi wasn't too bothered. 'Relax dude, we've just arrived. Let's think about courses later. We need to finalize our apartment first.'

'Of course. Abhijit suggested we get some rest today, and go check out apartments tomorrow.'

'Yups man, will do.'

'Boss, I am already feeling sleepy. I guess this must be jet lag. I'll go take a nap. Let's catch up tomorrow.'

'Alrighty bud. See you tomorrow.' Jazz was out in action, the local slang flowing smoothly.

'Beta Jaspreet, hold on for a minute.' Mr Arora grabbed a bewildered Jassi by his shoulder and took him into the balcony, closing the sliding glass door behind them. He was going to make sure Jassi was a worthy roommate for the apple of his eyes, the fruit of his loins, Akhil.

Akhil winced. He had clearly told dad that his to-be-roommate Jaspreet Singh preferred to be called Jassi.

He grilled Jassi for the next thirty minutes. By the end of the session, dad knew all there was to him. He knew Jassi's parents' names, their parents' names, employment details of his entire extended family, his food preferences, his drinking habits, the type of clothes he liked wearing, his marks in the 10th and 12th standard and every semester of college, and a whole lot more. Jassi had balked at the question about his dad's tax returns, and threatened to walk out of the interview when asked if he had ever had sex.

Through the glass door of the balcony, Akhil saw his dad shake hands with Jassi and pat him on the shoulder. The door opened and Jassi walked out, shaking his head in disgust. He stepped out of the apartment without looking at anybody.

Mr Arora came to Akhil and announced his verdict. 'Jaspreet is a little immature, but he should make for a good roommate. I don't think he will bother you much.'

Akhil smiled nervously. After this, he wasn't sure Jassi would even want to be his roommate anymore.

Luckily, Jassi laughed it off when Akhil stopped by his apartment in the evening to apologize for the interview. He had just one question for Akhil. 'When does your dad return to India, dude?'

'Get up, Akhil. I have been waiting for twenty minutes for you to get up. How much do you sleep?'

Akhil groggily rubbed his eyes to see his dad sitting next to him on the bed. He was wearing his blue Nike pyjamas and a striped yellow polo shirt. A green cap adorned his head. The excitement on his face was unmistakable. Akhil knew something wasn't right.

Akhil checked the time in his watch.

'Dad, what's wrong? It is just 7.'

The smile on Mr Arora's face grew wider. The last time Akhil had seen him this happy was when he had heard of his sworn enemy and lifelong competitor Bhallaji's son getting a campus job that paid half of Akhil's annual package.

'I made a new friend today. An American friend.'

As a bewildered Akhil rubbed his eyes trying to gain consciousness, Mr Arora started reciting his story. 'I woke up at 5. There was nothing to do, so I thought I would go out and get some fresh air. I crossed the road and walked for a little bit and came across a nice road with lots of lawns and flowers. I think it was your university. The buildings were old and had red brick exteriors that reminded me of Delhi University's North Campus. The place was deserted, but suddenly I saw a tall, strongly built man with a bald head and green eyes come jogging towards me. As he passed me, he waved and said "Hello, how are you doing?" Strangely, he did not even stop to hear my answer.'

'Now Akhil, if a nice man asks a question, I can't be rude and not answer. Maybe he thought that I was not going to reply which was why he kept going. I was so embarrassed. I am not rude, everybody knows that.'

'So I ran behind him. However, he was fast. Finally I managed to catch up with him, but I was out of breath by then.'

'I then shook his hand, said "Hi" and answered "I am doing fine, thank you for asking."'

'He smiled at me, but I think he was confused. I thought of making some more conversation, and told him that I was feeling a little constipated. I also told him that I couldn't sleep well last night, as the air-conditioner was very cold,' Mr Arora continued.

'At this he started laughing loudly, but Akhil, is it my fault if the airline food gave me constipation? You tell me?'

Akhil's jaw had dropped to the floor. He was seeing a new side of dad this week. Back home, he had been a drab person who had over the years talked to Akhil only when there was need to praise or scold him. Mostly the latter.

Mr Arora went on. 'We then sat on a bench and had a nice long talk. I forget his name. It was something with a 'd'. David? No, Douglas. I can't remember, and what's in a name anyway. He said he is a professor in the university. He is a very nice guy—jovial and fun loving. He told me a lot of stories about his students and the kind of things they do.'

Akhil was stunned. 'What department, dad? Tell me he is not in the Computer Science department. Oh God.'

'I don't know, Akhil. I will meet him again tomorrow. I will check then.'

Akhil's heart was thumping away like a Mahindra tractor gone wild.

Dad got up and rubbed his stomach. 'Okay I think I will have my motions now. Your mother's trick always works. Tea.'

Akhil sank back into his bed in horror as his dad went to complete his unfinished business.

Later in the morning, Akhil called up Priyank, their obnoxious neighbour Goyalji's famous son. The phone rang three times and an automated message came up. 'Hi, you've reached Perry.

Leave me a message and I'll call you right back.' Priyank was now 'Perry' with an American accent.

Akhil hung up. He had never encountered voice mail before, and wasn't quite prepared for the surprise. Ten minutes later, his phone rang. It was Priyank.

'Hi, I just got a call from this number.' Priyank said in a strong American accent.

'Hi Priyank, this is Akhil.'

'Oh, hi Akhil. How's it going, buddy? And don't call me Priyank, dude. I go by Perry now.'

'Oh I'm so sorry, Priyank...I mean PERRY. How have you been, man?' Akhil rolled his eyes. *THIS is the guy my parents want me to emulate?*

'I am well. So how goes the American experience, dude?' Perry's accent worked okay, save for some words that slipped past the Indian side of his tongue.

'It is okay, man. Just got here. Still figuring out things.' Akhil replied.

'That's awesome, dude. Well, good luck with your studies. Dad told me about your university. I hope that it is not entirely crappy, and you will get to learn some stuff. If not, what the hell dude? Even low ranked universities have hot chicks. Just find one and party, dude.'

Akhil sighed. A 'dude' per sentence! 'Sure Priyank. That's just the plan.' He didn't want to get into an argument with this guy. Their conversation was going to get filtered down to the Goyal household, where it would be spiced up before the Aroras were assaulted with deadly effect.

'Okay dude. Talk to you later,' said Perry and hung up.

Akhil smiled to himself. Perry sounded exactly what he

did not want to become. *Goyalji can keep singing songs praising his son.*

After lunch, Jassi's host Suresh suggested a trip to Walmart for their weekly groceries. Jassi had just woken up from his nap, and readily agreed. Akhil and his dad came by. They decided to drive to the Walmart store 10 miles away in Suresh's beat-up 1992 Toyota Corolla that he had bought from a senior for 1200 dollars for graduate students didn't have the money to spend on luxuries such as cars less than 10-years-old. This one was twelve.

Suresh looked at the boys gaping at his car and said, 'Space shuttle Discovery flew for 150 million miles. This baby's one lakh miles are nothing in comparison.'

The drive to Walmart took fifteen minutes. In the back seat, Akhil's dad had his eyes glued to the window, marvelling at the colourful signs, disciplined traffic, and fancy stores along the way. Jassi was on the window on the right side. Akhil spent his time alternating between observing his dad and his to-be-roommate go giddy with excitement.

Their collective jaws dropped as they entered the store. Walmart blew their minds away. Jassi whistled, 'Whoa! You could fit in a hundred small stores in here man. This place is huge.'

Suresh asked everybody to stay together. 'Don't stray too far. I don't want to spend an hour searching the store for you guys.'

Akhil and Jassi spent the next hour wide-eyed. Just the section on fruits and vegetables was massive. They were amazed at how big American fruits were. The apples were the size of tennis balls while tomatoes were as red as Pamela's swimsuit from *Baywatch*, and big like…well, never mind.

Mr Arora had disappeared somewhere, but Akhil was sure he would find his way back to the car eventually.

'Akhil. Here. Look at this, dude, this carton of 24 Coca-Cola cans for 2.5 dollars. About 120 rupees. One can for 5 rupees! Pinch me dude. Am I still alive, or have I gone to heaven?' shouted Jassi. Having heard so many stories about Walmart, for him this was a pilgrimage coming true.

Walmart had everything. EVERYTHING. Clothes. Stuff for pets. Electronics. Cycles. Paint. Guns. Jassi picked up a 5 dollars 'Go Noles' T-shirt referring to the FSU football team. (The Florida State Seminoles are the university's sport teams. Seminoles gets shortened to 'Noles' by cheering fans.) 'I will always treasure this as my first American purchase.'

Suresh rounded up his purchases. The bill came to 150 dollars for two weeks' worth of groceries.

'That's close to 7500 rupees for two weeks of supplies,' Akhil gasped. Jassi sighed. Suresh smiled, and addressed the newbies. 'You'll soon learn to stop converting dollars to rupees everytime you buy something.'

'What if we don't?'

'Then buddy, may God save you.'

Mr Arora joined them as they left the counter. He had a bulky shopping bag in his hand. 'Can't return to India empty-handed, can I? Your mom will kill me,' he winked.

In the evening, the boys attended an informal get-together for new students at Abhijit's apartment. Not everybody had come in yet, but there were already about twenty odd freshers, ready to embark on their American dream. The first round of instructions over, Akhil tried to recollect all their names in his head.

There was a couple from Mumbai—Leena Patel and Ambuj Gandhi. They were both in the Computer Science programme, and only seemed to talk to each other. They looked like they were either married, or uncomfortably close siblings. No one knew yet.

Kedar Godbole was another Mumbai boy. He had a triangular face with a prominent nose that stood tall like a proud skyscraper. He was tall and muscular, and could almost pass off as a hunk in some Tier-2 Indian city.

Then there was Priya Srinivasan, a tamil-brahmin girl from conservative Chennai. Just out of college. Shy.

Some seniors were also present. Dilpreet Singh had completed his Masters two years ago and was now working at one of the few technology companies in Tallahasseee. Nandita's friend Rashmi Chakraborty was close to completing her PhD in Geology.

Punjabis were in a minority in the room. Akhil could already see three distinct lobbies forming—the North-Indians, Andhraites, and Tamils. The Tamils outnumbered everybody else.

And there was Nandita herself who gave Akhil a warm hug as soon as she saw him, leaving him somewhat flustered. Akhil hadn't seen Nandita since they landed, and had been wondering about her whereabouts. Turned out she was staying with Rashmi, whose roommate had just graduated and moved from Tallahasseee.

Looking at the variety around him, Akhil thought, *This should be an interesting cultural experience.* Jassi smirked. 'So many madrasis, dude!'

The next morning, Sundar took Akhil and Jassi to the apartment leasing office. Akhil's dad went along.

The lady at the office was so white, her veins showed through her pale skin. She was talking on the phone with someone. They waited a few minutes, but the call dragged on. It sounded like an unhappy resident complaining about a clogged toilet.

After waiting for five minutes, Akhil's dad started getting restless. He cleared his throat. No response. He shuffled his feet, making as much noise as possible. She still didn't look at them.

Finally, he cut her conversation short and said, 'Hello Miss.'

Startled by the interruption, she looked up and said irritatedly, 'Sir, can you please wait outside? I'll be right with you.'

But Akhil's dad was pissed at her insolence. 'This is how they talk to paying customers?' He wanted to walk out immediately and try out the neighbouring apartment block, but Sundar reminded them that this was the cheapest option in the area. The four waited patiently outside her office.

A few minutes later, she appeared. 'Sorry to keep you guys waiting. Please come inside.' They followed her in. Her office had that smell from Sundar's apartment, the same unique mix of varnish, carpet, and wood.

'My name is Mindy. How can I help you guys?'

'Good morning, Miss Bhindi. My son here needs to rent an apartment.'

'I am sorry sir, it's Mindy.'

'Oh okay okay. I am sorry. I thought it was Bhindi.' Akhil and Jassi exchanged glances. Akhil knew this was just dad's way of showing his annoyance.

'It's okay, sir. Sure, we have a couple of apartments that just got vacated. Do you guys want to take a look now?'

'Sure,' Akhil and Jassi spoke up in chorus before Mr Arora could cause any more damage. Mindy got took out the keys from her desk drawer and led the rest out to show them the available apartments.

They passed by the swimming pool. There were a few people splashing about. They waved at Mindy and the boys. She waved back, flashing a wide ear-to-ear smile, and pearly whites. 'Looking good guys. How are you today?'

'Friends?' asked Akhil. By the affectionate display, Akhil guessed she must be close to them.

'Oh no, I don't even know them. They're probably visiting someone here.'

Akhil didn't get the show of emotion to strangers, but decided against probing further.

Mindy showed them the laundry room. It was right by the swimming pool, equipped with a bunch of washing machines and dryers. *No need for nagging maids who ran away without bothering to give any notice. No lines to leave clothes to dry. No hassle. Full convenience,* thought Akhil.

There was a Coke vending machine outside the washing room. Jassi was already looking forward to washing clothes while sipping the carbonated water and teasing the babes lounging in the pool anxiously waiting for him to join them.

Mindy stopped in front of an apartment.

'Here's the first option. It's a one-bedroom apartment. Nice and cozy, with a view of the pool, centrally air conditioned with heating, and a balcony, all for 600 dollars per month.'

They looked around. It was indeed a nice looking apartment. However, it had a single bedroom, so one person would have to live in the living room. Akhil didn't want to do it. Neither did Jassi.

'Do you have something bigger?' Akhil asked her.

'Yes, there's a two bedroom that just got vacated. I think it will be perfect for you. Let's check it out.'

The boys left the apartment and followed Mindy to the second one, located in the adjoining block of the building.

The two-bedroom apartment was big. There was a massive master bedroom with an attached bath, a smaller second bedroom, a living room, and a dining area which could easily serve as a third room. The rent was 800 dollars per month.

Jassi took Akhil aside. 'Dude, the apartment seems nice, but the rent is a bit high to share between two people. Maybe we can find more people to share the apartment. We get company, and the per-person cost will be lower.'

Akhil agreed with Jassi. 'I was thinking the same thing. There's enough space in here for three to four people. Let's check if there's anybody else willing to join in.' Sundar mentioned that Kedar was checking around for roommates. Problem solved.

Just one thing remained. Akhil's dad smiled confidently and gestured to them to let him do the talking now.

'We will take it. How much?'

Mindy looked confused for a second before realizing he was talking about the rent. 'Oh, the rent? It's going to be 800 dollars a month.'

'We will give 700.'

'I am sorry sir?'

'No no, there is no need to be sorry. 700.'

Mindy seemed clueless for a second. She rolled her eyes so high, Akhil feared she might cause irreparable damage to her vision. Luckily, they came back.

'All right sir. I can offer you 750.'

'720,' Mr Arora persisted.

'750.' She sounded confused by the impromptu round of negotiations, but held her ground

Mr Arora was going to make one last attempt, but Akhil spoke before things got any more awkward. 'We will take it. Thanks Mindy.'

'Great!' She heaved a sigh of relief. Mr Arora looked disappointed.

Two hours later, three co-renters signed the rental agreement. Kedar happily agreed to share the place. As per the negotiated deal, Jassi would take the master bedroom. Akhil would get the other bedroom, while Kedar would take the third semi-room. They could move into their apartment in two days. Mr Arora was annoyed at Akhil. He was sure he had Mindy. 'She would have gone down to at least 740, if not 730,' he said.

The roomies decided to go out to celebrate their new apartment. There was a Subway restaurant nearby. Akhil's dad did not come along. He was busy checking the construction quality of their to-be apartment. He had a lurking suspicion that Miss Bhindi was withholding some crucial information from them.

The Subway restaurant was a 5-minute walk from their apartment. It was their first time outside the University Club and the boys were dazzled by how refreshingly new everything was. Kedar and Akhil were excited about all the new things around them. Jassi was mesmerized. He reminded himself of his target to learn the American national anthem, *The Star Spangled Banner*, before classes started.

They finally made it to Subway and saw two hefty black girls behind the counter. Intimidated by their bulky frames and the nasty stories he had heard about black people, mostly on the online forums he loved to spend time on, Jassi almost ran out the door before Kedar restrained him.

The first girl approached them and spoke in a loud, manly voice, 'Is everything alright? How may I help you guys?'

Akhil opened his mouth to answer. It took his brain five seconds to register the accent, and then his English failed him. The words out of his mouth were a cryptic, 'Ummhgfdhr.'

Jassi was used to talking to Americans back at his Chandigarh office, though he wasn't quite sure if there were any African-Americans he had talked to. That girl's accent did seem a bit different.

'Hi. Are you having any vegetarian options?' Jassi asked her in his falting English. All those years of practice had failed to get his grammar perfectly up to speed.

'Sure. You could go for the Veggie Patty or the Veggie Delite.'

Jassi got about half of that sentence. The word 'delight' sounded better, so he asked for a Veggie Delite. The others nodded in approval.

'What bread, sir?'

'No no, that is fine. We will just be having Veggie Delite.'

'Sir, what bread would you like the Veggie Delite on?' She spoke with particular emphasis on the word 'sir' and her voice was now mildly threatening, as she pointed to the chart with a list of whole wheat, parmesan oregano, and other equally fancy sounding names.

Jassi selected the one that he thought she'd understand best. 'Italian.'

'Excellent. What veggies would you like?'

Tomato was easy. Onion was easy. Then there were a whole lot of things he hadn't seen ever.

He spotted something else he knew. 'I'll have capsicum as well.'

She sounded clueless. 'I am sorry?'

'Capsicum. Cap-see-cum?' Akhil pointed out with his fingers.

'Oh, you mean bell peppers?' Over the last five minutes, the tone of her voice had changed from threatening to amused, and now she just sounded sympathetic.

'Bloody angrez! They always say that Americans are uneducated. But I never knew they don't even know names of vegetables,' Jassi mumbled to himself in anger.

'Thanks.' Akhil made a mental note of saying bell peppers in the future. .

'Where are you guys from?'

'India.'

'Oh, new to the United States?'

'Yes. How did you know?'

She laughed loudly. 'Who's next?'

Kedar didn't waste much thought. 'I'll have the same.' This was enough excitement for the day.

The total came to fifteen dollars and forty-three cents. Akhil handed over a twenty-dollar bill and watched her patiently collect the change and hand back the precise balance amount, down to the last penny. It reminded him of the neighbourhood kirana store back home where the shopkeeper would hand back Cadbury eclairs candy instead of returning one or two rupee balances.

All three had the same sandwich. There wasn't much in it, thanks to the communication breakdown. Akhil nearly wept. 'Bloody, I paid 5 dollars for that. AND I AM STILL HUNGRY.' Nobody said anything. They just nodded in silent defeat. 'Let's not mention this to anybody, okay?'

The three pledged to avoid this place for at least a month. 'By then Beyonce will hopefully forget as well,' Jassi threw in a nickname for familiarity.

The next day the three MSketeers, which was the name Akhil came up with for their budding household, made their first trip to the University campus, which was a ten-minute walk from their apartment. Orientation was a few days away. The session would start officially on Monday after the orientation.

They soon reached the campus which wore a deserted look. Most people were still away for the break. The picturesque campus was spread over a significant area. Tree lined paths, buildings built in the Victorian style, manicured lawns, flowers they had never seen before, birds chirping away happily—it was beautiful.

They passed by a happy family presumably out to drop off their child to college. Husband, wife, and four kids. The happy white people smiled at the desi boys. The man wished them good morning.

The MSketeers looked around, surprised to see random strangers talking to them. Nobody back in India smiled at random, unknown people, unless they wanted to sell them something. The boys figured they must have made a mistake, and moved on, carefully avoiding the smiling family.

'Look at these people! Did you see how many kids they had? And people say that Indians don't know how to use birth control.' Kedar hadn't talked much till then, but now he was slowly opening up to his roomies.

They soon found the Computer Science building. The building also housed the Math department, which was Kedar's major. Over the next four hours, they finished off their paperwork, submitted health insurance documentation, vaccination records, got their first American bank accounts, and deposited their traveller checks in the bank.

The official work done, the three walked about the campus for some more time before heading back to the relative familiarity of University Club apartments. Their legs were creaking by the time they got home. America may be nice and shiny, but turned out you got tired here as much as you did back in India.

✈

'And I told him that I am the prince of a small Indian state of three million people, and he was so impressed, I thought his green eyes would drop out of their sockets.'

The room roared with laughter. Akhil's dad was describing

the account of his meeting with his American friend. It seemed like he had been on an exaggeration overdrive. Kedar, Jassi, Sundar, and Venkat were lapping it up. They had got together for tea at the MSketeers' new apartment.

'I told him we have a palace that is spread over two hundred acres, there are ten Rolls Royce cars in the garage, and that we have palenquins to take us from one room to the next. He believed everything I told him. My God, it was so funny.'

Akhil was scandalized. 'Dad, you can't do that. People are not that stupid here.'

'No no, Akhil. He was totally convinced. You underestimate your old man, son.'

'Dad, did you find out what department he is in? Or his name, at least?'

'Come on, Akhil. The details are not important. I have just two more days before I return. Let me develop a lasting relationship with my friend. Maybe he will become my pen friend and write letters to me once I have gone back to my kingdom in India.'

The room erupted once again. Akhil noticed Kedar wiping tears from his eyes. They were having fun, but Akhil was worried. This didn't seem right.

'He asked me if I travelled on an elephant. I, of course, said yes. His next question was if we had electricity in India yet. I never thought that people here would be so ignorant of our country. It took all my will-power to resist laughing when he asked if I had a harem.'

'Harem!' he exclaimed. 'I can't handle one wife, how will I handle a whole harem of bickering ladies?'

Akhil's eyebrows went up, but the rest of the audience

applauded. His dad was putting up a show tonight, and the boys were sure having fun.

Akhil looked at the group of people assembled around the room. His dad and Jassi were sitting on their new green coloured sofa with a long tear on the side. The same sofa they had transferred from the trash area a few hours back. It stuck out like a sore thumb against the cream-coloured walls of the room and light brown carpet, but it was free. For now, it was the only piece of furniture in their living room.

It was Venkat's suggestion. New furniture was too expensive, and people here discarded perfectly usable stuff for the smallest of flaws. This discarded stuff went on to adorn the houses of desi students.

Someone had whistled en route as they were transporting the heavy sofa, and Jassi wanted the earth to open up and swallow him. He did not want to be seen indulging in such cheap desi activities. 'How embarrassing is this, guys! We are people from respectable families.'

The next items the boys needed to procure from the trash were mattresses and tables. Until then they would continue to sleep on the carpet, which was hopefully thick enough for a good night's sleep.

✈

That evening, the three roommates went to a neighbouring Indian departmental store with Dilpreet, the friendly sardar next door. Warm and cordial, he had offered to take the boys along to Walmart and the Indian store everytime he went for his groceries.

His frozen paranthas had run out that day, so he asked the boys if they wanted to come along for their groceries. The Indian store was some 15 miles away, in a quaint market on the other side of town, flanked by a nail spa on one side, and a pet store on the other.

Dilpreet had one piece of advice before entering. 'Be nice to the owner, you'll be dependant on him for the next two years.'

'Sure sir,' the three responded in near-chorus and entered the store. Dad marched ahead of the group. He had a notepad out in his hand. There was serious work to be done.

The place was four full aisles of India bursting at the seams. Parle-G biscuits. Dettol soap. Godrej shaving cream. Coriander chutneys. They had everything. The boys had their lot of toiletries brought from home, but they attacked the food aisle with a vengeance. Frozen aloo paranthas were picked up, as were plain paranthas, chapatis, palak paneer, and dal makhani. Jassi picked up a chicken curry. They soon had two basket loads of foodstuff.

The Gujarati lady at the checkout counter smiled at them. 'Hello. New in town?'

'Hi! Yes, we just came to Tallahasseee,' Akhil replied.

'Oh okay. Welcome. We will hope to see you here often.'

The bill came to 160 dollars. *A little over 7000 rupees*, Akhil mentally calculated. Jassi whistled. Akhil's knees trembled, but he held onto the counter.

Kedar paid up. 'Let's settle the bill once we get home.'

'Just one minute.' Akhil's dad came to the counter, his notepad held high like a trophy.

'You guys are fleecing the poor kids. Thums Up bottles for 2 dollars? A packet of Maggi for 1 dollar? DVDs for 15 dollars?

Everything way above the retail price, even if you take into account some margin for import etc. Why don't you just make the students write blank checks to you every month? This is extortion!'

Dilpreet looked like he had just been hit by a truck. He knew you couldn't mess with the Indian store and live in this town. He and Akhil quickly took Mr Arora outside just when he was about to start reading from the list of prices he had compiled, with conversion to rupee prices and their printed MRPs.

Just one more day, and Mr Gyaneshwar Arora would be flying back to India, FOR GOOD.

Akhil spent the next day helping dad pack for his trip back to India. He was mellow. Even though his dad had a 'different' way of doing things, he had a knack for invariably being right in his judgement of things and people. Akhil remembered how he had always supported him and his sister in everything they did. All those fears of being alone, of his parents missing him and crying about him, came rushing back to Akhil. It was still less than a week since he had left home. He already used to wonder if his mom was still crying all the time. His last image was of her trying to hide her sobbing face in her sari pallu. He knew that dad was made of harder stuff though. He was the steadying influence in the family.

America was great, but it wasn't his country. People here were different. They talked differently. They behaved differently. Everything seemed sugar coated. Akhil hoped that one day he would get that sense of belonging in America, though he felt sure it would never be 100 percent. America may be his adopted home, but he would always be an Indian first.

The orientation session was to happen on Monday, still a couple of days away. Classes would start thereafter. He hoped that they would keep him busy enough not to leave any time for homesickness.

They managed to complete packing shortly before noon, and then went for lunch at Taco Bell, the famous Mexican fast food joint. It was a Saturday so Dilpreet came by to join them. On his recommendation, everybody opted for Burritos.

Dad took a bite of his Burrito and his bushy brows (it was clear where Akhil had inherited his thick Persian carpet eyebrows from) got within touching distance of each other. He laid the Burrito on his tray and opened up the wrap.

'Ha, I knew it! This is just Rajma wrapped in a roti. Dilpreet, you said they serve Mexican food here? So you're telling me we just paid 5 dollars for rajma wrapped in a lousy roti? This is so disappointing. Such a waste of money.'

Dilpreet smiled and wondered what he would say when he found out that Taco Bell also served kidney beans with rice. Rajma chawal. One of his classmates had once referred to the chain as Taco *Balle Balle*, for its closeness to Punjabi tradition.

Dad's flight was at 7 pm. Dilpreet and Akhil dropped him off to the airport. He was dressed in a hoodie he had purchased from Walmart, and formal black pinstriped trousers, held in place by a belt with a huge Harley Davidson buckle.

Just before departing, Akhil touched his dad's feet seeking his blessings for the journey ahead. Dilpreet followed suit. Dad hugged both of them. 'Dilpreet, I am leaving my little boy with you. Take care of him. The poor boy has never lived alone. I just can't stop worrying about him.'

Dilpreet promptly responded with, 'No worry, sir. I will take care of him.' Akhil couldn't help notice the earnest look on Dilpreet's face and thought he would do well in an elder brother role in one of those Bollywood family movies.

Mr Arora turned and quickly walked towards the security check before the two could see the solitary drop of tear that had made its way out of a corner of his eyes.

Dilpreet kept a friendly arm on Akhil's shoulder and they walked away. Farewells were the most heartbreaking aspect of American life, and this was just the start for Akhil. There would be many more to come.

Masters of Science

It was August 20, 2004. The Fall semester formally began with a departmental orientation session. Akhil, Jassi, and Kedar reached Love Building, which housed the Math and Computer Science departments. Jassi was sure the name of the building was a sign of things to come. The roommates wished each other luck and headed for their respective auditoriums.

Jassi and Akhil took their seats near the back of the hall. It wasn't too large, big enough for about 300 people. The session was going to begin in fifteen minutes. The hall was just about half-full, with people still trickling in. Some of the kids came in with loud music blaring from their headphones, some others were busy texting on their phones, and a girl came in with a head as colourful as a peacock's feathers, while there was another one with her left arm covered by a massive serpent tattoo.

Akhil was excited. 'This is great, yaar. I just hope the coursework is not going to be too tough.'

Jassi was excited as well, but for a different reason. He had already counted seventeen pretty girls with whom he wouldn't mind forming a study group. In his mind, he had them ranked and set up a priority list already.

Akhil noticed Jassi drooling, and nudged him. 'Oye Jassi, stop it man. Leave some girls for the others too.'

Jassi sheepishly responded with, 'Dude, is it my fault if the girls here are so pretty?'

Priya, the shy girl from Chennai, took the seat next to them. Jassi promptly shut up. Akhil noticed the seemingly inseparable Leena Patel and Ambuj Gandhi sitting together in a corner, whispering to each other.

It was time for the session to start. The hall was nearly full. The faculty members took seats in the front two rows. This gathering included both undergraduate and graduate students (In America, post-graduate students are referred to as graduate students). Akhil noticed a group of kids giggling away. They were Indian looking, but with pronounced American accents.

Must be ABCDs, he thought.

American Born Confused Desis. Second generation Indian-Americans who looked Indian but spoke and behaved like Americans. They weren't entirely American because of their brown colour and Indian upbringing by their first/second generation Indian parents, but they weren't really Indian because they didn't identify with the values Indian people talked of (including very often, their own parents). This gave rise to the whole conflict between their American and Indian identities.

Dilpreet had given Akhil, Jassi, Kedar, and Sundar a full lowdown on the terminology. The two-hour session had ended with an explicit warning never to use the ABCD term in public. 'People don't take kindly to that reference,' was his strict warning to the newbies.

Talking of terminology, Akhil and Jassi were FOBs. Fresh off the Boat. They didn't come by boats anymore, but the term had stuck.

The Indian overseas diaspora was primarily split into these two groups—FOBs and ABCDs. Young kids like Akhil came in with dreams in their eyes, but not much idea of how things worked in the US, and were known as FOBs. Most of what FOBs knew of America was knowledge gleaned from *Friends* reruns and Hollywood movies. Typical FOB behaviour consisted of converting any costs into rupees before making the final purchasing decision, speaking in accents and languages that nobody could understand, and a strict faithfulness to Indian food regardless of the remote corner of the country in which they may be present. All the dollar-to-rupee conversion also meant that FOBs were great at mental-maths, and could easily multiply three digit numbers in less than ten seconds.

Over the years, FOBs got assimilated into American society. They got their green cards, learnt the American national anthem, waited a few more years, gained political insights (and generally turned into Democrats), and became citizens. Meanwhile they had ABCD kids who were proud American citizens. It was technically impossible to go from FOB to ABCD. To be an ABCD, you had to be born in America. It was a bit baffling to newcomers, but it all made sense.

A sharp nudge in the shoulder from Jassi brought Akhil back to the present. Dr Sumit Singh, Head of the Computer Science department, had begun delivering his welcome speech to the students. Singh was something of a superstar in the local Indian community. Came to the US in the 70s, completed his PhD in a record three years, and hadn't looked back since.

He had dozens of patents in the field of computer architecture and his books were used as textbooks at colleges across the US.

Singh didn't waste much time speaking. He did a quick 'Welcome to FSU' followed by an introduction of himself and the department. He then handed over the mic to Dr Elizabeth Connor, a smiling old lady with wrinkled skin.

'She must be over a 100-years-old,' Jassi whispered to Akhil.

Wrinkled skin apart, Prof. Connor was warm yet professional in her address. As graduate advisor, she was the one who helped the entire batch plan out their coursework and eventually checked that they had fulfilled the criteria to get their degrees. She explained how the programme worked and gave out details of the criteria required to graduate.

The other professors were a mix of American, Chinese, and Indian—a racial distribution quite similar to the audience present. The session ended in an hour. All students were advised to schedule appointments with Prof. Connor to go over their coursework and plan the semester.

✈

Akhil met Prof. Connor at 1 pm. Fifteen minutes later, he walked out of her office looking like Sachin Tendulkar walking back to the pavilion after the ignominy of a first ball dismissal. Butterfiles were flying around his eyes, and he had no idea where they had come from.

Prof. Connor had gone through Akhil's college coursework and transcripts and identified some additional coursework that he would need to take at FSU as pre-requisites, given he hadn't studied those subjects as part of his Electrical Engineering.

This was a sudden and unexpected twist in the tale. She had mercilessly handed Akhil a list of seven undergraduate courses he would need to take in addition to his regular coursework. This effectively meant that his degree was now going to take at least two more semesters. He would need three years to complete his degree. All plans of graduating in less than two years had gone out the window. As Prof. Connor added each course to the list, a new butterfly started flying around Akhil's head. By the end of the meeting, he was numb to any more shock.

That evening, the group got together for dinner at Sundar's place. Everybody seemed happy. Jassi had managed to get a teaching assistantship position, as had Priya and Kedar. Jassi was going with the option of taking straight courses without doing a thesis and finish off his Masters next spring. Akhil seemed uninterested in the conversation. He was thinking of a plan to get out of the mess he had landed in.

Suddenly he had an idea.

The next morning, Akhil paid a trip to Prof. Connor's office armed with a bunch of certificates from his GATE exam (an apt name for an exam that served as the entrance test for admission into post-graduate enginering courses in India), that proved that he had indeed studied many of the extra courses she had asked him to take. As he walked the five hundred metres to Love building with heavy steps, his heart went through emotions of anxiety, hope, nervousness, and misery, on loop. The last time he had felt this nervousness was when those ruffians at IT-BHU had called him over for those fateful few hours to room no. 43 in the hostel. He hoped the outcome would be different this time, and nobody would make him do a striptease and then perform a naked mujra to Michael Jackson's *Thriller*.

Over in her office, Prof. Connor went through his list, and struck off four of the pre-requisite courses she had assigned to Akhil based on the evidence supplied to her. 'Looks like you have indeed covered much of the material for these courses,' was her comment to a delighted Akhil.

From his now misty eyes, Connor suddenly seemed like the kind Goddess Lakshmi. Akhil nearly got up to touch her feet as a mark of respect, but figured she might not understand what he meant, and stuck to a relatively cold 'Thanks a lot Professor.'

'For the database course, I want you to meet Professor Apostolov. He takes the course and will be able to confirm if he is okay for it to be waived.'

Akhil was hesitant. He had heard from other students that Prof. Apostolov had the demeanour of an African lion that had just escaped from captivity. He seemed like the type who would bite off your head in an instant.

He reasoned with himself. *Who knows? Appearances are deceptive. He may just turn out to be a friendly chap who will immediately sign off on the course waiver once I tell him that I have studied it all myself.*

Akhil knocked on the door of room no. 105, Apostolov's office.

'Come in.' The gruff voice sounded like a mix between Sylvestor Stallone and Amitabh Bachchan.

Akhil entered his office. 'Hello sir. My name is Akhil Arora. Professor Connor asked me to talk to you.'

'Oh sure. She talked to me about your case. How can I help you?' Rays of light reflected off his smooth, bald head.

Akhil told him of his problem and mentioned to him that he had worked on a couple of database intensive projects during his engineering, and that he had brushed up on the standard textbooks as self-study.

Apostolov looked at Akhil intently before answering, 'You know what Akhil; the problem is that self-study cannot substitute formal education. You miss many concepts. Besides, assignments and tests play a vital part in ensuring your grasp on the subject.'

'Sir, please. This might end up delaying my graduation by a semester. Is there anything we can do?'

'Okay, let me ask you a question. If you answer it correctly, I will waive the course requirement,' Apostolov offered with the look of a benevolent hunter throwing a piece of bait at a hapless animal blisfully unaware of what was going to happen next.

He continued, 'What is the second normalization form of relational databases?'

Akhil was not prepared for this. He had last picked up a textbook many months back, and all definitions were gone from his head. He hesitated as his brain refused to bring up the exact detail, whispered a silent prayer to lord Rama, licked his dry lips, and answered in a voice that wavered like a candle stranded in Hurricane Charley's path.

'The second normal form indicates a relationship between columns of a table and the primary key. I can't recall the exact definition though.'

Apostolov made a disappointed face, and answered his own question. 'A table is in the second normal form if every non-key field depends on the entire primary key.' The tone was triumphant and unmistakably sarcastic.

Akhil replied in a shaky voice, 'Yes, you are right. That's what I was trying to say.'

'Of course I know I am right. You didn't know the definition, so I think you should take the required course. It will help brush up on your concepts.'

'Please sir,' Akhil pleaded.

'I think we are done.'

'Sir, please. If you can give me some more time, I'll brush up on my definitions and we could do this again.'

Apostolov's face turned grim, and Akhil felt his green eyes drilling holes inside his body. 'Listen, buddy. I don't know how things work where you come from, but here a NO means a NO. I've told you what my decision is already and I'm afraid I won't be able to change it. You need to take this course and pleading with me can't help do anything about it.'

Akhil got up and muttered a dissapointed 'Thanks.' He felt ashamed of himself. The desperation to get the course waived had got the better of him. *This won't happen again*, he told himself. For now, whatever happened in Apostolov's office was going to stay here. It was too embarrassing to share with anyone.

The mission was not a total failure though. Akhil now had only three pre-requisite courses to take on top of his graduate course work. He could probably still cover up by taking a few additional courses, and working through the summer semester.

Akhil next met the instructor for the Computer Literacy course for which he was going to be a teaching assistant. Things were finally falling in place. There was a week to register for courses for the semester. He was going to 'proctor' tests for the

Computer Literacy course, which was just a fancy word for supervizing students while they took the test. The assistantship would pay most of the tuition fees, while his stipend would cover his living expenses and some more to spare.

Over the next few days, the seniors helped the incoming batch decide on their courses.

'Advanced Unix Programming is going to be very tough. Keep it for later.'

'Advanced Operating Systems is not available in spring, so plan accordingly.'

'Professor Amit Kumar has funding available for a research assistantship. Try to impress him in his Algorithms course this semester, which will help get that Research Assistant position in spring.'

'Computer Security is an easy course, so expect all the hot chicks to be there.'

It was all a bit chaotic for the newcomers. Not only did they need to come to terms to life in a new country and culture, they also had to balance the nuances of a new educational system where one decided one's coursework and had to do some strategic planning for the entire programme. Back home, most colleges still had mostly fixed syllabi, except for a few optional subjects. This was stressful, to say the least. A wrong move here could easily come back to bite you later when you were trying to graduate.

Among the senior batch, Anil Sisodia was turning out to be a very helpful mentor to the Computer Sciences group. Akhil, Priya, and Jassi had their courses planned out. Akhil had gone for two of his pre-requisite courses on Databases and Algorithms. His third course was Computer Networks, taught by Prof. David Yu. Jassi took Computer Security and was quite looking forward to it, in anticipation of all the ladies expected to be in the class. He would also be on the Computer Networks course, which was one of the mandatory courses. Priya was in that course as well.

Registration completed. Fees deposited. Classes would begin in a week.

On the first day of classes, Akhil woke up at seven, got ready, and had a sumptuous breakfast of a microwaved hashbrown patty inside two slices of the multi-grain bread they had got from Walmart, topped up with a cheese slice, tomatoes, and a pinch of the MDH chat masala Jassi had brought from home. His first class was for the Algorithms course, at nine.

He bowed before the idols of Rama and Sita he had installed in his room as a makeshift temple and prayed to the Gods to make this a worthwhile experience. Jassi was still snoring away in his room. His first class was later in the afternoon.

As Akhil walked on the road to the campus, he approached a small intersection. Just as he was about to cross, a pickup truck pulled up. Akhil hesitated and moved back. The truck also stopped. Akhil was confused what to do, so he waited. Nobody moved for a minute. Akhil decided to wave to the truck to drive past first. An angry head emerged out of the driver's window. It was a heavily built white guy with a shaved head. He shouted a profanity at Akhil and asked him to cross first. 'Move, you asshole,' were the carefully thought out words.

American drivers are paranoid of pedestrians. Most of them would rather stop and wait for them to cross the road than risk hitting them and going bankrupt paying damages.

Akhil hesitatingly crossed the road. The angry car driver honked loudly and drove on, giving Akhil the middle finger as he breezed away from sight.

Akhil was in the campus now, which bore a much different look from last week. The place was buzzing with activity. Young girls and boys were rushing for their classes. Some were talking on their mobiles as they walked, and there were many others with headphones plugged in their ears. Some of the girls were wearing barely-there shorts that revealed their slender, smooth legs, and walking in what closely resembled the hawai-chappals from back home. They called them flip-flops here.

Akhil heard a voice in front of him.

'Mom, Aparna can go to hell. I don't care how much she scored on her SAT test. Ten points more than me is not such a big deal.'

Akhil had found the source of the voice. It was a girl walking a few feet ahead of him talking to someone on her phone. She was clearly of Indian origin, likely an ABCD. She was very different from the fashionable crowd around her though. She had a tired look on her face and her eyes seemed swollen, perhaps from a night spent studying. She was wearing a crumpled T-shirt and plain blue jeans and walked with about as much grace as a polio-afflicted deer. She looked like she had slept in the same clothes, woken up and headed straight to college.

'No mom, I am not being disrespectful. Why must you keep comparing me with her? Maybe I *should* turn into Aparna and find a white boy to sleep around with? You have no idea of the sort of stuff that girl does.'

Akhil was listening intently, his curiosity piqued.

'Okay ma, no need to get so worked up. I am getting late for class. I have to go now. Sat Sri Akal.'

She sighed and kept her phone in the back pocket of her jeans. She turned around slightly and saw Akhil staring at her. She gave a nervous smile and quickened her pace.

Akhil reached his classroom and settled into a desk in the second-last row. People were still trickling in. The room itself wasn't much different from the classrooms back home. There was an overhead projector for presentations, a blackboard, and a table for the professor. His classmates were an eclectic mix. He noticed a very pretty Indian girl fidling with her phone. There was a group of Chinese students in the front row nervously awaiting the start of the class, and a couple of other Indian kids busy discussing *American Idol*.

The door opened and in walked two huge white guys. They were both over six feet tall, their heads were shaved and they were built like wild buffaloes. Akhil recognized one of them with a dismayed look. He had met him about half an hour back, while crossing the road en route to class. He was that pickup driver from the road intersection.

The two surveyed the room. *He* noticed Akhil, laughed loudly, and whispered something in the ear of his mate, who then turned to stare at Akhil. He came up to Akhil, bowed slightly in mock respect and did a *namaste*. As the entire class watched the show, he said 'thank you, come again' in what was a poorly imitated Indian accent. He then laughed loudly and did a high-five with his mate.

At that moment, the professor entered the class and closed the door behind him. The two took seats next to Akhil.

'Good morning class. My name is Amit Kumar and I will be your instructor for the Algorithms course.' The professor was young and had a mild Indian accent. He was an FOB.

The Buffalo Brothers

'I am going crazy, man. This is bloody hard.'

Akhil and Priya turned to Jassi, who was about to slam his head into the flat-screen monitor of the computer lab PC. It was two in the morning and the three were working on a networking assignment due for submission the day after. Two weeks into the first semester, and they had their hands full of homework.

Classes had started in full earnest. The Chinese professor Yu seemed jovial, but he was in reality a hard taskmaster. For his first lecture, he had walked into the class, run through a thirty slide long presentation, assigned two chapters to read for the next class in two days, and next week they had an assignment to implement the TCP Internet protocol in five days.

This was very different from his experience of Indian colleges. Akhil remembered his classes back in Delhi as monologues so boring, they put the drab regional songs and dance shows on Doordarshan to shame. Just about three people in the class of eighty would pay attention, and the others would copy the assignments of these dedicated few when due. A week before the exam, textbooks would be opened, digested over successive night-out sessions, and then regurgitated on the exam papers. The students got their degrees, the teachers thought they were teaching, and everybody was happy as long as the kids got through campus placement season with a confirmed job offer.

America was diametrically opposite. The professors were young and energetic, laying a lot of emphasis on research. Courses were not as much about cramming theory as applying it. Students were made to work hard for their degrees. Plagiarism was a strict no-no that led to disciplinary action against offenders. More importantly, most people were in college because they wanted to, and not because their parents had a competition going on with a Bhallaji or a Goyalji.

Akhil had been going to the lab every night after dinner and staying on until the wee hours, working on his never-ending coding assignments. The seniors had asked them to wait until Thanksgiving to buy a laptop. They told them one could get some good deals on merchandize on that day, even if it meant lining up outside stores in the dead of the night, and struggling to avoid being trampled in stampedes once the sale opened. Until then, the computer lab was to be his second home.

The practical nature of assignments was turning out to be the problem for the moment. 'This Yu, he is making me go crazy. Will he make us implement all the concepts he teaches? Is this a bloody joke?' Jassi was fuming now. 'How am I going to find time for all those pretty ladies if this continues?'

Priya sighed. At her college back in Chennai, she had spent four years studying Computer Science and had never had to write software code. Not a single time. Now suddenly faced with this mammoth assignment, she was nearly in tears. It was not without reason that the major Indian technology companies cribbed about freshly graduated engineers being unemployable.

'Guys, it is quite late. Let's head back and resume tomorrow.' Akhil was tired now, and having a couple of frustrated people in the lab was not helping. Jassi had already started mumbling Punjabi curses.

The harried geeks walked back to their apartments. The 10-minute walk was quite pleasant at this time. The tree-lined paths were calm and serene. There was an exhilarating nip in the air. As expected, the campus was empty, except for a couple of girls in athletic gear who suddenly ran past them, out for a 2 am jog.

'Dude, look at these girls running at this time! These people are crazy.' Jassi watched the girls with a dreamy look in his eyes as they ran into the distance, their ponytails bouncing behind them.

That night, Akhil dreamed of getting perfect grades in all of his courses that semester. Jassi had a dream where the ponytailed girls running on campus stopped by their apartment asking for a Coca-Cola. One thing led to another, and soon they were naked in bed with the Jazzminator.

✈

'Yo Akeel, do you guys have electricity in India yet? Do you have cars?' Akhil shook his head in dismay. Algorithms classes had turned out into ragging sessions for him. He had managed to find out the names of the Buffalo Brothers—Jim and Brad. The two sat through the class like bored zombies at a Sunday mass, but came prepared with a new topic to deride Akhil before every class. Last week they wanted to check if he was *Moslem* ('Your guys are all Moslems, aren't they?' they had asked), and wanted to know why he wasn't wearing a turban.

The week before that, they came in curious about how Indians did their morning business. They had apparently seen an instructional video on YouTube and had been fascinated by the white-expat demonstrating how to squat on an Indian-style toilet seat.

Akhil noticed that the two never messed with the other Indians in class. He thought maybe it was because they were all ABCDs, and he was the only one who spoke with an Indian accent, besides the young professor Kumar, who had also come from India for his PhD from Columbia University, before joining as a faculty member here a year ago. Or maybe they had a special love for Akhil.

'Yo dude, cat got your tongue? You don't like us? Why aren't you answering?' Brad prodded him.

The cat reference stumped him, but Akhil responded. 'No Brad, we don't have electricity in India. My life changed after coming to America. Thanks to lamps, I am seeing the world in a new light now.' Akhil shrugged his shoulders in mock dismay. He knew there was no point explaining anything to these guys. The two went silent for a minute as they contemplated their next move.

Akhil noticed the pretty ABCD girl in the class giggle as she fiddled with her mobile phone. Brad finally came up with a response a minute later, in that ridiculous Indian accent. 'Thank you. Come again.'

After the class, the Indian girl walked up to Akhil and introduced herself. 'Hi, my name is Aparna.'

'Hi. Myself Akhil,' he replied. You can take an Indian out of India, but it's extremely hard to take Indian-English out of Indians.

'Nice to meet you, Akhil. I see you're doing quite well in the class.'

Akhil smiled. She was even prettier up close.

'Listen, don't mind Jim and Brad. I known them very well. They behave like dicks sometimes, but they mean no harm. They're just messing with you, having watched that stupid *Harold and Kumar* movie a bit too many times.'

'Okay thanks. That's good to know. To be honest, those guys do scare me sometimes.'

She laughed. 'No silly. Don't worry about those two. They are just paper tigers. All bark, no bite.'

Her phone rang. She looked at the flashing screen and waved a goodbye to Akhil, 'I'll talk to you later.' Akhil was suddenly reminded of the ABCD girl he had overheard arguing with her mom on the first day of classes.

✈

That evening Akhil stopped by Dilpreet's place with some questions around his courses and there *she* was, the girl from the first day, still bearing that same beaten down, crumpled look from the first time he had seen her. Akhil had a lurking suspicion she was still wearing the same clothes from that day.

Dilpreet introduced her. 'Akhil, this is Devika Singh. She is a good friend of mine, and is currently in the pre-med programme, preparing to be the best doctor in America.'

Akhil smiled at her. She recognized him, and returned a nervous smile.

Turned out Devika's dad was a prominent surgeon in Atlanta. Her mother was a housewife. They were from India, and had met Dilpreet at one of the Sikh community gatherings at the local gurudwara. Dilpreet had known Devika for the last two years, and she regarded him like an elder brother.

Devika was worked up over something, and was cribbing about her parents to Dilpreet.

'I scored 1590 out of 1600 in my SAT tests, and mom still hasn't got over it. "Why wasn't it 1600? How could you goof up? How will you become a surgeon now?" she says. Nothing is enough for them. If I get an A grade, they ask me why I didn't get an A+. If I get an A-, it's like someone died in the family.'

'I told them I need independence to make my decisions, and guess what dad told me? He said "Sure Devika you can become anything you want, as long as it is a type of surgeon."'

Dilpreet laughed loudly. 'I think all Indian parents are like that. My mom nearly killed me when I suggested that I try becoming a journalist.' He chuckled at the thought of what might have been.

'I sometimes feel like I live in a madhouse. Then they keep comparing me to that stupid Aparna, whose father came to the US with my dad. He is also a surgeon and my parents have some sort of contest going with them, constantly comparing our grades and performance in anything we do. But they conveniently forget that Aparna's parents let her choose Computer Science and not kill herself to get into medical school.'

Her voice was getting louder with each sentence. This was clearly a touchy topic for her.

'Today, she called me again with news about this paper that Aparna has apparently got published in an academic journal, asking when was I going to *start showing some results*. That's when I got really pissed and threw up a storm, which ended in her hanging up on me with another of her dramatic lines — "I can't understand where we went wrong in our upbringing to land up with this disrespectful child."'

Devika sighed loudly. 'She is crazy. Do you know what she said when she saw an Indian kid on *American Idol*? "Who are these kids wasting time singing on reality shows? Don't they have to prepare for their SAT? How do their parents let them waste their lives on this stupid song and dance?" She just can't think beyond SAT and med school.'

Devika managed a slight laugh at the hilarity of the situation.

Akhil let out a soft whistle, thinking that Devika's mom made his mother look tame in comparison, though he had his share of similar frustrated moments with her. He soon realized that Devika was probably talking about the same Aparna in his Algorithms class. It was turning out to be a small world after all, with Indian parents in India and America having a lot in common with each other.

✈

Two weeks later, Jassi was in love.

He had taken a fancy to one of his classmates in the Computer Security class. He didn't know her name yet, but he was smitten. She had the face of a happy angel just returned from a secret misson to save a small planet in a remote galaxy. Her skin was as smooth as the satin sheets on which Jassi imagined himself rolling around with her. His heart nearly stopped every time she laughed while talking to her friends. The only problem was, Jassi was never able to eavesdrop on their conversations. He did not understand Chinese. She hardly spoke English.

Luck was on his side. The kind professor split up the class into groups of three for a semester long ongoing project. Jassi got paired with Nigel, a smiling black man, and *her*. Jassi was sure that this was a sign. Things were just meant to be.

The three stayed back after class for a discussion to plan the project work. Her name was Vivian. 'Such a beautiful name,' Jassi told her. He was a bit disappointed that they couldn't just be two people in the group. But he had to be courteous to the black man too.

'Hi dude. My name is Jazz.'

'Yo Jazz, 'sup Bud? I am Nigel.' Nigel had a musical tone to his deep voice, like he had come with a factory-fitted subwoofer in his throat.

They got talking.

'So Jazz. Where you from?' Nigel asked.

'India.' Jassi answered, and turned to his ladylove. 'Where are you from Vivian?'

She smiled nervously. 'I am from Chh-ina.' The English was broken and heavily accented.

Nigel again interrupted, as Jassi anxiously waited for Vivian to confess her love for him. 'So Jazz, how do you like it here?'

'It's cool, dude. America is much better than India.' Jassi replied to Nigel in a slightly annoyed tone while staring at

Vivian, who was tying up her hair. He had half a mind to ask her not to, *they look better that way*. He wasn't here to chit-chat with the dude about India, or anything for that matter, especially when there was Miss China sitting in front of him.

'Okay dude. I've gotta scoot for another class now. Laters.' Nigel got the hint, and was off. Jassi was finally alone with Vivian. The classroom was now empty. He moved closer to her.

She got up. 'I have go. Friend waiting.'

Jassi smiled. *She likes me, but is just playing hard to get.*

✈

Akhil was sittting in the living room watching *Everybody Loves Raymond* with a cup of tea, when there was a loud knock on the door.

It was Nigel.

'Yo dude. Wassup? Is Jazz around?' Nigel spoke in that musical voice of his.

Jassi stepped out of his room. Since that first meeting a few weeks ago, he had gotten along well with Nigel.

On this day, Nigel had stopped by to hand over some notes to Jassi. Akhil invited him to tea, and he happily accepted the offer. 'Sure man. If that ain't too much bother for you.'

'Oh no problem. There's some more tea in the kitchen. Let me get some for you.'

Akhil returned with tea for Nigel, along with a bowl of chocolate chip cookies. These were a recent discovery, and Akhil had not yet had his fill of the delicious but calorie-rich snack.

'Thanks dude. I appreciate it.' Nigel grabbed his cup of tea and a cookie.

They got talking, starting with introductions.

'Well, myself Akhil. I passed out of my college back in India this year and am now here for my Masters,' Akhil beamed.

Nigel made an awkward face, and soon burst out laughing. 'Christ. Dude, what was that? You passed out of college? We generally just graduate. Your school must've been pretty bad.'

He noticed Akhil's stung face and apologized. 'I am sorry guys. Guess it must be a cultural thing. You'll learn,' he smiled.

'Gosh, it must be tough for you guys to stay so far from your homes in an alien country,' He said breaking the awkward silence a minute later.

Jassi replied, 'Dude, I don't miss India at all. America is everything India is not. Everyone is so nice here. The water is clean. The air is clean. The police does its job efficiently. In India, there is so much crime, so much dirt, corruption, and what not. The whole system is rotten. If I had my way, I would line up all the politicians and shoot them. They are the ones to blame for the state the country is in at the moment.'

'Besides, the girls are all so hot here,' Jassi winked at the others.

'Yea man, I saw you got eyes for that Asian chick,' said Nigel laughing out loudly.

He continued, 'Surely it can't be that bad. America has its own problems, you know.'

Akhil spoke now. 'I'm with you on this, Nigel. America is great, but it is difficult acclimatizing to a new culture. There are so many differences in how things work here. America is nice and welcoming, but I miss India. Despite its problems, it is the country where I have lived all my life. Besides, like you said, every country has its problems. India just got independence

57 years ago. We will get there eventually.'

'That's my man.' Nigel high-fived Akhil.

Strangely, Akhil felt an obligation to defend India. This was a new feeling for him. He had himself felt some helplessness about the pathetic conditions back home, but now he felt like he had to come to his country's aid. Now suddenly, it was like he was representing India and had to ensure that Americans had the correct picture of the country in their minds.

'Whatever, dude. India sucks.' Jassi obviously had no such expectations of himself.

They were a month into the semester. Akhil's expenses had increased manifold due to one thing mainly—coffee. It let him turn into a nocturnal creature that slept every night after three and then woke up by seven to go for classes. His eyes had turned a permanent shade of red.

He had been doing about average until now. His assignment submissions had been good, but not great. There was a lot of ground to be covered. FSU was testing him thoroughly.

The Buffalo Brothers had toned down after the initial few weeks, though occasionally they came up with stupid jibes at Akhil. Just yesterday, Brad had stopped Akhil in the building corridor. 'Yo Akeel, how do you say "I have a huge dick" in Indian?' Akhil had walked past him without a response, as the two high-fived each other behind him.

Straight 'A' grades weren't going to come easy. There was a lot of work required to get there. Goyal uncle's obnoxious smirk was still fresh in his memory. He had to prove him wrong.

He had to prove his parents wrong. He just had to succeed.

Meanwhile, his teaching assistant work had begun. For now his only responsibilities included supervising the Computer Literacy tests and grading answer sheets. This was supposed to take twenty hours of his time every week, but in reality, it took slightly less effort. He also got a room as his office, shared with another teaching assistant. Not a bad deal in exchange for not having to pay any tuition fees, and getting a salary in addition.

It was the day of the test on MS Excel skills. Akhil entered the test lab. He knew students would start trooping in soon. He was supposed to check their names against the day's schedule, look at their IDs to match their photos, assign them a workstation, and start the test. An hour later, he would collect answer sheets, lock the room, and be done with it.

It was an easy batch. Just about 10 students. Akhil was glad that there were no 'weirdos'. No one coming in with loud music blaring out of headphones. Nobody with even a pierced tongue.

The hour went by slowly. Akhil tried reading up on news from back home on rediff.com but got exasperated by the abundance of stories on murders, rapes, and road rage related incidents. He closed the browser and sat back in his chair, looking at the students busy taking their tests. His mind soon wandered elsewhere.

Nandita had dropped in yesterday evening for a quick tea session. She was doing well, busy with her work and assignments, and getting along nicely with her roommate Rashmi. Akhil had been content watching her speak. Others might have found her loud and boisterous, but to Akhil every word coming out of her mouth was like a joyous note from the flute of world-renowned Hariprasad Chaurasia. As she gorged on the chocolate chip cookies Akhil had served, he had felt the sweet taste in his mouth. It was a wonderful feeling for him.

He already looked forward to meeting her at next week's Freshers' Party.

His first two months in America had been an interesting experience. He thought of the various characters he had come across so far. He had met ABCD girls—Devika and Aparna—and discovered their strenuous ties. There were the Buffalo Brothers, Brad and Jim, who had taken a fancy to him, never losing an opportunity to ridicule him. The inseparable Ambuj and Leena had still not opened up, though Akhil saw them often in the department. He still wondered if they were siblings, or dating each other.

He had called up home last night and spoken to mom and dad. Dad's first question had been, 'So how is your Miss Bhindi?' He recalled the crazy moments in the first week with dad. Akhil still didn't know the identity of the professor his dad had befriended.

Akhil and the others had received their Social Security Number (SSN) cards in the mail within a few weeks of applying for them. One's entire life history could be tracked with this one number. Everything was connected to the SSN number utilities account—mobile phone, credit cards, banking, employment history etc. Contrastingly in India, it had taken Akhil five months to receive his passport after numerous visits to the passport office, chai-paani (aka bribes) to sundry babus, and a trip to the police station to prove his existence. There had been a point where he had wondered if after all the hard work gone in getting his admission to FSU, he might not be able to travel to the US because a babu in the passport office had developed a liking for his file and didn't want to let go of it.

Akhil came back to his senses with a start as someone clapped loudly in his ears. A bored looking student was standing in front of him, staring at the Indian teaching assistant slumped into his chair deep in thoughts. The rest of the class was now giggling. Akhil told the students to focus on their tests, collected the answer sheet of this student, and he marched out of the room humming a Pink Floyd song.

Gradually the room emptied. Akhil was done for the day.

✈

Jassi got up feeling good. He had dreamed of being in that summer house by the beach in *American Pie 2*. The party was rocking and all the girls seemed to have picked him for the night. It had got a bit wild and Jassi had to work hard to satisfy all of them, but he managed all right. Nothing was impossible for the Jazzminator.

As he walked to campus wearing a T-shirt that read 'I'm so great, I am jealous of myself', there was a spring in Jassi's step. America was awesome and he was loving the experience so far. It had been an excellent initial couple of months. Every girl he had met so far seemed to hit on him, flashing warm smiles as soon as they saw him look at them. He knew they were all going to be crazy about him. Now all Jassi had to do was stand with open arms, and the girls were going to just line up.

He looked around him. Maybe it was his sense of dressing or his confidence and charming personality, but there were already half a dozen pretty girls that Jassi was sure were eyeing him with hungry looks. He sized them all up. First there was this Chinese girl in pink stockings and foot high heels, pretty but walking funny, like there was a rat inside those stockings. A hot white girl with the body of a slim hourglass. Another sexy Latino wearing a short skirt that revealed her gorgeous, buttery-smooth legs.

The stars were lining up. He was meeting Vivian at the library in thirty minutes.

Nigel had come up with a master plan. The three were to get together for a project discussion, and Nigel offered not to show up to give Jassi that opportunity to make a move on the pretty Chinese girl.

Jassi had been waiting for about ten minutes when he noticed Vivian approaching in the distance and waved at her. He had taken one of the tables meant for students who wanted to work together on projects or assignments.

Vivian came over to the table. She looked around anxiously. 'No Nigel?' she asked.

'Umm, no he had some work but asked us to carry on.'

'We reschedule?' She didn't seem very excited.

'No, no, it is okay. I will share our notes with him.'

'Okay,' she replied nervously.

They opened their notebooks and continued from where they had left off the last time. Vivian had many smart ideas, but her English was a problem. Jassi had to pick up her broken words and extrapolate them to form sentences.

An hour passed. Jassi was getting bored now. She was business-like, and brushed aside any personal questions with monosyllables.

Jassi got up to stretch his legs. 'I am tired. Let's resume next week'

'Okay, that fine.'

'I am hungry. Let's grab a coffee?' Jassi made one last try.

'Uhh...' She looked worried. Jassi thought he saw a spot of bother on her divine face.

'Okay we go,' she finally said after thinking for a minute.

They got out of the library and started walking to the nearest Starbucks outlet.

A few feet away from the Starbucks, a Chinese man appeared out of nowhere and started talking to Vivian. Jassi had no idea what he was saying. It was all Chinese, but he sounded angry. Vivian retorted, again in anger. He got quite mad. Vivian also seemed angry.

He said something, and Vivian stormed off. The angry man followed her, still mumbling something.

Jassi had watched all this, his mouth wide open. The angry man had pointed at him once while shouting at Vivian, but apart from that he had ignored Jassi throughout the discussion. *Could have at least had a round of introductions?* he wondered.

Jassi was confused about what had just happened. *Maybe the man was her father and was against inter-racial marriages.*

Later that week Vivian got her study group changed to another one comprising three bumbling Chinese girls. Jassi apologized to himself for his lack of judgment. *Should have stuck to American women. You just can't trust anything made in China.*

When in Rome

It was September 28, 2004, the day of the rather belated freshers' party organized by the Indian Student Association. The University ballroom had been booked for the party, which was one of the biggest events conducted by the Indian Student Association all year.

Akhil and the rest of the gang decided to go dressed in traditional wear. Akhil had brought along a couple of fancy kurta pajamas especially for such occasions. Jassi had nothing to do with it. He had left Indian wear behind, and was wearing his Levi's jeans with a black T-shirt that said in big white letters, 'FBI—Female Body Inspector'.

Akhil got dressed in his red kurta with embroidered patterns and a churidar pajama along with the kolhapuri chappals he had bought from Chandni Chowk just for such desi occasions. The pajama had a zipper, and Akhil marvelled at this fine example of human innovation. Kedar also found a kurta pajama for the occasion, though not as elaborate as Akhil's.

The roomies were standing outside their apartment waiting

to be transported to the venue by the seniors plying their cars back and forth. A group of pretty girls in workout gear passed by. One of them remarked, 'Wow, you look like Indian princes.' Akhil blushed, Jassi mumbled, and Kedar shouted 'Thanks' behind them.

The party was fun. The organisers had arranged a full dinner for which everybody had contributed 10 dollars. The incoming batch was about fifty strong, and each one of them got a chance to come on the stage and give a quick introduction.

Akhil hadn't met many of the people there. He knew the ones in University club, but there were many others who lived in other parts of the campus. In all, the gathering was an eclectic mix of people from all parts of India, majoring in mostly science and engineering subjects, with some MBAs thrown in the mix. The Tamil and Telugu camps seemed stronger than Akhil had thought earlier. There were barely a handful of North-Indians in the gathering. He already knew all of them.

He was more interested in one person though. Nandita came in late, and took Akhil's breath away. She was wearing a blue silk sari with zardozi work on it. She waved at Akhil from the entrance. Kedar let out a soft whistle. She came over to their group. Akhil was thankful she didn't grab him like she had at the last get-together.

'So, who is this handsome guy I can't even recognize?' she winked at Akhil.

'So says the woman who has come dressed like it's her wedding?' Kedar teased Nandita.

'Don't worry guys. You'll probably see me dressed up like this only once a year or so. Gosh, I can't even breathe in this heavy sari.' Nandita grabbed the glass of Coca-Cola Akhil was sipping from and gulped the drink down in one go.

'Don't think I'll be able to stay for long. There's this stupid assignment due on Monday that I need to complete, but I had to come see you,' Nandita said to Akhil, whose face turned a delicate shade of pink matching her nails. He was not used to pretty girls talking about him like this. Or, in fact, talking about him at all.

Akhil was disappointed. He had hoped to spend some time with her that evening. 'Miss Busybee, try finding some time for me sometime.'

'Sure, let's get together some weekend. Maybe a movie?' she replied.

'Cool.' This worked for him.

Dinner was a sumptuous spread comprising shahi paneer, rajma masala, tandoori chicken, aloo gobhi, and vegetarian biryani courtesy the local Indian restaurant.

The dance floor was now open. One of the seniors was manning the station, playing standard Bollywood hits from his laptop. A bhangra number came up. Nandita grabbed Akhil's hand and took him to the dance floor. They danced for a little while before she realized it was time to leave, and Rashmi was waiting outside.

Nandita looked at a profusely sweating Akhil and teased him, 'Oye hoye, My Punjabi hero. How many left feet do you have? Was this the first time you have danced? Akhil was a bit embarrassed at her observation as he dropped her off to the parking lot, where Rashmi was impatiently smoking a cigarette while awaiting her roommate.

When in Rome

Akhil had indeed never danced before, but with Nandita, he wanted to try out everything.

✈

The next morning as Akhil got out of the apartment to walk to the computer lab to work on those never-ending assignments, he met the dashing senior, Anil Sisodia, loading his car.

'Hi Anil, where are you off to?'

'Oh hi Akhil. Just a quick day trip to St George's beach. We spend too much time studying, but don't realize that we need some off time as well. There's still some space in the car. Do you want to come along?'

'Umm...'

'Come dude. There's always going to be time to study. And you look like you could use a break.'

'Uh okay. I'll come.' Akhil had a splitting headache from last evening's party, which had ended up in an impromptu drinking session at Venkat's place. Akhil had tasted the first beer of his life. He was no more the *beergin* he used to be in India. The drums banging away in his head told him that he could surely use an outing.

In the car were Anil's flatmates, Akhilesh and Ruksh. All three were Computer Science majors. Anil and Akhilesh were the brightest of the batch. Akhilesh had just got back from a summer internship with Microsoft at Seattle and the desi residents of University Club had turned up at his apartment half-expecting to see a halo around his head.

'Akhil, check with your roommates also if anyone wants to come. We can take one more person.'

When Akhil told Jassi about the plan, he jumped at the opportunity and agreed to come. In a month, the only outings they had were the trips to Walmart and the Indian store. Besides, they were going to a beach. Beaches were the reason he was in Florida.

The boys were off. En route, Ruksh stopped the car at a gas station and returned with two 6-packs of beer and assorted snacks. 'Refreshments,' he winked.

The drive was a couple of hours long. Akhil and Jassi got some useful advice from the seniors along the way.

Anil started off with his thoughts. 'Course work, research, everything is fine, but at the end of the day, you need to find a job. Make sure that is your target. Focus on programming skills. Brush up your analytical skills for interviews. Network with people.'

Ruksh offered more pragmatic advice. 'Don't take very tough courses if you want to have a life. There are plenty of easy courses you can take that will let you graduate comfortably.'

'Sure, take your pick between comfort, chasing girls, and having a future,' Akhilesh added.

'Dude, you live the life of a hermit. Locked away in your room all day, coding, coding, coding. Hope you have heard the saying, Use it or lose it? ' Ruksh winked at Akhilesh and smiled at his own joke.

'Ruksh, Akhilesh does live like a sadhu from the Himalayas, but don't forget he is the one who landed with an internship at Microsoft, and is almost certain of getting a job there as well.' Anil piped in.

'Guys, stop it. Let's focus on the drive.' Akhilesh pointed out to the scenic countryside they were driving along. The highway was four-lane each side, flanked by rich greenery. Beautiful trees as far as the eye could go. They were driving along at nearly 80 mph.

'Almost 150 kmph, and it still feels so smooth. In India, there are hardly any roads where you can reach that speed. Even the highways have potholes and sudden holes in the road,' Jassi exclaimed. In his eyes, there was nothing America could do wrong.

'Dude, this is the United States of America. One of the first good things they did after the last World War was developing their road network. They say these roads are a big part of their growth,' Anil replied.

'Anyway, so what are your plans?' Anil asked Akhil.

'Plans?'

'Generally, what do you want to do in life?'

'For now, I am just focusing on the course work. Then get a nice job, work for a few years, and move back to India.'

Ruksh nearly crashed into a passing car, whose driver honked angrily, and threw them a middle finger salute as he swerved to avoid them. 'What?'

'Why, did I say something wrong? I plan to move back to India eventually.'

'Dude, why would you do that after all the hard work? People would kill to be in your position and you are already talking of going back?' Anil was having trouble believing Akhil.

'I don't know how to explain it. Anyway, that's the plan for now. Let's see how things shape up.'

Ruksh smiled. 'I can bet my painstakingly compiled collection of 'Girls Gone Wild' videos that you are not going to go anywhere. I have seen too many idealistic people start off like you, then get into their pursuit of the American dream, get married, have kids, and soon they are married to this country forever.'

'We will see.' Akhil smiled.

Halfway through the drive, Ruksh suggested a lunch of traditional, authentic American food. Ten minutes later, he pulled into a McDonald's.

Everybody ordered chicken sandwiches. Akhil went through the menu. He did a second pass, slower this time.

'What the hell is this?'

'What happened dude?' Anil asked the bewildered Akhil.

'I don't see any vegetarian burger here. Not even an aloo-tikki burger.'

Ruksh laughed. 'Dude, you will not find an aloo-tikki burger here. We are in America, remember?'

Anil came over. 'Sorry Akhil, I didn't realize that you were a vegetarian. Unfortunately, McDonald's here doesn't serve any vegetarian burgers.'

'So what am I supposed to do? I am dying of hunger here.'

'Umm…do you want to…?' Anil hesitated, but everyone realized what he was going to suggest.

'What the hell, the chicken is already dead. It's not like my not eating it will bring it back to life.' Hunger pangs had just added one more to the count of people converted from vegetarian to the dark side.

'Way to go dude,' Anil winked at Akhil.

Akhil got his sandwich, unpacked it, and took a bite. 'It tastes like paneer.'

Another bite. 'Not bad.'

When in Rome

He finished it off in a couple of minutes.

Ruksh whistled. Anil gave Akhil a high-five. 'You remind me of myself when I came here. I was a God-fearing, non-smoking, non-drinking, vegetarian Brahmin. The first day in the US, I went to this restaurant and ate a slice of pepperoni pizza thinking those red circles were tomatoes. It was meat. The rest, as they say, is history. When in Rome, do as the Romans do, I guess.'

Akhil smiled sheepishly. He had already risked ex-communication from his religion by drinking alcohol. They couldn't possibly kick him out twice for a second violation.

An hour later, they were at St George's Island. The sky suddenly turned dark. It was going to rain. Jassi was disappointed. He had come looking forward to see a sea of bikinis. The young students finished off their stock of beer at the beach, sat there for a little while, and soon it was time to go back. Jassi had seen exactly one bikini the whole day, on a woman so old that her wrinkled skin was going to give him nightmares for a few weeks. Jassi imagined his grandma in a bikini and shuddered.

There was just one unfinished business before they left.

However, there were no restrooms in sight. 'Guys, just find a vacant corner and be done with it,' was Ruksh's suggestion. They found what seemed like a deserted spot near a trash dump. With the sea wind rustling in their hair, birds chirping away, and only the open skies for witness, the five young lads from India relieved themselves right there in the open.

Kedar was ecstatic. 'God, this feels so good.'

'I can't believe we took a leak in the open in America of all places.' Akhil was a bit disgusted, though slightly excited about what must have been a criminal act in the eyes of the United States government.

'Look Akhil, the grass already looks greener. It says thank you for the fertilizer.' Ruksh patted Akhil's shoulder.

'Okay guys, let's run now before someone reports us and we spend the night in a police lockup.'

Ruksh took out the car, and they fled without any more words being exchanged. Two hours later, they pulled up into the University Club parking lot.

'Thanks guys. I had a fun day.'

'No worries Akhil. We will try to do this more often.'

'Alright dudes. Thanks.' Jassi looked tipsy from the beer, as he stumbled inside the apartment behind Akhil. Their first road trip of America had been fun. Akhil and Jassi couldn't wait for the next one. For now, there were assignments to be completed.

✈

Jassi could not take his eyes off the girls. They were pretty, athletic, and wearing skimpy clothes. He felt a pang of jealousy for the boys who were holding them, touching them all over their bodies, lifting them, catching them.

Nigel nudged him. 'Yo man, here's a beer. Whatchu oglin at? Ah...' He noticed the direction Jassi was looking at. 'Don't worry dude. You'll get used to it soon. This is nothin'.'

Jassi looked up from the cheerleaders. He checked the scene around him. The stadium was full of almost a lakh screaming football fans. Most of them had that now-familiar red plastic cup full of beer in their hands. The atmosphere was electric. The noise deafening.

He had come to see his first football game with Nigel and some others. American football, not the one Indians knew. That was soccer. The campus wore a different look that day. Families were camping in the grounds. People sat in the open in tents, while cooking various types of meats on their barbeques. The air smelled of beer and slow cooking meat, which Nigel joked, was the national smell of America. Jassi couldn't help wondering that even cricket matches didn't inspire this kind of madness back home. This wasn't even an international match—just an inter-university game.

Nigel had insisted that Jassi come along. 'You'll love it dude.' They had been getting along well, and Jassi had been spending many of his evenings at Nigel's dorm room as he thought Nigel was way more fun than his desi roommates.

Jassi had no idea about what was happening on the ground. Nigel explained the rules of the game briefly, but it didn't make much sense to him. All Jassi saw was dozens of bulky men in big costumes with padded shoulders. They would huddle together, a ball would appear, everybody would pile on top of one person, the crowd would roar, they would walk away, only to repeat the exercise all over again.

'I don't get it. The ball isn't going anywhere. They are just beating each other up, aren't they?' Jassi asked Nigel.

'Just hang on dude. Things will move eventually.'

Suddenly the stadium erupted. A man was running holding the ball for dear life. He reached the end of the field and everybody went berserk. FSU had a 'touchdown', even though Jassi had no clue what that meant.

Jassi heard the screaming voice of a girl nearby. She sounded distinctly Indian from her accent. He turned to see Lavina Fernandes, the pretty MBA student from Goa a few rows away. She was with a handsome white guy who he thought must be a friend. The guy had an arm around her waist. She was wearing a short, revealing top that would have been frowned upon back in India. Suddenly she turned around, he grabbed her by the waist, and they kissed. The way they were going at each other, to Jassi it appeared more like they were charting the insides of each other's throats.

Obviously not just a friend, he thought.

The football game ended and Jassi heaved a sigh of relief. He didn't get much of what was going on, except he had consumed half a dozen glasses of beer and had gone to a different planet after the fourth one. He had also noticed Lavina kissing her friend every few minutes, and by the end of the game, he could tell that the dude definitely had his hands inside her top.

'Slut', Jassi wanted to shout out to Lavina. 'Spoiling the good name of Indian girls.'

'Girls are evil. Most of the ones I know are skanks.' Devika was ranting away as Dilpreet drove his car along the tree-lined streets of Tallahasseee. She had just returned from a trip to meet her parents at their place in Atlanta over the weekend.

'Most of my friends have American boyfriends and very active sex lives, but tell that to my mom, who thinks I am the worst possible daughter who will never be good enough for her. She throws a party last night for some friends and relatives and then goes—don't wear that short dress. Don't reveal your legs. Don't dance to that item song. You're not a whore. Don't dance like that.'

'She keeps going on and on about that Aparna. I wonder what will happen when she finds out that girl changes boyfriends like her underwear. Last I heard she was going with a redneck from her class. Someone called Brad. But at home, she's the most saintly woman there ever was.'

Dilpreet had been invited to a prayer at the house of a Sikh faculty in the university and he had asked Akhil if he wanted to come along. Devika had also joined in. They were about five minutes away from their house, but for now Devika was busy letting her frustrations out.

She sighed loudly. 'Then of course, she uses some other favourites on me. "Don't talk to boys. Don't talk to black people or Mexicans. Learn to make round rotis or you will never get married." Jesus Christ man, she drives me up the wall. At this rate I will become Spiderman one day.'

She giggled at the comparison, but she was clearly annoyed. 'I say anything and she shuts me up with a—"Don't be disrespectful. We didn't raise you to see this day."'

'Back when I was home, she would wake me up every morning to the sound of the grinder making a mint and chilli chutney, and aloo paranthas being cooked in high cholesterol desi ghee. So unhealthy. And then she wants me to become a doctor.'

Dilpreet smiled at her. 'Calm down, bachche. She is a typical Indian mom who wants what's best for her child.'

Devika threw up her hands in despair. 'Of course, now you

take her side, but please tell her that it is okay to sometimes watch a basketball game on TV. Even if the spelling bee is on. I already gave a few years of my life preparing for the stupid competition just because my parents thought it would make them look cool in front of their friends if I won. In their eyes, I *only* made it to the regional finals beating ten thousand kids, and they reminded me of my failure to reach the nationals for the next many years.'

Akhil laughed loudly. 'I've seen a few of those. It's crazy, with young kids spending a dozen hours every day mugging up words they will never use again in their life. It's a bit like IIT JEE coaching back in India. These days some coaching centres have started programmes for children studying in 7th standard. Six years of not having a life, just to get into IIT! In a few years, people will start offering IIT coaching discounts for unborn children along with hospital maternity packages.'

Devika chuckled. She had more.

'And you know what she gave me for my birthday last year? A box full of Fair and Lovely cream. Says I need to get fairer if I want to get married to a half-decent guy. I was like, give me a break ma.'

'I tell her to give me some space, and she goes—"We have a 5,000 square foot house. You can have as much space as you want." Thank God she doesn't live in Tallahassee, or I would have gone cuckoo by now.'

Dilpreet laughed as he pulled into the driveway of an impressive two-storey house with roses in the garden and a Mercedes parked outside. They were at the home of Professor Kuldip Singh, one of the senior faculty at the College of Engineering.

For the next three hours, Akhil, Devika, and Dilpreet sat with their heads bowed, listening to the reading from Guru Granth Sahib. Akhil felt at peace with himself. It didn't matter that he was not Sikh, or that he didn't understand any of the words in Gurmukhi. The house exuded warmth of family, and Akhil felt happy to be a part of it. In a foreign land, the smallest gestures help.

The excellent lunch spread that followed was the icing on the cake.

The Janitor's Son

The air had started getting cooler. Trees were gradually getting naked as their leaves deserted the branches. October was upon Tallahasseee. Akhil's life had settled into a schedule. His three courses had two lectures each week, and the teaching-assistant work required him to supervise tests during the evenings. He would leave home early morning, attend lectures, spend time in the library studying or working from his office, be home in the evening, grab dinner, and return to the lab on most nights.

Back home in India he had spent numerous sleepless nights due to power-cuts. Here there was 24-hour electricity but he didn't have time to sleep. The irony Gods were working overtime. Primetime no longer meant watching a recent Bollywood blockbuster at 9 pm, but slogging away on an assignment due the next morning.

Tonight he was supervising yet another Computer Literacy test. All 20 students had been seated and had begun their tests when Nandita dropped by.

'Hi Akhil, how are you?' She flashed that brilliant smile of hers. Akhil's heart skipped a beat.

'Hi Nandita, what are you doing here?'

'Nothing. Just thought I'll see how you are doing, and what your tests look like.'

'Yaar, I am at work right now. Let's catch up later.'

'Oh come on buddy, don't worry. I will not make too much noise. Anyway, you are the boss here. These kids cannot complain.'

'See what I brought for you.' She handed him a Godiva chocolate bar. 'These are very tasty. Eat wisely.'

'Thanks Nandita. Now go. I don't want to lose my job over someone complaining.'

'Okay okay. I'll go. See you later.' Akhil watched her leave, though his heart didn't want her to go anywhere. He thanked God for Nandita, the girl who was making him feel emotions he never knew existed. They were officially just friends, but Akhil wanted more. This was bigger than any of his numerous crushes on pretty girls over the years. Way bigger.

✈

Later that night, as Akhil was returning home from his office, he walked past the janitor mopping the corridors. He smiled at Akhil. Akhil had noticed him quite a few times, but they had never talked.

'Good night, son,' he said.

Akhil looked at the black man. A tag on his chest mentioned his name as Joe. He was a hefty guy, over six feet tall. Must have been over 50-years-old, but he would have made a handsome young man back in the day.

'Hi.' Akhil smiled at him.

'You work very late man. I don't see no one stay later in the building than you.' He thought for a second before adding, 'except for us janitors sometimes.'

Akhil grinned, not sure what to say. He was tired, and hungry. It had been a long day.

'Where you from?' Joe asked him.

Akhil looked at his peaceful expression. The man genuinely seemed interested in talking. He decided dinner could wait another ten minutes. 'India,' he replied.

'Ah, thought so. You Indian people are very smart. Indian and Chinese. That's all I see in the building these days.'

Akhil wondered how to respond to that.

Joe continued. 'I have a boy. 15-years-old. I want him to be smart like you Indians. Hopefully he will be able to get into FSU, but he doesn't study.' He looked on wistfully. He went on for the next fifteen minutes, talking about his dreams for his son, who didn't seem to care too much about studies.

Akhil listened to Joe patiently, answering questions about his own background, and how he happened to come to FSU.

He didn't know how to ask him, but went for it eventually. 'I had always heard that American parents don't worry about their children. But you are so different.'

He laughed. 'Where did you hear that, son? Some movie? This is not true. American parents are like any other parents. We care about our kids. We just make sure they become independent, and then it is their life.'

Akhil probed further. 'But then they move out and old

parents are left to live alone. In India, we take care of our parents.'

Joe replied, 'Yes, that is a bit different. But again, it ain't a bad thing. People here prefer their independence. There are good facilities to take care of old people here, so it ain't as bad as you think.'

Some myths surrounding America were getting shattered for Akhil.

He looked at his watch. It was closing in on 11. He had been talking to Joe for an hour without realizing it. He turned to Joe. 'Thanks Joe. It was great talking to you. I sure learnt many new things today. Thanks for sharing your thoughts.'

Joe smiled. 'No worries man. You're a good kid. Good night. Go get some rest.'

Akhil walked the ten minutes to University Club in silence, mulling over the just concluded discussion. He wondered why American culture was so maligned back home. The American people were clearly not as strange as everyone made them out to be.

✈

'So, what country are you from?' She spoke softly, with great emphasis on each word.

'I am from India' Jassi replied, in the same soft tone.

'Oh wow. How do you like it here in the States?' the girl talking to Jassi asked him. She had a reasonably pretty face, though with a bit too many pimples for his liking. He rated her a 6 on 10, but figured she was *good enough for practice*.

'It is great. I had heard that the US is the world's greatest country, and in my experience so far, there is no doubt about that. India does not even come close.' He sniggered, amused by the audacity of the comparison.

Suresh, their neighbour and Jassi's first acquaintance in the US, had told him about the International Center, where they organized regular sessions to help foreign students with their English skills. 'The girls are cute, and with some effort, you can easily *land* one,' had been the advice. 'Just be smooth and play along. Get a number on some pretext, and then we can take it from there.' Suresh had promised Jassi this worked.

'Ah. India has Taj Mahal, no? It is very beautiful. I hope to see it one day,' she replied.

'Yes, it is very pretty. Just like you,' Jassi winked at her. In his mind there was no doubt she would not be able to resist his charm.

'So what is your good name?' he asked.

'I am sorry? My what name?'

'Your name? I am Jazz.'

'Jazz! That's a cool name. I am Victoria.'

'Good to meet you, Victoria.'

'Thanks. I see you speak very good English already. '

'Well, just a little I have learnt. But still there is a lot to learn, with your help.'

'Oh, I am sure you'll do well. Just give it some time.' Victoria touched Jassi's shoulder and Jassi's brain immediately sent him a barrage of excited signals. He was convinced that she wanted to sleep with him right now.

She got up to talk to the next person, a lost looking Korean guy who looked like he was asleep. Jassi grabbed her hand.

'Wait a minute, Victoria. Can we maybe meet once a week

to help me practice? All my friends speak horrible English like me, so I would be appreciating it if you could help me out.' Jassi had learnt the 'appreciate' expression from Nigel, though clearly he could use a grammar teacher.

Victoria seemed confused. She glared at Jassi for a minute, and then a faint smile appeared. She said, 'Yes, sure.'

Jassi had won the battle. The war was still to be fought, on his mattress, he hoped. He got her number and they agreed to meet in the library every Wednesday at 6 pm.

Jassi felt like Alexander the Great must have after his first victory. He was ready to rule American women.

✈

Next Wednesday, Jassi had his second meeting with Victoria. He called her up and asked if they could meet at Starbucks instead. She agreed. Jassi's sly twist worked. The library would have been too formal a setting. As 'love guru' Suresh told him, 'the stepping stones to success with women are—coffee shops, restaurants, clubs, and bedrooms.'

Jassi went for the 'date' in his coolest clothes—a Calvin Klein ripped jeans he had bought at the mall last month for 60 dollars, and a T-shirt with John Lennon's face on it. He had read on the Internet that girls digged it. Then there was his spiked hair that took him a good thirty minutes to get right.

He was already there when Victoria walked into Starbucks. Jassi tried giving her a hug just as she bowed and did a namaste. *WTF dude, no one does namaste even in India anymore.* Jassi sighed but kept his thoughts to himself.

Once seated, Victoria asked Jassi, 'How do you say "Hi" in Indian?'

Jassi smiled. 'Well, there is really no 'Indian' language. We have over 20 major languages, and thousands of dialects. We just say Hi. Like that.'

Victoria laughed. Jassi felt even more confident of his chances with this woman.

They talked for the next hour. Victoria was doing her Masters in Anthropology and had an interest in learning about various cultures, which was also the reason she worked with the International Center. Through the course of their conversation, he also learnt that she belly-danced as a hobby, and occasionally performed at a nearby lounge. Her next performance was due to take place in a few weeks.

'I will surely be there,' Jassi promised. She left with a hug.

Back home, Jassi reported his progress to Suresh, who had become his guru in these matters.

'I am proud of you, Jassi.' Suresh patted Jassi's back in admiration. It had taken him a year to land his first date. Jassi had been here barely a couple of months.

✈

The phone rang. The caller-id said Priyank Goyal. Akhil grimaced.

'Hi dude, this is Perry.' The voice was loud and boisterous, the accent still fake.

'Hi Priyank,' Akhil refused to call him by that name.

'Akhil, dude I told you not to call me that. Anyways, what's up buddy? How are you doing?'

'Yes, doing well. Classes are going on. It's getting hectic day by day.'

'Oh okay. Are you just attending classes or doing anything useful also?'

'What do you mean, Priyank?'

'Come on, dude. You are still that boring fellow everybody loved to rag back in Delhi. You need to change with the times. I mean, c'mon…you are in the US for chrissake. Use the time well. Go out. Have some fun. Hang out with the girls. FSU is one of the biggest party schools in the country. Don't waste your time on classes.'

'Sure Priyank. Bye.' Akhil hung up. He didn't need to go out with girls. He had his eyes set on one, and Priyank had no need to know.

A week later Akhil had the group over for dinner. It was one of the rare evenings when he had some time for socializing, thanks to the just concluded mid-terms. Akhil had done well, getting good grades on his tests. If he kept up the pace, he was on track for A-grades on all of his courses.

Akhil, Jassi, and Kedar had been getting along cordially. Akhil was the pragmatic one. Jassi was the outgoing extrovert who seemed to know a lot more about local traditions and slangs, though Akhil failed to understand some of the things he did. Jassi seemed to be two different people to him.

Kedar was the joker, always clowning around and cracking jokes. Venkat and Sundar lived two houses down, but when not busy on assignments the group was at either of the apartments together. Akhil didn't quite get Venkat at times. His behaviour ranged between extremes of aloofness and friendliness. Priya occasionally joined in.

Then of course, there was Nandita, whose mere sight used to warm up Akhil's heart.

For someone who had not cooked even a simple dal in India, Akhil was now able to whip up full meals. Like Kedar told him, the good news was that even if he failed to get a technology job after his MS, he could get hired by a restaurant as a chef. Jassi was also getting there, priding himself on his ability to make Maggi noodles and boiled eggs without burning them.

Between mouthfuls of rajma chawal, egg curry, and frozen paranthas, the group was discussing the semester so far. Soon the discussion shifted to broader topics of America and its people. Kedar said something about Americans having no values when Akhil recited Joe, the janitor's story.

Dilpreet spoke first when Akhil finished. 'I completely agree. I have also always felt our people have so many misconceptions about Americans. I think their system is better than ours. It gives everybody their space to live.'

He continued, as everybody listened to the veteran in rapt attention. Dilpreet led the life of a sage and was full of wise, practical advice for his fellow FOBs.

'These people have it all worked out. Unlike what we think, parents here love their kids with their lives. But they will only do that till a stage. Once the children are able to take care of themselves, they are supposed to move on. This ensures they gain some sense of responsibility, while the parents get their lives back. In India, parents worry about their kids even after the kids have kids of their own. It may seem a bit impersonal to us, but it does make sense if you think of it. These people like to live for themselves. No compromises. If a mother needs her time, she will find a babysitter and go out. In India she'll be called names if she even thinks of leaving her child like that.'

Venkat spoke next. 'Yes, I agree with what you say. However, it is not all good. People here sometimes seem so dumb. I take classes as a teaching assistant, and half of my students are idiots. They don't know anything. Some of them can't even spell basic English words properly.'

Priya giggled. 'One of my classmates today asked me if India was near Spain. I was like, yes, just about 10,000 kilometres away.'

Dilpreet added. 'Guys, never forget that everything has a good and bad side. America has a lot of good things. The resources are aplenty, people are courteous and disciplined, and everything is nice and clean. Most importantly, they welcome immigrants with open arms, or we won't be here living happily.'

'At the same time, there are bad things as well. There isn't enough focus on education. While everyone thinks that this country is amazing, the economy is not in a good shape. There is corruption here as well, though it is more sophisticated and at much higher levels.'

'As for people, there are all types of people everywhere. I have had people stare at me and ask what is inside my turban. After 9/11, people regularly used to shout at me and call me Osama, because in their minds that's what a turban got associated with. What can you do about it? Nothing is perfect, especially people. But I should not tell you everything. You guys will learn in due course.'

He looked at his watch. 'It is 9. All right, kids. It is bedtime for me. Akhil, thanks for the food, man. You should do this more often.'

Dilpreet patted Akhil's shoulder and he was off. Gradually the gathering dispersed. Kedar helped Akhil clean up the dishes, and Akhil was back to his assignments.

The next evening Jassi was at the Sheesha Lounge, a middle-eastern hookah-lounge close to campus. Victoria had invited him to see her belly-dance performance. Jassi wondered if any girls from decent families back in India would indulge in such a 'disgraceful' dance form, as people back in the motherland would call it. He was having doubts if his mom would ever approve of their marriage, if it came to it.

He reached barely five minutes before the dance performance. The lounge was filled mostly with students. They actually had hookahs going around. Jassi wondered why they would do that. *Hookahs belonged to Indian villages. What are they doing here?*

Victoria stopped by. She was wearing the traditional harem pants worn by belly dancers, and looked stunning. In his mind, Jassi increased her rating from 6 to 8. She gave him a quick hug and was off to the stage.

The dance was somewhat sensuous, but not slutty like Jassi had thought.

Victoria stopped by his table after completing her dance. She was soaked with sweat from the exertion.

'So, did you like it?' She asked Jassi.

'It was great. You looked fantastic.' Jassi was earnest for once.

'Dinner? I am starving.' She got up.

'Sure.' Jassi followed.

They drove to a diner a short distance away in Victoria's car. Dinner got over early and Jassi didn't even notice what he ate, mainly because he was already imagining going back to his apartment with her, followed by some rolling around on his trash-retrieved mattress. *Tonight was going to be 'the' night*, he was confident.

They got to the car. Instead of taking the passenger's seat, Jassi went to the driver's side and opened Victoria's door for her. As she moved to get in the car, Jassi gave her a hug. He then leaned in, his lips outstretched and eyes closed in anticipation. She gave him a confused look.

'Do I at least get a kiss?' he said disappointed.

Victoria laughed, and gave him a peck on the cheek. She got into the car.

Jassi was embarrassed. This is not how it was supposed to be. He couldn't let go this easily.

'Well, this was not what I had in mind.' He stood his ground by the car door.

Victoria was taken aback. 'Let's just head back. It is getting late.'

Jassi got in the car. He had no words to say. He had failed.

Victoria broke the silence. 'I am sorry. I wasn't thinking of you romantically, but more like a friend.'

'Yea sure.' Jassi couldn't bring himself to say much else. He had been declined by a woman who was a mere 6 on his scale. This was not good. Maybe she already had a boyfriend.

Or maybe she was into women. America had lots of those.

Nobody spoke anything for the next twenty minutes. They reached University Club. Jassi got off the car.

'Good night Jazz. I had a fun night today,' said Victoria and drove off.

November had started. The Algorithms class was getting harder with every week. On this day, the topic was a particularly complicated one, known to the professor as Dynamic Programming. The class might have called it The Great Indian Rope Trick, for all they cared. It didn't make much sense to most of them. The professor operated in a different orbit as compared to the students, who were mostly befuddled by the pace of the proceedings.

The class was trying to answer the question on the blackboard. It pertained to finding the maximum possible sum of any possible sequence in a given list of numbers, in the most optimum manner. Simple as it sounded, the problem was quite complex to solve. Akhil was scratching his head frantically. He knew he was close to the solution.

Suddenly he had the answer. As he got up and gave out the solution, the entire class watched in admiration. The professor grinned, gave him a thumbs up, and the class broke out in applause. Akhil saw Brad cast a glance from across the aisle and smile at him, for what must be the first time in the semester.

At the end of the class, the professor handed out assignments from last week. Akhil saw his assignment and broke into a wide grin. He had scored 89 out of 100, his best performance in the semester so far. This was very likely the highest score in the class.

From his seat, Brad cast a look at Akhil's desk and let out a soft whistle. He had scored a 54 and had been feeling quite happy with his performance. The Indian dude was making everybody else look mediocre in comparison.

As Akhil headed out of the class, Brad caught up with him.

'Hey dude. Great work there on that problem.'

Akhil was pleasantly surprised at the friendly tone. He had half-expected another jibe.

'Thanks man.'

'Dude, at this rate you're going to spoil the bell-curve for everybody. This is not fair.'

Akhil grinned.

'Hey listen, we're heading up to the union to grab some grub. Wanna join us?'

Akhil assumed he was referring to lunch at the University food-court. He had planned to go home for his lunch, but now that Brad was extending a hand of friendship, he couldn't say no. 'Sure. I'd love to,' he answered.

'Awesome. Thanks bud.'

Jim, the second half of the 'Buffalo Brothers' joined them, and Akhil headed off for lunch with the two. They were walking on each side of Akhil, who felt like a pygmy in comparison to the two giants. They reached the food court and Akhil found Aparna was already waiting there. She waved to the three, came by and kissed Brad on the lips. Akhil suddenly remembered Devika mentioning Aparna currently going out with a Brad. He hadn't realized it was *this* Brad she was talking about.

Everybody took seats and placed their orders. Akhil

noticed a Cheese Burger on the menu and went for it, happily unaware that it wasn't quite the only vegetarian choice on the menu like he had thought, but it was in fact beef. He might have tasted chicken already, but wasn't yet ready to be referred to as a cow-murderer, as mom would invariably call him if she found out.

'So I see you guys finally became friends?' Devika looked at Brad and Akhil.

Brad smiled. 'Ah it was nothing. We were just yanking his chain. The guy's a genius, man. You saw what he did in today's class?'

Devika nodded. 'That was pretty cool, Akhil. You seriously make us all look bad.'

Akhil blushed.

As Akhil took a bite of his sandwich, he saw Brad looking at him. His eyes were wide open in horror, like he had seen a ghost.

'What happened, Brad?'

'Dude, don't you have a religious thing or something where you aren't allowed to eat cows?'

'What?'

'That sandwich. It is beef. Hope you know that.'

'Oh shit. It said cheese burger so I thought it was vegetarian.'

The three people seated at his table laughed so loud, people at nearby tables turned around to see what the commotion was all about.

'Aww Akhil. I can't tell you how many times I have heard people do this. This is such a classical rookie mistake.' Aparna spoke between bites of her chicken sandwich.

'Oh well. I am not too religious, so I guess it is okay. Though my mom probably won't let me enter the house again if she finds out.'

'That's cool then.' Brad heaved a sigh of relief. He didn't want a crazy Akhil going about on a killing spree to avenge his loss of religion.

'You know Akhil, I spent a month in India last summer backpacking with some friends. I guess I got taken in by all those documentaries about India. You know, the ones that start with a tabla playing while they show a shot of the Taj Mahal. Boy, it's a funny country. One the one hand, you guys say that cows are sacred and then you leave them to roam around on the roads, getting hit by cars, eating crap etc. Talking of roads, what's with the open urination, man? I even saw some kids taking a dump on the roadside. There's so much squalor, so much filth, so much chaos. How do you guys manage, man?' Brad shuddered, recalling the visuals from his trip.

'I apologize if this offends you, but I am being honest. It is what it is. I am not even exaggerating. My experience was particularly horrible. We didn't have much money to spend, so travelled by trains, buses etc. In India, it is all out there. It hits you in the face, dude. In Delhi, I took one of those tuk-tuks from the railway station and he took me on an hour-long ride across the entire city, for what I know was a 2 kilometre distance. He then asked for the equivalent of fifty dollars, and wouldn't show me anything to justify that charge. No meter. No tariff chart. Nothing. It was extortion. A day later, someone stole my wallet in the middle of the market. Jeez. I doubt I'll ever go back to your country.'

Akhil didn't know what to say. There was nothing wrong in what Brad had mentioned. Foreigners were routinely taken for a ride, over-charged, and abused by people who thought everybody with white skin was a rich person with massive bank accounts back home.

'Anyway, it's not like it is your fault. Every country has its dark underbelly. Let's talk about more important stuff. We're planning a little party tonight. You game for some weed? You know, weed? Grass?'

Akhil was confused. 'Weed? You will do gardening in your party?'

Jim snorted so hard, Akhil saw drops of Coca-Cola come out of his nostrils. Brad got up and clapped his hands in delight.

Aparna stepped in. 'Stop it, guys. Akhil, you are so naïve. These guys are certainly not planning on doing any gardening. Brad is talking about marijuana. You smoke it and get high.'

Brad made a gesture of smoking, exhaling an imaginary smoke ring. 'Yo dude. We'll do a nice bong. It'll be fun.'

Another new term. Akhil wondered how a Bengali person came into this picture. Maybe their dealer was a bong? But he dare not ask, for fear of another embarrassment. Dilpreet might know.'

'So you up for it?' Brad asked him.

'No man. I think you guys carry on. Tell your bong friend I said hi.' He got up and walked off, as Brad and Jim looked at each other perplexed.

Shall We Dance?

'Guys, Pooja is outside. She wants to talk about tonight's Diwali party.'

Kedar and Akhil looked up at Jassi. Pooja was Priya's roommate, an IITian, and in the Math PhD programme. She had a pleasant personality and used to get along well with the others. Akhil had seen her walking about the campus with Kedar a few times.

'Yaar, this is awkward. Can't we just ask her to come back later?' Akhil covered his bare torso with a towel.

They heard someone walking through the apartment, and Pooja opened the door of Akhil's room, filling it up with the smell of Aloe. She took a look at the boys, and an amused expression formed on her pretty, dusky face.

She kept her hands on her prominent hips, and asked Kedar, 'Whoa guys. What's going on here?'

Akhil was startled by her sudden appearance. 'Pooja! How did you come in?'

'Well, the door was open and I walked in. I am sorry, am I

not allowed in your apartment anymore? Kedar, Akhil, what are you guys upto? Is that a hair trimmer?'

She took out her mobile from the pocket of her dangerously low-rise jeans and took a picture before anyone could move. 'This will make for interesting dinner time conversation with the girls tonight.'

Akhil got up from his position on the ground and put on his T-shirt. Kedar also got up and covered himself.

'Okay okay. We bought this hair trimmer from Amazon and Kedar was just giving me a haircut. It's so damn expensive getting your haircut outside. The trimmer cost less than a single haircut.' Akhil explained.

She laughed, 'You guys are crazy. To save money, you are risking your hair getting ruined at the hands of each other?'

'Well, you don't need a PhD to cut hair, but what would you know? You girls spend 50 dollars on a haircut and your hair ends up still looking the same.' Akhil replied.

'Whatever, you guys. I just dropped by to check your plan for tonight's Diwali potluck.'

'Well, I was thinking of Rajma, jeera pulao, and a nice kheer.'

'Okay, great. You boys carry on then. I'll see you tonight.' Pooja left. Kedar picked up the trimmer to complete the unfinished job on Akhil's hair.

It was Akhil's idea. Last month he had got a haircut at Walmart that had cost him 15 dollars. He hadn't been able to sleep that night after realizing that he had spent the equivalent of 650 rupees on what would cost 20 rupees back in India. He and Kedar could buy a trimmer for that much, cut each other's hair, and save a lot of money in the bargain. Jassi wasn't interested. He couldn't risk getting it done by complete novices; there were girls relying on him to look good.

It was Diwali and the desi residents of the University Club had organized a celebration of sorts. There would be a puja, followed by a potluck. The concept of a potluck was simple. Everybody came in with some food to add to the dinner table.

By now, Akhil was acknowledged as the best cook in their house, and his enthusiasm for such occasions was a blessing for his roommates. They just had to transport the finished goods, and themselves to the party.

The kheer was simmering on low flame. It would continue to do so for the next hour or so to give it that rich, creamy taste. He had given the rajma eight to ten whistles in the pressure cooker, but the beans still seemed a little raw. Murphy's Law was at work, manifesting itself through obstinate kidney beans. He would cook the pulao at the last minute, to keep the rice steaming hot.

Akhil's day had begun with a phone call from home, followed by more calls to other members of the extended family. Mamas. Chachas. Cousins. Diwali was the time to socialize with relatives, and thanks to Alexander Graham Bell's invention of the telephone, distances were immaterial in modern times. Everybody was happy back home. Everybody talked about how much they missed his presence. Luckily, no one cried.

Mom had asked him to give some food to a cow, in keeping with the auspicious nature of the occasion. Akhil was not sure what to do about this. Where was he supposed to find a stray cow in America? He promised her he'd find one, or something close to it. Jassi had put on a lot of weight in recent days and could almost count as one.

'Okay beta, if you can't find a cow, at least find a beggar and give him some alms.'

'Sure mom.' Akhil wasn't sure if this helped. He was yet to come across any beggar at any of Tallahasseee's road crossings. There were no beggars. There were no vendors selling pornographic magazines, assorted snacks like papads, coconut slices, or cut cucumber. Road travel wasn't much fun in the US compared to Indian roads, which were like a thrilling roller-coaster ride through pockets of angry drivers, potholes, urinating people, and colonies of jaundice, typhoid, and cholera. India made you thankful for reaching home safely every night. America was relatively lame in comparison.

Akhil thought of checking with the one homeless person he had seen around campus a few times, but he wasn't sure if he would appreciate a plate of rajma chawal and kheer.

At Dilpreet's house, everybody had pooled in their statues of various Gods, which were now assembled into a mini temple. Nandita had project work to complete tonight, but she had promised Akhil a movie outing this weekend, now that the mid-semesters were over.

The puja commenced at 7 pm, and the girls took over. The only problem was that no one knew the entire Lakshmi Aarti by heart. Luckily, Google did, and the puja was performed with the 20-odd Indian heads bowed in reverence as Anoop Jalota sang praises of Goddess Lakshmi on YouTube.

Pooja handed out the halwa as prasad to everybody, and it was time for what everybody was waiting for. Food. For the next one hour, everybody ate, and ate some more. Dilpreet handed out Hajmolas at the end.

Venkat burped loudly. 'Oops. Sundar, that's a compliment

for your sambar. It was too good, man. Too good.'

Sundar went red. 'Nonsense, man. Stop it.'

Everybody slowly dispersed after enjoying the sumptuous spread.

It was about 11 pm when Akhil, Kedar, and Priya decided to head to Venkat's place for the after-party. Sundar had lit up the stairs and front of the apartment with little diyas, like they would do back in India.

Kedar was impressed. 'Wow Sundar. NOW this feels like Diwali.'

'Sundar cooks great. He keeps the house clean. He is religious and punctual. He never gets angry. Priya, you should think about marrying Sundar.' Venkat was his usual outspoken self.

Priya didn't know where to look.

'Shut up Venkat. Priya, ignore the useless fellow.' Sundar went red, for the second time that night.

'Okay okay, relax guys. But seriously Sundar, if I were a girl, I would marry you.' Kedar added.

'Alrite Kedar, that's good to know. Now let's go inside.'

Venkat grabbed a couple of beer bottles from the fridge, and handed them out.

It was almost 3 am when the group broke up and left for their respective homes.

✈

The next few days passed by in a blur for Akhil. He wanted time to fast forward to the weekend. He couldn't wait to spend an evening with Nandita.

It was Saturday. Akhil was making himself a cup of tea when the phone rang. It was Nandita.

'Hi Akhil!'

'Hi Nandita.' Akhil's face lit up. Just hearing her voice filled him with joy.

'So handsome, what time do we leave?' Nandita asked. Akhil blushed.

The two decided to leave in the evening. They would take the bus to the mall. None of them had a car. A cab would be too expensive.

At five, Akhil was outside Nandita's apartment to pick her up. She took a couple of minutes before finally answering the door bell. Akhil held his breath as he saw her. She looked mesmerizing. It was only the second time Akhil had seen her with her hair left open, after the Freshers' party. He wasn't even sure he had ever seen her wearing lipstick before. The bashful woman from the Air France flight had turned into an angel from heaven in a couple of months.

Akhil was speechless. He wanted to grab her right there and do things to her he had never done before.

'Stop staring, will you?' she said to the now gaping Akhil.

'Oh, sorry. I was thinking about something else.' Akhil tried covering up.

'Sure.' Her smile told Akhil his lie hadn't worked.

They walked to the bus stop. Akhil felt conscious of their desi neighbours watching them from their apartment windows. Nandita possibly sensed it too, for she quickened her step.

About five minutes of awkward silence followed. Akhil had never been on a date before, and had no idea what to do or say. Walking straight while looking at his feet seemed like a reasonable option. He had spent a couple of hours last evening polishing the leather boots enough to reflect light. It was a good thing that he only owned a single pair, so there wasn't much to choose from, because he had tried half a dozen shirts before settling on one with blue checks, his idea of romantic clothing.

Nandita broke the silence eventually. 'So, what movie are you showing me?'

'*Shall We Dance?*' Akhil replied, referring to a new romantic movie that had been released a week ago.

'What? Here?' Nandita exclaimed.

Akhil laughed. 'Arre baba, that's the name of the movie. There are some other options as well. We can watch whatever you wish.' He was suddenly sweating with nervousness.

Half an hour later, they were at the mall. Akhil bought the tickets, popcorn, a Coca-Cola and they got in the auditorium.

The movie was fun, though Akhil spent most of the time looking at Nandita. Her high-pitched laughter sounded like an A.R. Rehman symphony to him. He wanted her to never stop smiling.

As Richard Gere bent in to kiss his wife in the end, Akhil's pulse rose. He wanted to kiss Nandita right then and there. His legs started shaking with the river of adrenaline running through them. He grabbed them. The moment was gone.

The movie ended and Nandita got up to leave. Akhil thought he saw disappointment in her eyes. *Maybe I am just imagining things*, he told himself. Nandita grabbed his hand and they left the auditorium.

Dinner was at an Italian joint in the mall. Nandita couldn't stop talking about the movie, the dance sequences, about how romantic it all was. Akhil couldn't take his eyes off her.

Akhil was head over heels in love. Nandita had enchanted him.

Time flew by quickly. This had been the best evening of his life. Akhil was doing a butterfly stroke on cloud nine. Nandita had parted with a short embrace, and Akhil could still feel her breath, her fragrance, her quickened pulse.

He thought he noticed a fleeting look of disappointment on her otherwise angelic face as she left. There was smoke on both sides of the fence.

Back at the apartment, Akhil drank a glass of water and lay down on his bed for a minute, thinking of the assignments that were yet to be finished.

He woke up the next morning at nine.

As he went to the restroom, Akhil peeked into Jassi's room to check on him but saw nobody. Akhil remembered he had gone for a party last night. *But why is he still not back?* he thought. Akhil was worried, but had no idea where to check. Jassi had left no contact information about the people he was going out with.

An hour later, the phone rang. It was from the Tallahasseee Memorial Hospital. Akhil listened to the caller in dismay and called up Dilpreet immediately after hanging up.

'Dilpreet sir, need some help from you. Last night Jassi was admitted in the hospital. He had gone to a club with some friends. He must have had too many drinks and passed out on the road outside the club. The people at the club found him unconscious and took him to the hospital in an ambulance. Just got a call from the hospital. Can you please take us there?'

Shall We Dance?

'Sure Akhil. Come over and we will go.' Luckily, it was a Saturday and Dilpreet was home.

Akhil and Kedar ran to Dilpreet's house from where they went to the hospital. They found Jassi lying on a bed in the Emergency Room. He was conscious but looked pale. He had a drip on.

A doctor came by. 'He's fine now. We'll have him ready to go home in a couple of hours.'

By noon, they were ready for the discharge. Akhil and Kedar went to settle the dues. Akhil's heart sank on seeing the final bill—3000 dollars. Nearly 1,45,500 rupees for a few hours' stay in the hospital!

Apparently, emergency services came at a premium. Jassi paid with his credit card and walked to Dilpreet's car with heavy steps, his beer belly wobbling with the exertion.

'Bloody rascals. It would have been better if they had just left me there for a few hours. I was just drunk, not dead. This amount is almost a year's worth of living expenses for me.' Jassi was close to sobbing now. His American accent was gone.

'Relax Jassi. You have insurance, right? They might just cover the ambulance charges,' Dilpreet pointed that all was not lost yet.

'Though I am not sure they would cover hospitalization due to someone getting drunk,' he added as an afterthought. He was serious.

Kedar couldn't control a wisecrack. 'So next time Jassi, try having a heart attack or some real ailment that insurance covers. We look bad sharing an apartment with a sardar who had to go to hospital because he couldn't take a few beers.'

'Shut up Kedar. So what exactly happened, Jassi?' Akhil asked.

Jassi spoke slowly. 'We were out drinking. It was awesome. The club was massive. The girls were so hot. I danced with a couple of chicks who were giggling throughout. They definitely loved my moves. Then these guys called me for a round of tequila shots. We did 2, 3, maybe 5 shots. I don't know. I was already drunk when we started the shots. I went out with Nigel for a smoke, and that's all I remember. I must have passed out. Next thing I remember, I was in the Emergency Room. Bloody people thought I was dead or something. As if they never get drunk.'

'Chal anyway. All's well that ends well. Cheer up.' Akhil placed a friendly arm on Jassi's shoulder.

'What cheer up man? I am down 3000 dollars for those bloody tequila shots. This is a disaster.' Jassi was close to sobbing.

Jassi took a day to recover from the physical stress. The mental trauma of the financial loss would take much longer to go away.

✈

It was November 24. It was the day of the great American celebration called Thanksgiving. Jassi had finally managed to get out of the shock of his hospital bill. He had attended Thanksgiving Day parties at his Indian office, but Akhil couldn't get his head around it.

'So they have a special day set aside for eating dinner with your family? But aren't you supposed to do that everyday?

Shall We Dance?

I know back home we would wait for everybody to be home before having dinner together.'

'Dude, you are crazy!' Jassi didn't get his roommate at times.

Akhil suddenly felt a lurking suspicion that he may just never fully understand America. There were just too many things they did differently.

Thanksgiving as such didn't affect Akhil and his roommates, but the massive Black Friday sale the next day did. On that day, everything is supposed to be heavily discounted, so much so that people start lining up outside stores in the night.

It was the day students looked forward to all year to buy their electronics and a lot of other stuff. Priya and Akhil had done extensive research for the best deals, and had narrowed down on a couple of laptops they wanted from Best Buy. They checked around to see who all were planning to go shopping. Dilpreet was.

The group left for the mall at around 1 am in Dilpreet's car. The store would open at 6 am, but they had to be there early if they wanted to get hold of any of the decent stuff. First come, first serve.

The Best Buy parking lot was bursting at the seams. Dilpreet parked his car in the adjoining parking lot, and Akhil, Priya, and Kedar joined the line. They had underestimated the crowd. The line was already half a mile long. There were people who seemed like they had been camping there for days. A group had a small tent setup. Many others were snuggled up inside sleeping bags.

The temperature was a chilly 35 °F. The desi group had gone unprepared, wearing only light jackets.

'Guys, this is tough. What are we going to do in this cold

for the next five hours?' Akhil wondered.

Dilpreet patted him on his shoulder. 'Relax Akhil. It will be daybreak in no time. Trust me, I've done this for many years now. Just watch the people around.'

They all took Dilpreet's word. He was the veteran among them after all.

Akhil looked around. Most people in the line were Black or Latino. He wondered if race had anything to do with the Black Friday nomenclature and thought of asking Dilpreet, but decided against doing so.

The store opened before time, at about 4.30 am and people stormed in like a hurricane. It was like a melee of people trying to board the unreserved compartment of an Indian train. Utter chaos.

The lady who opened the door moved aside just in the nick of time, and saved herself from getting trampled. The store was soon swarming with people who seemed to be picking up whatever they could lay their hands on. It was crowded and people were pushing each other. The place was beginning to smell as the air conditioners creaked under the load. It was like everybody had been magically transferred back to India, on a 'free entry day' at the Delhi Trade Fair.

Dilpreet had a suggestion. 'Guys, we know who wants what. Let's spread out in the store and pick up any of those things we can find. We can then always sync up in the checkout line.'

'Great idea, sirjee. Would have been even better if we had a set of walkie-talkies to coordinate,' said Kedar.

'Sure Kedar, why don't you buy a set today? Will come in handy next year,' Dilpreet winked.

Three hours later, the harried desi group was out of the store. Akhil had been able to get hold of a laptop, a digital camera, and a printer. Kedar and Priya had also picked up their laptops.

They reached back home just as the sun was rising. The air had that invigorating nip about it. Akhil was excited about his new laptop. No more nights to be spent at the lab.

The excitement of the Black Friday sale didn't last long. The finals were just around the corner. There were assignments to be completed, and books and presentations to be reviewed. The group was spending more and more time on work, mostly at the cost of sleep and personal time.

Akhil slept an average of four hours every night in the week before the finals. He *had* to get those perfect A-grades. Nothing less would do. He could never forget Goyal uncle's condescending tone. It egged him on whenever his motivation levels went down.

He talked to Nandita every night for comfort. Just hearing her voice eased his troubles and gave him the energy to carry on. But she had her own set of worries. She had bombed on one of her mid-terms and was struggling to make up in the finals.

Eventually Akhil wrote his tests to the best of his ability. When the results were announced a week later, Akhil was delighted to find that he had achieved his target. He had secured the first set of A grades. Nandita had scored good grades too. They had a two-week break before the Spring semester, so Akhil and Nandita decided to celebrate it with a party. Life seemed good.

Hope floats

Anil proposed a week-long road trip to Miami over the break. Jassi was more than willing to come along. Also coming along were Anil's roommates, Akhilesh and Ruksh. Kedar refused to go saying he needed to complete an important project.

Nandita was going to stay with one of her cousins in Seattle for a week. The last night at the club had been fantastic. Akhil had seen yet another of Nandita's avatars. She had come in a short red skirt and Akhil could barely take his eyes off her glorious legs. They had both had a few drinks and danced like crazy, returning home only in the wee hours of the morning.

It had taken all of Akhil's will power to keep his hands off her, but he wasn't sure how long he would be able to control himself. He had looked forward to spending the break with her, but she had family obligations. He reluctantly agreed to come along to Miami with the rest of the group while she was gone.

Anil had rented an SUV. It could seat almost seven people in total. The more the merrier, as it meant less shared cost for everybody.

Sundar joined in as well. A couple of comforters were laid out in the trunk of the massive car, packets of snacks and a crate of Corona was procured, and the desi gang was out on the first major road trip for the newcomers. They would travel down to Tampa and then on to Orlando where they planned to spend a couple of days at Disney World. From Orlando they would drive to Miami and Key West, and return to Tallahasseee. The whole trip would take five days.

Soon they were out on the highway. Everybody was in a great mood. *Linkin Park* was playing on the stereo, Pringles were being passed around, and Anil and Jassi already had their beer bottles open. The car was flying through the light traffic on the smooth 4-lane expressway.

Anil asked Ruksh to slow down. 'Dude, the speed limit is 75. You are going at 90. You don't want to get a ticket for overspeeding.'

He had barely completed the sentence when the familiar police siren blared, and a state trooper car sprung into action from its hideout in the central verge between the two carriageways. Everybody froze. Anil called out to everybody to hide the beer bottles immediately, and for Sundar to hide in his dugout in the trunk. They were committing at least two offenses in addition to overspeeding—consuming alcohol in a moving vehicle, and overloading the car with passengers in the trunk. Ruksh shouted at everybody for distracting him. They were all in danger of getting arrested. Beads of sweat started forming on his forehead. Akhil felt his own heart thumping away.

The police car was right behind them and gaining speed. Suddenly it moved to the adjoining lane and sped away. The cops were going after someone else. The boys had just been saved by the skin of their Rupa underpants.

For the rest of the journey, Ruksh drove the car at atleast 5 mph below the speed limit. Nobody spoke for an hour after the scare. They discarded the alcohol at the next rest stop, which was another new American concept to the car's Indian passengers. Back home they had only seen creaky dhabas along highways to stretch their legs.

It was lunch time by the time they reached the town of Tampa. They decided to stop at an Indian restaurant, get lunch, and then head to the beach. Ruksh drove them to the restaurant for which he had taken directions before hand. It was a pre-GPS era, so they were travelling with printed Google Maps for directions.

'Jewel of India' was a reasonable, quaint little Indian restaurant a few miles from the beach. Anil quipped that between the words 'Jewel', 'India', 'Taj', 'Spices', and 'Kohinoor', one could probably cover the names of 90 percent of the Indian restaurants in the US.

They were just in time for the lunch buffet, which featured chicken tikka, paneer butter masala, dal makhani, and gulab jamun for dessert. The defacto universal buffet menu for Indian restaurants in America, as Anil explained to the others.

At 12 dollars per head, it didn't seem particularly cheap to Akhil, but the sight of the sumptous gulab jamuns made him hesitatingly agree to part with his dad's hard-earned money for this meal. Ruksh looked at the chicken tikka and sighed. It looked tantalizing.

'I don't eat non-veg on Tuesdays,' he lamented. It was a Tuesday.

A 'three-by-six' tomato soup kicked off proceedings for the group. Half an hour later, the six graduate students had extracted their money's worth. Their table now resembled a scene from a war zone. The restaurant staff watched helplessly as the group devoured everything in sight.

'Holy crap, dudes. I am stuffed.' Ruksh said wiping the sweat off his forehead. He had compensated for the chicken with the vegetarian stuff on offer.

'Ruksh, you did great. That you must never be able to get up straight from a buffet meal is one of the basic tenets of Indian culture.' Anil offered the one left-over gulab jamun to Ruksh, who winced. Anil finished it off with one surgical strike.

They paid. No tip was left, because as per Ruksh, 'Who the hell gives tips for a buffet meal!' The waiter made a face as they left. 'Thank you, sir. Please come again.' He didn't look like he meant it though. Akhil thought he heard him add a *'don't'* at the end of his sentence.

They reached the beach. It was not too crowded at this time of the year as there was a very slight nip in the air. Some people were loitering about, but there weren't too many in the water. Jassi felt massive disappointment. There were hardly any swimsuits on display. It all seemed like the second wasted effort after that futile trip to St George's. He had now been in Florida for five months and not seen a single bikini clad hot woman. This was worse than all the fruitless Saturday nights he had spent back home, waiting for the cable operator to telecast, you know, *that* stuff. Or, to use the term allegedly conjured by the good people of the Harappa civilization—KLPD.

Anil pointed out that though the day was a cool one, the weather forecast over the next few days predicted it would be warm. 'Miami will likely be very hot by the time we reach there, so don't worry too much. You boys will get tired of looking at bikinis.'

Despite the relatively cool weather, Akhil was keen on getting in the water. The others joined in, took off their T-shirts and played about for a little bit in the water. Some other people at the beach noticed the crazy Indians shouting about in the cold, and joined in the water.

The four-hour drive on to Orlando was uneventful. After the scare in the morning, Anil carefully drove below the speed limit, which ended up annoying some fellow drivers on the road. Road rage was clearly not limited only to Indian roads. They reached by 8 pm, and checked into a small motel.

The lady at the front desk was Indian. As were the bellboys. The boys discovered that this was a hotel run by a single Gujarati family. All the staff were members of the extended family. The manager, receptionist, janitorial staff, everyone was a Patel.

As an aside, Gujaratis own over 40 percent of all the hotels in the US. In fact, they are so ubiquitous that a new term has been coined for Patel owned Motels—Potels. Akhil was fascinated by how a hard-working, entrepreneurial community, had achieved its American dream by providing Americans comfortable places to dream.

The hotel was nice and clean, as much as one could expect from a 40 dollars per night budget hotel. The boys took two adjoining rooms. Nobody felt like having dinner after the heavy lunch. Akhil felt like he had eaten enough to last him a couple of days. They watched TV, and tired from all the driving, soon everybody dozed off. The next morning they planned to leave early for Disney World to ensure they had enough time during the day to cover all the attractions the place had to offer.

The night passed by in a blur and Anil's phone alarm went off at 6 am. Half an hour later, everybody was up. By 8 am, everybody was scrubbed and bathed. Before leaving, they planned to make the best use of the complimentary breakfast that came with the room booking. The boys finished their breakfast and headed onwards to Disney World. A day's ticket cost around 50 dollars, though they got a 50 percent discount for being Florida residents. Akhil gasped on hearing the ticket prices, though the discount made him feel better.

The money turned out to be well-spent. Disney World was a revelation. It was huge, with more than enough options for just a single day. The food was terribly expensive though, and Akhil nearly skipped lunch after finding out that the vegetarian burger cost 15 dollars.

Disney World rounded off the day with a daily fireworks display. Jassi was awestruck. 'Guys, this makes our Diwali rockets look like giggling teenagers at an annual conference of nuclear physicists. This is out of the world! And they do this everyday?'

Anil laughed. 'This is America, dude. Every day is a celebration.'

Jassi nodded in silent admiration.

By the time the boys reached the hotel, it was past 10 pm. Everybody crashed on the king-size beds, exhausted. Early next morning the boys set off for Miami—the city of sun, sand, South Beach, and hot Latino women. It was a warm day, but the sun felt nice in the December weather.

They stopped for some snacks at a rest area a short distance from Miami city. The rest area was massive. There was a gas station for 18-wheeler trucks as well as passenger cars, a food court, toilets, vending machines, and some green area with benches.

Akhil went to relieve himself. While mid-stream, a Latino man came to the next urinal and said something to Akhil in a foreign lanugage.

'Sorry?' Akhil was bewildered.

He again said something that did not sound like English. Then it struck Akhil. He was talking in Spanish!

'He thought I was Latino,' lamented Akhil to the others when they met at the food court.

'Hah. We Indians do look like Latinos, thanks to the brown skin tone. Happens to everybody. You can't live in Florida and not face this problem,' Ruksh said remembering his own initial days.

An hour later, they passed a sign welcoming them to Miami. No Potel this time; they were going to stay with a friend of Akhilesh who was doing his PhD from the University of Miami.

Hardik Reddy was Akhilesh's friend from his undergrad days. An offspring of a Gujarati mother and Keralite father, he had chosen University of Miami for his doctorate, simply because he was a much more advanced version of Jassi. Enroute, Akhilesh had regaled his fellow passengers with stories of how Hardik used to walk up to girls in clubs and announce, 'I am Hardik, and I am Reddy. Your place or mine?' (Try speaking it out loud, and you'll understand). The strategy produced guaranteed results. Eighty percent of the time he got slapped, laughed at, or just given an incredulous stare, followed by the bouncers moving in. The remainder of the

20 percent times was what helped him sleep with a new girl every few weeks, and made all the humiliation worth it.

Hardik lived alone, but he was going to travel to Orlando overnight for a conference, so Akhil and the boys had the run of the entire apartment. The place was setup in the 'Harddick' theme. There were Kamasutra posters on the walls, an unusually graphic shower curtain, and a weird phallic table lamp in the living room. Akhil could see why he was lived alone. Or why nobody would want to live with him, in this sex dungeon.

Hardik had to leave for his conference, but asked his guests to help themselves to whatever was in the kitchen, cautioning them against touching any of his 'personal' belongings. A hungry Akhil opened the fridge. The shelves were bare. There were two slices of white bread, no jam, no butter, no fruit, nothing. It was like someone had cleaned up the fridge in advance. There is no such thing in America as a free lunch.

Akhil sighed. His stomach grumbled.

The boys had breakfast at a Bagel place they found nearby, and then went out for sightseeing. South Beach was the destination for the day. One of the most famous beaches in the world, where the high-heeled celebrities went to party and to be photographed for magazines. The beach was nice, the weather was just right, and the clean water was a fine shade of green-blue. It was quite crowded, and the boys roamed around in full clothes, camera straps in their necks, sticking out like sore brown thumbs in a sea of green, yellow, and blue bikinis. Jassi was in heaven. Akhil felt guilty looking at anyone other than Nandita. The experienced seniors were careful not to ogle too openly, but Jassi was oblivious to anything that day. Sundar was busy taking pictures of the sea and getting giddy at the sight of clear blue waters.

They noticed another group of Indian students nearby, also staring at the ladies and taking photos sneakily. Careful to avoid eye contact, both groups marked their territories, and moved to different parts of the beach.

The boys spent a few hours on the beach and returned home, after a dinner of Subway sandwiches. Since that first trip in Tallahasseee, the boys had now gotten familiar with how Subway worked.

The next morning, as Anil drove the car out of the parking lot to drive to Florida Keys, a drop of rain fell splat on the windshield. Within five minutes, it was pouring heavily as they reached the highway to drive down to the southernmost part of mainland USA.

The drive from Miami turned out to be a splendid one, with numerous bridges over the sea, connecting the various islands in the Florida 'Keys'. The last island in the chain is Key West, officially the southernmost point of the US. The plan was to reach by afernoon, spend the rest of the day there, sleep the night in a hotel, and then head back for Tallahasseee the next morning.

As they drove down the iconic 'Seven-Mile Bridge', Beyonce singing on the car stereo, windows rolled down, the gentle breeze in their hair, and water all around them save for the stretch of road in the middle of the sea, Akhil and Jassi gasped. They had seen a lot of pretty sights in the past few days, but this had to be one of the highlights of their trip. It was like they were driving among the clouds, on top of the prettiest shade of water there could ever be.

They reached Key West and the hungry boys found an Indian restaurant there. A sumptuous buffet was devoured, followed by a trip around the happening part of the tiny island. Akhil took the customary photographs with the stone monument in stripes of red, yellow, and black that marked it as the 'Southernmost point of the United States of America'. A Latino man approached them and asked if they were interested in a sunset cruise.

The regular price was 20 dollars per head for the 45-minute trip where they would take people out to sea on a speedboat. They would show some sights along the shore, one could see the sunset in the open waters, and come back safely to shore. The man offered the desi students a 30 percent discount. They took it. The offer of unlimited free beer onboard played its part in helping the boys make the decision.

The cruise was fun. Each of the 20 odd people onboard got a plastic glass, which the crew promptly filled with beer even before they had left for sea. 'This is going to be fun.' Ruksh was excited.

Anil held his glass up. 'Three cheers to Florida'

'Three cheers to bikinis.' Jassi added.

The captain took the boat out to sea, pointing out a few sights along the shore. Fifteen minutes later, they were in the middle of nowhere, with only water all around them. Akhil had never been this far out in open water. The best he had done till now was a boat ride near India Gate back in Delhi. Not exactly open water.

The dozen odd sunset seekers on the boat had already consumed copious amounts of beer. A few were now getting dizzy, and the seasickness wasn't helping matters.

All of a sudden, there was the loud sound of thunder. The skies turned a couple of shades darker, and Akhil felt a tiny drop of water strike his face and trickle all the way down to his neck. The sea turned violent. The captain shouted something loudly in Spanish. They stopped refilling the beer glasses.

Over the next ten minutes, the winds got faster, the skies darkened, and the crew visibly seemed to be in a state of panic.

They were in a rickety boat, many miles out at sea in the Gulf of Mexico, in the midst of a storm that was getting worse by the minute. The boat was now tossing around in the sea, as the crew shouted at each other in a language that none of the boys understood. They seemed terrified, so the passengers could clearly guess they weren't exchanging compliments.

Akhil saw lightning flashes around them. He could spot what seemed like small tornadoes forming in the distance. This was turning out to be a nightmare. He did not want to die this way. They would likely never be found if they drowned here.

Everybody was praying. This was the best they could do in this situation.

For the next half an hour they tossed and turned in the sea. No land was in sight for miles. Some people were openly sobbing now. Ruksh threw up, likely from the half a dozen glasses of beer he had consumed until now.

Akhil saw his life flashing before his eyes. His mom wiping her tears with her sari pallu at the airport, the flight to the US, that tea with dad on his first morning in the US, those mattresses they had lugged from trash bins to their apartment. Nandita. Their movie date. The night at the club.

The storm abated slightly. Someone shouted 'I see land!'

Night had fallen by now, but Akhil could see lights in the distance. They were back on track. There was hope.

Ten minutes later they landed back at Key West. Everybody got off the boat. The crew handed out towels to dry themselves up, and a cup of hot chocolate to each passenger. Someone murmured that the captain had lost the way and gone out way more than he should have.

Akhil saw the name painted on the side of the boat. 'Hope'. Hope had certainly saved them.

They finished the hot chocolate and went off to their hotel. The day had taken a dramatic turn from the exhilaration of the drive from Miami. The 45-minute cruise had ended up being two hours long. In the melee, they didn't even notice when the sun had set.

The boys checked in to the hotel and went to bed. Nobody had the appetite to eat anything after the ordeal of the sunset cruise.

Next morning they woke up early. The drive back to Tallahasseee was at least twelve hours long, and they wanted to cover as much distance during the day as possible. By 9 am, their car was on the road. The three seniors would take turns between them to cover the long drive back home.

They were at University Club apartments at 10 pm.

'This was the most action-packed trip of my life. Thanks guys, though next time I could do with a little less adventure,' Akhil said laughing, though he knew things could have been much worse.

'No worries dude. Glad to be alive after the scare yesterday. You guys take care now and get some rest. I'll see you later.' Anil drove off.

As Jassi and Akhil approached, they noticed someone in the distance, coming out of their apartment. It was a female, but they couldn't see the face in the dark. She was gone by the time they could get any closer.

Too tired afer the long drive to give it much thought, Akhil and Jassi crashed in their beds.

✈

The next morning Akhil called up Nandita on her mobile. She was still in Seattle, but due to return in two days. They spoke for a couple of hours. Akhil described the entire road trip, from the police scare to the wonders of Disney World, the drive to Key West, and finally the adventure aboard that fateful cruise. Nandita was horrified when Akhil described the cruise.

'Oh my God, Akhil. No more cruises for you. Also next time I will go with you.' She sounded genuinely terrified.

'Thanks Nandita. I sure could use your company. You should have just told your stupid cousin that you have a project to work on, or some excuse.' Akhil replied.

'Just another couple of days, and I'll be there. Keep some of your precious time free for me.'

'Of course, Nandita. All my time is for you.' Akhil smiled. His heart skipped a beat and a few more.

'Liar,' she said. Akhil could feel Nandita flashing that heart-warming smile on the other end.

'See you then.' Akhil's heartbeat took a few minutes to stabilize after the call.

Condom Balloons

The break was over. It was time to return to the grind for the Spring 2005 semester. Fall had proved excruciatingly rigorous for Akhil, and this semester didn't seem any less punishing. The only redeeming feature might be the beautiful flowers expected to blossom during the season, and Spring Break later in March.

Akhil also looked forward to the blossoming of his budding relationship with the adorable Nandita who had returned from Seattle last week. They had the entire week to themselves, and had roamed all over town. The two had been to the Capitol building, housing the Florida government. The 360° view of the entire town from the top of Tallahasseee's tallest building had been fantastic. Then there was the 3D movie at the massive IMAX theater. It had taken Nandita an hour to recover from seeing fighter pilots zoom around, while Akhil couldn't stop apologizing for getting her into the dizzying film.

The two had covered the entire campus, discovering all the beautiful, ancient buildings, some of which dated back to the 1800s. Every day would start with Akhil going to Nandita's apartment to pick her up. She would greet him with the warmest of hugs and they would head out for their adventures, returning once they got tired. Akhil had forgotten all about the scare at Key West by now. He was living a blessed life, in the company of the woman he adored.

The week had ended far too quickly. This semester he had ended up again taking some of the most challenging courses on offer, and promptly bought a massive pack of instant coffee. Caffeine would continue to fuel his quest for perfect scores. He would need to burn a lot of midnight oil to stay on track for those elusive 'A' grades.

The first day of classes, Akhil got a massive shock on finding out that the book for the Advanced Algorithms course was going to cost him 100 dollars. The equivalent of 4900 rupees then. There was no way Akhil wanted to spend that much on a book if he could avoid it.

He called up home that evening and asked his dad if he could check if they had an Indian edition of the book at Chandni Chowk's 'Nai Sarak'. Those were invariably a fraction of the cost of the US versions. They could speed-post the book and he would have it in a couple of weeks. Even with the cost of shipping, it would be a good bargain. Until then he could manage with photocopies. Akhil's thoughts went back to his college in India, where some students had actually proposed building a temple dedicated to the photocopier machine on campus. After the placement office and the cafeteria, it was the most important spot for budding engineers.

The next evening, a crowd of around twenty Indian students gathered at apartment 201 in the University Club. Pooja had individually called them all up for Kedar's birthday party.

She had spent the day helping Akhil and Jassi lay out a sumptuous spread for the party. Akhil was frying his last lot of Gulab Jamuns when Jassi came in the kitchen and proceeded to fill up a pack full of condoms with turmeric water.

Priya soon walked in with what looked like a puffed up can of milk. 'This milk turned sour last week. I saved it for the occasion.'

Kedar had no idea about this party and Venkat had invited him over on the pretext of discussing something important over a couple of beers. Akhil gave a missed call to Venkat's mobile, which was the signal for them to walk Kedar back to the apartment.

Kedar entered to a rousing welcome from the assembled people. The apartment was heavily decorated, besides being heavily populated. Kedar was pleasantly surprised. He had been quite disappointed all day that no one had bothered to wish him on his birthday.

Kedar cut the cake and Jassi took the creamiest part of the cake and smothered Kedar's face in the chocolate cream. What followed was a free-for-all, with everybody joining in the fun and ensuring that every inch of Kedar's head was covered in cake. Jassi brought his condom water balloons and threw them splat on the head of the poor birthday boy.

There was no cake anymore. It was all either in Kedar's hair, on the carpet, or wet.

Priya brought her can of rotten milk and Jassi had a crate of eggs in his hands.

Dilpreet intervened. 'Guys, it would be better to take this outside if you are going to create more mess.'

The group led Kedar outside. Over the next ten minutes, the wild desis fired eggs at him from all angles. For the grand finale, Priya opened the can of rotten milk and handed it over to Akhil to do the honours. Akhil brought the can up to Kedar's head and was overwhelmed by the smell of the milk combined with all the egg yokes peeking out of his hair.

Akhil's stomach did a cartwheel and, unable to bear the smell any longer, he threw up on Kedar's left leg.

At that moment, a police patrol car drove up outside, and two officers got out, hands on their holsters. The neighbours had called the cops after hearing the commotion outside. They probably thought that the hapless Indian dude was being sacrificed to one of the several million Indian Gods in some weird ritual.

Dilpreet handled the cops and explained the situation to them. They hung around for half an hour, asked everyone to return to the apartment, and eventually left once they were convinced it was just a bunch of hyper desi kids with a misguided sense of adventure.

It took a glass of Limca for Akhil and three rounds of shampoo for Kedar to get back to their normal selves. The party had made Akhil puke, the carpet was most likely ruined, Kedar was still stinking, and everybody was very hungry. Nobody was going to forget this birthday party for a while.

After the party, the boys got together at Venkat's apartment. Akhil mentioned how Pooja had worked doubly hard preparing for the party and had tirelessly decorated the entire apartment.

Kedar revealed that he had a thing going with Pooja. His face was a light shade of red by the time he was done.

Akhil was surprised. He had not seen this coming. Pooja had apparently been visiting Kedar for late-night encounters. Now they knew why Kedar refused to go for the Miami trip. Akhil could now guess who was the mysterious figure they had seen emerging from their apartment when they had got back from the trip.

✈

It was one of the quieter January evenings. It had been two weeks since Kedar's infamous birthday. Sundar was over for a cup of tea.

If there was one grounded man in the entire Indian population in the university, it was Sundar. In the last few months, Akhil had never seen him stressed or angry. He was always at peace with himself, kind to others, and with a smile on his Chiranjeevi face. Akhil had experimented with alcohol and meat, but Sundar had stuck firm on his ideals. His cooking skills were already a legend. Akhil admired him though he could never resist pulling his leg.

Sundar was upset. 'Quite mad', by his own admission. It was their new roommate, Arnab.

'Man Akhil, this Arnab is crazy. You will not believe the kind of things he does. He found out that last month our electricity bill was a little high, and now he goes about the house turning off all the lights. I was cooking dinner yesterday and went to the bathroom for a minute. When I came back, he had turned off the kitchen light and told me to stop wasting electricity. If you leave your room for a minute, he will go in and switch off the light.'

'He's just so…weird. He creates a mess wherever he goes. I work at keeping the house tidy and he does the opposite. Besides, I suspect he steals from my stock of supplies. I am going crazy with this guy. I cannot even able to understand how we will live with him if he behaves like this. He will do all the stupid things only. Useless fellow.' Sundar spoke an endearing Tamil version of Indian-English.

Akhil laughed, but he knew he had roommate issues also just waiting to blow up.

Things were changing between the three roommates. Ever since the birthday party, Kedar had been spending a lot more time with Pooja. Jassi had never had time for the house or roommates. He was forever running after girls.

The house was a mess most of the times. Akhil had a cleanliness streak about him, and would end up cleaning the entire apartment. Kedar would complete his cooking and leave the kitchen a disaster, with utensils choking up the sink until someone took the effort of cleaning them. Akhil was no longer cool with being that lone Indian batsman who had to carry the weight of the entire team in every match. Things between the roomies were a bit strained, though still cordial.

The carpet's stains had not gone anywhere despite repeated attempts with different types of sprays procured from the Dollar Store. Ruksh had scared them with stories of another household who had been made to pay 1000 dollars towards replacement of the carpet because they had burnt a hole in it after an especially drunk night. Akhil had trouble sleeping for the next two nights after hearing the story.

'Alright Akhil, I'll leave now. Have to prepare dinner. Hopefully Arnab hasn't caused any new mess today.' Sundar got up to leave.

Jassi was at the University's fitness centre with Nigel. The two had come to the gym to work off all the beer they had been piling on their bellies.

Jassi was fascinated. The centre was huge and the machines were state of the art, with numerous options for working out each muscle in the body. More importantly, there were pretty girls in itsy-bitsy workout gear everywhere. Jassi cursed himself for missing out all these months.

An hour later, a thoroughly tired Jassi headed over to the locker room to get a shower, and change back into regular clothes from the workout gear. He was in pain. He wondered if this is what they meant when they told you to listen to your body, because he could clearly hear his body groaning. As he approached the lockers, he noticed a man weighing himself on the balance. Which was fine, except the guy was not in workout gear. He was naked. Jassi quickly moved away before it formed an image that would give him nightmares forever.

Nigel took off his clothes and walked into the showers. Jassi watched him get naked, his mouth open. He realized he was also expected to follow suit. In his birthday suit.

There were at least a dozen men in the open shower area. They were all naked. Jassi wondered for a second what mess he had landed himself into. He looked around him for a few minutes and then he took off his clothes and stepped into the shower. He took the quickest of showers, careful to avoid the gaze of anybody else. He then got dressed and quickly left the gym.

The next evening, Jassi was back to avail his free session with a certified instructor, who turned out to be a stunning woman by the name of Adriana. Adriana was gorgeous, with flawless golden skin, light brown hair, and the body of Scarlett Johansson. A 10 on his rating meter, Jassi had no doubt. She was going over an exercise routine for Jassi, while he was more interested in knowing her personal details. The charm wasn't working very well though, for she was focusing on completing the mandatory one hour, not responding to Jassi's questions about her birth date or, 'how did you manage to become so beautiful?'

The session was over. Adriana suggested he cool off in the sauna for a little bit to relax the sore muscles. The sauna was close to the Olympic sized pool. Jassi gingerly got into the hot water and heaved a sigh of relief as the heat worked its magic. There were a couple of girls in the sauna as well. They smiled at the Punjabi lad, who greeted them with a raised left eyebrow, a slight upwards movement of the head, and 'how you doin?' like Joey from *Friends*. They giggled. One of them turned over and kissed the other girl. Jassi cursed his luck. *Why do I have to get all the lesbians?*

Jassi felt slightly less shy in the shower that day. He hoped to get used to the idea in due course. If this is what being American meant, then he was all for public nudity.

Condom Balloons

The Florida sun dawned on February 14, 2005. Akhil was reminded of past Valentine's days. Back in his engineering college, there had been three girls in his class of eighty horny boys. The competition was intense for what was at best, mediocre reward. He had never even bought a rose in his life, leave alone give it to anyone. He had crushes on a number of girls over the years, but had never dared to speak to any of them. He knew they'd say no, or laugh. Or worse—say no *and* laugh.

This time was different. Akhil called up Nandita first thing in the morning and confirmed lunch at the International Center, where a hare-krishna guy from the local ISKCON temple, served sumptuous Indian lunches every day for five dollars each.

As Akhil was finishing his phone conversation, Kedar appeared from his room. Akhil asked Kedar what his plans for the day were. By now, everyone knew of his relationship with Pooja, though the two had never openly admitted to it, except to the very close friends.

'Nothing yaar. There are no plans.' The response was curt. Kedar looked like he hadn't slept all night. He returned to his room and slammed the door shut.

Akhil spent the afternoon roaming around campus with Nandita. They had lunch prepared by the ISKCON guy, a bald, white man dressed in a dhoti, who went by the name of Nityanand. The food was delicious and the helpings generous. They were thankful they didn't have classes to attend that afternoon or they'd have dozed off.

They decided to lounge around in the lawn outside the library. The weather was pleasant. The flowers were beautiful.

The stomachs were sated. Akhil was sitting on the grass. He had the love of his life lying in his lap.

'I love you Nandita,' Akhil finally mustered the courage to say the magic words. He could barely hear his own words over the loud racket his heart was making.

Nandita did not say anything. She pulled Akhil down to her and kissed him. The best of friends were now lovers.

Akhil walked on air for the remaining part of the day.

Later that night, Akhil had just finished his dinner and was watching TV in the living room when Kedar entered the apartment. His eyes were swollen, and he didn't seem to be in very good shape. He saw Akhil sitting in the living room and went straight to his room without saying anything. They hadn't talked all day. Akhil was stumped. Clearly all wasn't well between Kedar and Pooja.

✈

The Algorithms book had become a problem. It was not available in India, though the bookshop owner kept telling Akhil's dad that it was about to come out. After ten calls over the last two weeks, he had finally asked him to stop calling. 'We will call you once we get the book.'

The advice from headquarters had been a frustrated, 'Buy the book Akhil. It is okay. We'll get a loan for the 100 dollars if need be,' his dad had joked. Akhil had already spent more than a month without the book, using photocopies or sharing a copy from the young professor Amit Kumar. His performance on assignments was now slipping, so it was now a call between giving up the grade and spending the hundred dollars.

The next day Akhil went to the bookstore and bought the book. He shed a silent tear as the Asian guy at the checkout counter swiped his card for the 100 dollars, but he couldn't avoid it anymore. Not eating out for the next two semesters might help recoup the cost.

It was March 15, 2005. Akhil was in his office working on an assignment, when there was an urgent knock on the door. He opened the door and was surprised to see Pooja, who had never visited him in the department before. This was the first time he had seen her since she and Kedar broke up around Valentine's day.

She entered the door and closed it behind him.

'Hi Akhil.' She gave him a hug and took off her leather jacket revealing a low-cut top. Akhil's pulse quickened at the sight of the unexpected cleavage. *What is she here for?* he wondered.

Pooja moved close to where Akhil was sitting. He could smell her perfume, which reminded him of fresh jasmine flowers. She spoke in a soft, seductive tone. 'It had been such a long time since I talked to you, so thought of stopping by your office for a little bit. Hope you don't mind?'

She looked at the anxious look on Akhil's face and said, 'Why are you looking so scared? Relax dude, I am not going to molest you.'

'Not at all. Why would I be scared?' Akhil was the man here, he reminded himself.

'Akhil, I've been intending to talk to you for a while, but never got the chance. Are you avoiding me these days? What happened to our friendship?' They used to get along well until the last semester, and Akhil had found her company enjoyable, though now he had eyes only for Nandita.

'I don't know, Pooja. What happened between you and Kedar?'

'I don't want to go there. It is over with Kedar.' The tone was cold now.

The two sat in awkward silence for the next few minutes. Pooja eventually got up, wore her jacket, bade goodbye and left, her wide hips swinging behind her like a mini-pendulum, leaving Akhil wondering what to infer from her surprise visit.

That evening Akhil decided to talk to Kedar. They hadn't really got back on talking terms since Kedar broke up with Pooja, and Akhil had no idea what the grudge was. He made two cups of tea and walked into Kedar's room.

'Tea?' he offered the surprised Kedar.

'Sure, thanks buddy.' Kedar took the cup from Akhil and offered him a seat. No one spoke for a minute.

'It has been a while since we talked.' Akhil broke the silence eventually.

Kedar sighed. A wry smile emerged on his face.

'Did you get a haircut?' Akhil noticed Kedar's short hair.

'Haan *yaar*. They were getting long and unruly, and the one you gave me the last time was awful.' Kedar smiled, reminded of their *session*.

Akhil laughed. 'It wasn't much worse than what you did to me.'

They both laughed. The tension was gone. Kedar was back. All this while, he had just needed a little talking to.

'I am sorry for cutting off from you guys and being a

stupid idiot,' Kedar spoke after another minute long silence.

'No worries man. Good to have you back.' Akhil placed an arm on Kedar's shoulder and they sipped their tea like old buddies.

Kedar went over his story. Things had been going well with Pooja. She was the one who initiated things last semester. She would meet him after class every day. They'd have coffee. She would ask to have lunch with him. She visited him after dinner. She would call up every night to wish good night. Soon the charm started working. Kedar thought it was love. They got physical. Kedar thought things were moving in the right direction.

A day before Valentine's Day, Kedar had confessed his love for her. She had just stood like a statue, frozen. Then she walked off, saying 'sorry'.

Kedar said that he had no idea what happened, but after that day, he was too shattered to say anything. His studies had suffered. He was trailing in all of his courses. He had stopped talking to anyone.

'That woman played me.' Kedar was sobbing by the time he finished. 'And the bitch started going after Suresh's roommate Vijay, after dumping me. I saw her come out of their apartment around midnight every day for the next couple of weeks.' Kedar managed a wry smile.

Vijay had perfect grades, four papers accepted at conferences already, and close to a rockstar status in the math department. 'The irony is that I only introduced her to Vijay in the library, and he had mentioned that he was expecting a journal publication next month.' Kedar said with a sigh, adding 'There is no love. It is all about finding someone who has better grades, more papers, and who can make more money. Love is all bullshit.'

Akhil was unable to bring himself to tell Kedar about his encounter with Pooja earlier that day. There wasn't much point in adding to his hurt feelings by telling him that Pooja had tried to throw herself at him a few hours ago. She was obviously shopping around, and Kedar had been tried, tested, and dumped, much like people returned cameras at electronic stores after using them for a month. Clearly, Vijay had also not worked out for her either.

Akhil was glad they had this discussion. More than anybody else, Kedar needed it. He had been alone all this while.

The phone rang just as Akhil got off an hour-long call with Nandita. March had come to an end. The mid-terms were over. Nandita had also done well on her tests, and the two were very close to getting their A grades again. Things now didn't seem as stressful as last semester, when he had cried himself to sleep on several occasions after bouts of stress-induced self-doubt. His dad always used to say that love and girls distract one from studies, but Akhil felt otherwise now. Love was inspiring him to do well. It was getting the best out of him.

Kedar's performance had also picked up, and he had got good grades in his courses. No one knew about Jassi's scores though. Akhil did not have any common courses with him this time. He doubted anything good was happening there. Jassi was spending his entire time in extra-curricular activities.

It was Akhil's mom on the phone. She was upset about the Bengali family that had recently moved into the neighbouring house. The dad was retired and spent his days staring at anyone who went past, especially any visitors to the Arora household. Their daughter was approaching thirty, but was still unmarried.

'That man is so spooky, staring at us all the time. Then every other day they cook fish and the smell is nauseating. Just yesterday, as we sat down to watch *Kyunki Saas Bhi Kabhi Bahu Thi*, they started their cooking. Disgusting, I tell you. Just when Mihir was going to fight his mother to support his wife, your father vomitted, unable to bear the smell of their machchi. Now we can't even watch TV in peace. God, they are so weird. We must have done some sins in our previous life to deserve these Bengali people.'

Akhil sighed as he kept the phone. This did not augur well for the future, for whenever they found out that he had given his heart to a Bengali girl.

It was quite ironical. Just a day ago, Sundar had been complaining of people in his lab being racist and not talking to him nicely. Akhil wondered if white people looking down upon Indians was much different than Punjabis' dislike for Bengalis, or Tamil or Marathi people sticking among themselves, with an inherent distrust for anyone who didn't speak their language. Did Indian people have any right to talk about racist treatment abroad when they themselves were the biggest racists, at home or overseas?

✈

Jassi was at the gym. He had been coming regularly for a month now, trying to work out at least two to three times a week. He had gained a lot of weight ever since he landed in

Tallahasseee, and looking at all the fit people in campus had made him realize that he needed to be thin to be popular with the ladies.

It wasn't easy though. When you are approaching 85 kilos, every minute trying to run is torture worse than the one practiced in Indian jails on unsuspecting criminals. When he started the regime, he would run for thirty seconds and it would feel like his lungs were about to explode. The next couple of minutes would go by trying to regain his breath, panting and wheezing like he had just completed a marathon while being chased by rabid dogs that hadn't eaten for a week. The only thing that inspired Jassi to keep moving was all those pretty girls in stretchy spandex tights, running past him on the indoor running track at the gym. Each woman running past beckoned him to try harder, to run one lap more. Many days he had managed to extend his runs purely by imagining Pamelaji in front of him, wearing her Baywatch swimsuit, calling out to him with outstretched hands.

Things were much better now. He was able to run for five minutes at a stretch. Jassi was confident he was on the verge of breaking a world endurance record. He had one more month to lose all those rolls of fat on his tummy. Spring Break was coming up. Jassi was going to head out on a road trip with Nigel and his boys. This was the biggest party in the entire year. Jassi couldn't wait. However, he needed to be in beach-ready form first.

Jassi was going over his plans in his mind, when a familiar figure ran past. In tights, Victoria's body looked even slimmer. She had lost those pimples since their last encounter, the one of the desperate, failed kiss. Jassi looked at her shapely contours and wished that the government would make a law for hot women to only be allowed to wear tights. Or bikinis, which he felt would be even better.

Victoria had not noticed him, and was getting farther away. Jassi quickened his pace. This was about to get interesting.

She had started off with a light jog, and Jassi was able to close in fast. Gradually she increased her pace, and Jassi's breathing started getting laboured with the exertion. As he wheezed and huffed a few metres behind her, admiring the view, she turned around to check the source of the commotion.

She looked at him and her face broke into a smile. 'Jazz?'

Jassi stopped, but it was a minute before he could respond. His breathing finally came back to normal. He wiped the sweat on his forehead with the sleeve of his shirt while she looked on, hands on her hips, and an amused expression on her face.

'Hi Victoria,' he finally managed.

'Whoa there. Looks like somebody's working hard to get rid of the love handles.' Her face looked radiant, especially with the slight sweat that had begun to form before she stopped for Jassi.

'Love handles?' Jassi's ears stood at alert at the mention of love.

She laughed loudly. 'Oh, these.' She grabbed a tire of fat on Jassi's side.

She touched him, and Jassi knew that he was back in business. In his mind, there was no doubt that Victoria was definitely interested in him.

As he took his shower that evening, Jassi suddenly realized that Victoria was probably doing the same a few doors away, in the ladies' shower room. A shiver ran down his body as he imagined her bathing in all her naked glory, and he quickly rushed to wear his clothes. He was going to head to McDonald's to catch-up with her over dinner. Jassi had latched onto her suggestion to talk over dinner, and luckily she was free tonight. He had plans to work on an assignment due the next day, but dates with pretty girls override any other commitments for most boys.

Jassi had a great time at their dinner, in part because he was just so hungry from the workout. Victoria stopped him from going for a second burger, reminding him he would have to run about ten miles to make up for it. 'Mr Jazz, you need to watch your diet if you want to lose weight.'

The two decided to become workout partners, and meet at the gym every evening. Jassi was delighted. He knew it was just a matter of time before he moved their workouts from the gym to his bedroom.

'Alrighty then, I'll see you tomorrow.' She waved at him as she got into her car.

'Yes, I will give you a ring tomorrow when my classes are done.'

Her eyes opened up wide. 'You'll give me a ring?' Jassi realized the faux pas and gestured to his mobile phone.

'Ah, *that* ring!' She laughed loudly. This quirky Indian dude was crazy.

The evening ended with Jassi getting a peck on the cheek from Victoria.

Two Festivals

It was the much-awaited spring break. The campus wore a deserted look. All the students were away indulging in wanton pursuits of alcohol and sex at exotic beach destinations. Some had gone to the popular beach towns in Florida. The more adventurous ones went to Mexico or the Bahamas. The location probably didn't matter, because they were anyway going to be too drunk to comprehend their surroundings.

Akhil didn't have the luxury of taking the week off. He had assignments lined up to complete. He was studying outside the department building under the pleasant sun when two shadows emerged on the table from behind him. He looked up from his notes to see two young white guys smiling at him.

'Hi there. Sorry for interrupting you, but mind if we ask you a couple of questions?' asked the dude with the blonde hair and braces.

'How can I help you?' Akhil wasn't very happy about the sudden disruption.

'We are from the Church of Jesus Christ of Latter-day saints.

We noticed you sitting by yourself so thought of having a quick conversation with you.'

The boy in braces introduced himself. 'My name is Michael. This is George.' George waved at Akhil.

Akhil responded with a polite, 'Hi. I am Akhil.'

Michael continued, 'Hi Akhil. What country are you from?'

The 'quick' conversation ended up taking thirty minutes of Akhil's time. Michael and George grilled him with questions on his religion, his concept of God, how he prayed, and what he thought of Christianity.

Akhil tried his best to dodge their volley of questions. 'I think God is within us. I am not a very religious person as such, and believe that being true to yourself and your work is true worship.'

They didn't look happy with his answer and started talking about their church and its principles. Akhil realized where this might be headed and excused himself saying he had to get lunch. He walked off just as the young boys were about to hand him a pamphlet.

Akhil thought of the missionaries who ran the Buddies of International Students' association. They weren't directly under the ambit of the International Center, but Akhil had learnt about them from flyers that were circulated there. From ferrying students to and from Walmart for free every week, arranging English speakers to help non-native speakers improve their language skills, free donated furniture, to visits to American families to celebrate festivals such as Christmas and Thanksgiving with them, the association was doing a lot of good work for hapless international students.

Akhil thought if it was all too good to be true. *Why would they take so many pains for blabbering foreign kids?* He wondered if all this was just an open-hearted goodwill or did these people actually expect something in return?

He had no idea.

The next morning Ruksh called up Akhil. 'Dude, we are planning to go to Panama City beach today. Do you want to come?'

Akhil wasn't so sure. 'Man, there are some assignments I wanted to complete.'

'Trust me dude, this will be worth it.' Ruksh seemed very excited.

An hour later Anil's car was racing down the I-10 inter-state expressway towards Panama City, two hours away. Kedar had also come along.

'So Ruksh, what's the deal with Spring Break? And what did you mean it will be worth it?' Akhil had no idea what to expect.

Ruksh explained, as Anil drove singing along to *Linkin Park*. 'Dude, Spring Break is the one week in the year when kids here get completely reckless. They go to some fancy place, typically beach destinations, and spend the entire time drinking, hanging out by the beach, and in general being super horny. Everybody is so drunk; they don't even know who they are sleeping with. Which is great for us desis. Even we stand a chance, if we play it right.'

Anil smiled at his roommate's description.

Ruksh continued, 'Then there are a lot of events they have at the typical Spring Break destinations. There are wet T-shirt contests that you just have to see to believe. It'a *ALL* out there man, if you know what I mean. The beauty is, everybody knows what happens at these events. Even parents, who have to play cool with it.'

An hour later, Anil pulled into the parking of the biggest club in Panama City.

'This place has the wildest events in all of Florida,' Ruksh was having trouble hiding his excitement. 'The real parties happen at night but there's going to be plenty of action now as well.' It was 1 pm.

The club was massive and there was a little stage erected in the little island in the centre of the swimming pool. There were lots of pretty students all around. Hunky dudes in their swimming trunks and pretty girls in teeny bikinis. Acres upon acres of skin on display. The boys got a beer each. There was that ubiquitous red plastic cup in every hand all around them. Everybody was waiting in anticipation for the events of the day to start.

The master of ceremonies, a buff dude wearing a T-shirt and shorts, came on the stage. 'Boys and girls, bros and hos, welcome to Panama City, the hottest destination for Spring Break in all of Florida. Are you all drunk yet?'

Loud cheering followed. The guys high-fived. Girls screamed. The host continued above the racket, 'Alright then, we will start with the 'Handsome Hunk' contest in five minutes, which will be followed with the wet T-shirt contest. If you think you are a handsome hunk, come see me.'

The cheering continued. Akhil made a quick trip to the restroom to take a leak.

The contest started. One by one, handsome young boys

walked the makeshift 'ramp' across the water, strutting their stuff. Some flexed their muscles. Most of them made obscene, suggestive gestures. The girls hooted loudly in response.

The emcee announced the name of the next contestant, and out walked Jassi. He was there—a lone desi ranger in this sea of tanned white skin. Akhil gasped seeing his roommate here.

He seemed a bit nervous. The guys before him had all been devoid of hair on their bodies, while Jassi looked like a baby Gorilla, with a chest full of rich black hair that fluttered in the wind. The sound levels went down, as the cheering subdued. Jassi was an outsider crashing the party. He had managed to lose a lot of weight, but the 6-pack abs were still hiding under layers of fat. Someone booed as Jassi flexed his biceps. Akhil cheered for his roomie. Jassi smiled nervously at the unexpected support. But the booing grew louder and Jassi had to run off the stage.

The wet T-shirt competition was next. Girls lined up behind the stage, and changed into flimsy T-shirts that would become transparent once wet.

The contest started. It was crazy. They would come on the stage one by one, and someone would direct a burst of water from a pipe at them as the onlookers cheered. The girls were all too drunk to care. One of them took off her top and flung it into the crowd, where it landed a few feet from a delirious Ruksh. Another one took her bottom off, and was promptly escorted off the stage. The others stuck to raunchy dances denoting assorted sexual positions.

Akhil couldn't believe the absurdity of it all. He wondered if any Indian girls also participated in this orgy, and how their parents felt about it. He felt some shame in watching the proceedings and walked out.

The boys headed to the beach, which was full of pretty young things lying on beach chairs, getting tanned. Anil looked at Akhil, 'Look at these people. They'll lie here for hours at stretch. I stay fifteen minutes and my skin starts burning. Let's get in the water, shall we?'

The four Indian dudes were the only ones on the beach wearing T-shirts, just like they had in Miami back in December. They took off their T-shirts and got in the water. Akhil found the beach even more gorgeous than Miami. The sand was white. The clear waters a striking shade of blue.

They stayed on for a few more hours and headed back. Ruksh was interested in staying overnight for the *real* party, but Anil and Akhil vetoed it. They had seen enough already of this American *celebration* of youth.

Akhil spent the rest of the break studying and finishing off his assignments. He talked to Nandita every day on the phone, but they met just once during the entire week. She had started on her research and was spending more and more time in the lab. Akhil had his hands full as well.

Soon it was time for Holi, the festival of colours and alcohol. A bunch of Indian students showed up at Leon Country Public Park, dressed in their holi finery, or in other words, tattered clothes.

No water or rowdiness was permitted by the authorities, so the gathering had to limit themselves to good old dry organic gulal. The boys smeared each other's faces in various hues across the RGB colour spectrum. Akhil grabbed Nandita as soon as she arrived, and smothered pink gulal all over her face. Kedar whistled in the distance.

Sundar had brought along a couple of his American friends. 'Akhil, meet my labmates, John and Kathy.'

Akhil applied colour on John's cheeks. He looked at Kathy and hesitated. He felt a little apprehensive of applying colour on her pale skin. He had been told that American people were allergic to the strangest of things. Besides, India had taught him not to go around touching girls not related to you. He gave her a nervous smile and quickly retired to the company of the others.

The food was sumptuous. Akhil had never realized that the town had so many Indians who lived and worked in Tallahasseee. The fully sated boys were soon back home. Venkat had some new DVDs he had picked up from the Indian store. Akhil and Kedar joined him and Sundar to watch *Bunty aur Babli*.

Akhil felt grateful for Venkat and Sundar's company. While everybody else had changed around them, these two had remained their same warm selves since last year. Jassi by now was living his own life. They barely talked. Pooja was rumoured to be pursuing someone in the Chemistry department, after going after Kedar, Vijay, and Akhil briefly.

Akhil had been warned that this was coming. America was changing people. Money. Relationships. Ambition. The reasons were many, but people just didn't seem as straightforward as they used to when they had first landed off the boat.

Akhil noticed a lot of glitzy magazines in Sundar's living

room. He asked him if they had subscribed to all of them, and Sundar smiled.

'Our good friend, Arnab. Somebody told him that magazines here have a trial offer of a few free editions, and he has gone and subscribed to all of them. When the free versions stop, he subscribes with a different name and they restart. The guy knows all tricks to save money. Last week I saw him extinguish a cigarette after smoking half of it, to reuse. That boy is crazy.'

As Akhil picked up the latest version of *Cosmopolitan* and browsed through it, the door opened and in walked Arnab. As soon as he saw Akhil going through the magazine, the expression on his face changed. 'Sundar, please tell your friend to not go through my personal stuff. It is called stealing.'

Akhil's jaw dropped. He kept the magazine back on the rack.

'Thanks. Next time, please ask before using anything that belongs to me,' retorted Arnab and went into his room. Sundar made a frustrated expression.

'I am so sorry, Akhil. Please don't mind the idiot. He is just stupid. Just last week we had a big fight because he said the utilities bill is too high because Sundar and I use our laptops too much, and refused to pay his share. I don't know when he studies, because he spends all his time researching ways to save money. He probably knows the India calling rates of all companies by heart.'

As Akhil got up to leave for his apartment, Sundar had one last question. 'Akhil, why did you skip Kathy while applying colour at the Holi function? She felt left out and was asking me if I knew why.'

Two Festivals

Akhil was surprised. 'Sundar, back home, we never touch random women. It is considered rude. In Delhi, you'd get beaten up even for unintentionally brushing against a woman not known to you. I wasn't sure if it would be appropriate to touch her.'

He was embarrassed, but confused. He had meant well, but had never thought that he would turn out to be the person who was percieved as rude.

✈

It was May 2005 and the spring semester was winding up. Finals were starting in a couple of weeks. Akhil and Jassi were at Devika's home, for the momentous occasion of her 21st birthday party. She was now of legal age. She could officially go to bars. There was no more need for that fake ID that stated her age to be 22.

The apartment had 'student' written all over it. There were medical books on the shelves, a 32-inch LCD screen that her roommate had installed, and FSU memorabilia adorned the walls. Her roommate seemed like a big football fan. A large bowl of vodka laced fruit punch was in the kitchen. A keg of beer occupied prominent space in the living room. The place was swarming with people. The boys were a geeky bunch of Indians and Americans. The girls on the other hand, were mostly pretty and in dresses of various shapes and sizes. Jassi was going wild with imagination.

Last weekend he had a great idea. He called up Victoria and asked her if she was interested in a trip to the Panama City beach to catch some sun. That was his best chance of getting her into a bikini. The plan seemed infallible to him. They would get there, roll out the beach towels, and lie down on the sand. She would ask him to rub some sunscreen on her back like in the movies, and loosen her swimsuit to allow him access to the full real estate. One thing would lead to the other. Kissing was a given. Possibly more. The plan just had to work.

Unfortunately she said no, saying she had some work to complete.

The day presented another golden chance to him. The girls looked like they were all a couple of drinks down. He figured that soon they might get drunk enough and agree to go back with him for the after-party in his room.

As he sipped his vodka laced fruit punch, Jassi noticed an opportunity. There was this young Indian girl sitting by herself on the couch. She seemed shy, but looked quite stunning in her short black dress that ended a precious few inches above her knee. She was quite fair, unlike the other Indians present in the room. A solid 8 on his scale. He crossed the room and sat down next to her. She looked at him nervously and gave a slight smile, more out of courtesy than happiness at seeing him. However, to Jassi, this was his signal to move in for the kill.

'Hi, friends call me Nova, as in Cassanova.' Jassi went with his favourite pick-up line from *American Pie*.

She probably didn't get it, and looked at him with a confused expression. Jassi realized he needed to step it up. He tried again. 'If I say you have a gorgeous body, would you hold it against me?'

Two Festivals

Her eyebrows went up. Her glass seemed to have got stuck to her face, which she wasn't moving at all, lest she made eye contact with Jassi, who was equally determined.

She shifted in her seat and the sudden flash of her thigh encouraged Jassi, who decided it was time to pull out all stops. 'Nice top. Wanna fuck?'

She gulped down the entire drink, nearly choking in the process, and quickly got up from the couch to move to a group of peoples busy playing beer pong on Devika's study table. Jassi looked on nervously. She appeared to be whispering something to the group, and people turned to stare at Jassi.

At that moment, Akhil was outside with Devika and some of her Indian friends. They were discussing her favourite topic. Parents.

'Take a load of this. I got these awesome Calvin Klein ripped jeans. My mom looked at it and said, "What is this big hole? It is torn". She then proceeded to stitch up the jeans to *repair* it. My 200 dollar jeans ruined forever.'

One of her friends chipped in with her story. 'My dad once saw two lesbian chicks walking on the road, holding hands. He turned to me and said, "Look at them. Why can't you be this close with your sister?"'

An Indian girl came out and whispered something in Devika's ear. Devika's face turned red, she cursed loudly and stormed inside. Akhil followed behind, out of curiosity and a lurking suspicion that he might know the reason.

Once inside, she pointed to Jassi. 'There, that's him.'

Devika was stunned. She turned to Jassi. 'How dare you try to make a move on my kid sister? This is ridiculous.'

She then gestured to the door. 'Please leave right now.' Her face was red, and her hand shaking.

Akhil was embarrassed. He had asked Jassi to come along tonight, so he was partly to blame. The two walked out of the house, and returned to their apartment in silence. Jassi walked a couple of steps behind Akhil, like a rowdy child expelled from school for exploding firecrackers in the girls' toilet following his parent back home.

India Redux

The lady at the departure gate announced boarding to start in thirty minutes. Akhil found an empty seat in the waiting area and called up Nandita. It went to her voicemail. He hung up, well aware of his pathetic skills at leaving voice messages. That beep never failed to mess up his brain, and his mouth produced a garbled output even he couldn't recognize if played back to him.

She called back five minutes later.

'Hi Akhil.'

Akhil's eyes lit up. 'Hi Nandita. I was about to leave. Boarding is starting soon.'

'Have a safe flight, Akhil.' She wasn't her usual chirpy self. 'I'll miss you. Let's try if we can meet in India.'

Akhil had a lump in his throat the size of one of those tomatoes at Walmart. 'I'll miss you too, Nandita. This is going to be the hardest three months of my life.'

'I love you Nandu.'

'I love you too. Take care, Akhil.'

'Bye Nandita.' He hung up with a heavy heart.

Akhil sighed. It seemed like yesterday when he was terribly home sick, and now that he was going to India after being away for a year, he wanted to stay. Things had changed. He did not want to be away from Nandita.

The spring semester had ended. Akhil managed his 'A' grades in all courses. He was on track for his academic target. The summer semester was lighter and only a handful courses were on offer. People often took the semester off. Some people went to India. Some did internships, if they could find one. Akhil wanted to complete his degree as soon as he could, and was going to be taking courses this semester as well. For now, there was a two-week break before classes began in June, and he was travelling to India to be with his parents.

Nandita was taking the semester off, and would be travelling to India for the three months. Her flight back home was in a couple of days. Akhil wondered if he would be able to see her in India, given she would be in Kolkata and he in Delhi.

The boarding for the flight started, and with a heavy heart, Akhil got on the plane. Soon the massive Boeing 747 jet was airborne.

Looking dreamily out of the window-pane, Akhil went through the events of the past few months. His journey of self-discovery had been fruitful so far. He had done well academically. He had managed to live alone without killing himself. He could cook. He could wash his underwear. He had tasted alcohol. He had eaten meat. He had nearly died on that cruise in Key West. He could talk to strangers confidently. He had matured in the last nine odd months since he left Indian shores. America had turned out to be a worthy experience. That Noida startup job could have never taught him as much as America already had.

Then there was Nandita. Violins started playing in Akhil's head whenever she was around. He still remembered that first kiss. The silent acceptance of love. That feeling. The joy. Thanks to years of Bollywood influence, he had half expected a dozen dancers to jump out of the trees that day, and start dancing in formation, while Sonu Nigam sang a ballad.

Akhil wanted to write poems for Nandita. He wanted to give up everything and just watch her every day. He wanted to never be away from her. He was going to India, but felt like he was leaving behind a part of himself with the love of his life.

Meanwhile Jassi was also taking the semester off, but he had chosen to spend the three months in New York. With 'Perry' Priyank. Akhil sniggered. He had casually mentioned Jassi to Priyank. Jassi wanted to have some adventure over the summer. Priyank mentioned that he could use some company. The two dudes had hit it off instantly. Priyank invited Jassi to live with him. They were going to share costs, and Jassi had planned to take up a part time job in New York for the summer. Akhil wondered what stories were in store by the time Jassi *was through* with all the ladies in New York.

Akhil had spoken to Devika after the incident at her birthday party, and apologized for his roommate's behaviour. She in turn apologized to Akhil for being rude to him when it was not his fault. Akhil was glad to sort out things with her, though he was taken back by Jassi's brazenness when she told him what had actually transpired that night.

Akhil smiled thinking of Devika. He wondered if she was ranting to someone about the latest act of her mother at this time. Indian parents were really the same the world over, with their same worries, concerns, and demands from their children. *It was part of the Indian DNA, probably.*

Anil and Akhilesh had graduated and moved to Seattle to join Microsoft. The two had become the toast of the FSU desi community after getting lucrative job offers. Everybody wanted their advice on how to go about their careers. There were rumours that one of the girls in the batch had asked Akhilesh to marry her. Nobody seemed to know who it was, though Akhil felt certain it had to be Pooja. Ruksh had delayed his graduation by a semester to continue his job search.

The flight landed at New York. It was time for the onward flight to Delhi via London.

✈

At New York airport, the Air India staff announced that the Mumbai airport was flooded due to an especially nasty monsoon. The flight was going to be delayed as their jet was stuck in Mumbai. There were incredulous gasps at the check-in counter, especially from the Americans. The airline was going to accommodate the passengers overnight at a nearby hotel, and the flight would most likely leave for India the next day.

Akhil got together with some of his co-passengers and they were waiting outside the terminal for the shuttle to the hotel. Akhil suddenly noticed the air-train go past. He took out his camera and clicked a quick snap. A cop shouted at him. He was a black man with graying hair. He rushed to Akhil, grabbed him by the wrist, and took his camera.

'Sir, what are you doing? Photography is not permitted here.'

Akhil had heard many stories about police excesses post 9/11 and was stunned. He looked at the group of his co-passengers to come to his aid. They looked away in the other direction, trying to avoid trouble.

'Sir, I'll have to confiscate your camera and you will need to come with me.' He seemed serious.

Akhil panicked, and did the first thing that came to his mind. Apologize.

'I am sorry sir. I didn't see any sign that said that photography is not permitted.'

'Oh it is right there. I'll show it to you.'

'I am sorry. I am new here. Will take care in the future.' Akhil was shaking now. He did not want to go to jail.

The police officer looked at him in disgust. 'Son, why are you shivering? Come on man. What's the matter with you? Here take your camera and go.' He handed back Akhil's camera. Akhil ran back.

His fellow passengers all crowded around asking what happened. There was the hotelier from Alwar, returning from a business trip. A middle-aged couple from Mumbai. A very tall French-looking girl. Akhil was frightened, though annoyed. *Is this what they call racial abuse? From a black-American? How ironical!* He was also a bit ashamed about the shaking episode and wondered if it was getting out of hand, even though ultimately the shaking had come to his rescue.

Akhil spent a restless night tossing and turning on the queen-size bed in his hotel room. Early morning, a hotel shuttle dropped them off to the airport, where they were to wait for the next twelve hours for the flight to leave. Akhil was surprised to see the Americans just sprawled on the crowded airport floor wherever they could find place. In India, people considered sitting on the floor a lowly thing to do. American people continued to surprise him.

The 'French' girl turned out to be American. Her story was quite fascinating. She said that she was travelling to Delhi to be with her Assamese artist boyfriend, who lived somewhere in the crowded Paharganj part of the city. They had met at a music festival in Goa, and had fallen in love over bottles of the local liquor, Feni. Akhil was amazed to see an American girl travelling to India for love. He thought the love traffic was always in the other direction, a la Jassi.

He called up Nandita. They spoke for an hour. Nandita was worried. 'Hopefully there is no more excitement in store. Take care, Akhil. I'll miss you.'

Akhil promised to call her once he got home.

The flight took off late at night, more than twenty-four hours behind schedule.

Akhil had dozed off when there was a loud beep and the captain came on the speakers. 'Good morning ladies and gentlemen, we are currently circling over Mumbai. The rain Gods have been particularly happy this year, and it is still raining. We are awaiting clearance from the tower to land, as are two dozen other flights. We expect to land in about one hour.'

Two hours later, they landed at Mumbai airport. They were to offload a few passengers, pick up some, and then fly off to Delhi.

However, the weather Gods had other plans. The rains intensified. Twenty minutes after they landed, the airport was shut down for incoming and outgoing traffic. All incoming flights were to be diverted to other airports. Akhil cursed his luck. If this had happened twenty minutes back, they may well have been on the way to Delhi.

The airport was packed with people, some of whom had been waiting for over a day for their flights out of the city. Akhil found a vacant corner of the floor and sat down along with his newfound group.

They were to end up spending a full day here. The next morning Akhil was put on a flight to Delhi. He landed in Delhi, a full three days after leaving Tallahasseee. By now, Akhil's clothes were stinking, and his face was gradually disappearing under two days of overgrowth. He couldn't wait to take a nice shower and get into clean clothes.

As soon as the flight touched down at Delhi airport, the plane erupted with activity. People jumped up from their seats to collect their belongings from the overhead cabins, even though the seatbelt sign was still on. The middle-aged Punjabi uncle and aunty seated next to him got busy, packing their left-over paranthas and bhujias in their bags. The uncle looked at the inflight magazine. 'Should I take this?' He asked the missus. She nodded and he packed the safety instruction booklet as well. Someone a few seats behind jostled, trying to cut out of line in the packed aisle, and was promptly put in his place by an angry Sardarji.

A tired Akhil watched the pandemonium around him and sighed. 'Welcome to India,' he told himself. Everybody stood holding their bags in the aisle for almost half an hour before the doors opened. Akhil sat in his seat and was the last to get off.

Akhil was amazed at how different things seemed in India after being away for less than a year. To him, the staff at the airport looked malnourished compared to the hefty, filled-out bodies America had got him used to.

Soon he was outside the terminal where his dad had instructed him to wait. Shouting taxi drivers surrounded him. A sardarji came forward to take his trolley to his taxi. Akhil was having trouble breathing. The air was thick with dust and pollution. There was a non-stop orchestra of assorted horns trying their best to assure Akhil that he was back in Delhi.

Akhil found himself getting shocked at his reaction to India. He had always been amused by how obnoxious people returning from America sounded, and here he was—stressed, disappointed, and disgusted almost, with the same noise and dirt he had grown up with. He had become one of *them*.

He spotted his parents outside the airport and rushed to greet them. Finally, he felt some sense of belonging. Mom and dad seemed older than the one year since he had last been with them. Aarti was the same bubbly self.

Mom hugged him. There were tears in her eyes.

'Look at you, how thin you have become,' she said, and resolved to fix this during his short stay. America was obviously not providing enough nutrition to her thinning son.

India Redux

Jassi boarded his flight to New York. By a lucky coincidence, he had found about Priyank, who was Akhil's friend. Jassi wanted to get out of Florida for the summer and see more of America. He didn't know anyone in California, which was his first choice. After all, Pamelaji lived there. As luck would have it, Priyank asked if Jassi wanted to share his apartment for the summer. Jassi was only too happy to accept.

It had already started well. There was a hot girl sitting next to him. *At least an 8.5, if not 9.*

The flight stewardess came on the public address system. 'Ladies and Gentlemen, this is the United Airlines flight to New York. If any of you have boarded the wrong flight, this is your last chance to move before the doors of the jet are locked.'

Jassi thought of an opening and beamed at his pretty neighbour. 'This is crazy. What idiotic person would be getting into the wrong flight?' Only the words came out a bit fumbled. Jassi was not on top of his American accent of late.

She gave a polite smile and stared straight on without replying.

The speakers crackled again, a few minutes later. It was the flight stewardess. 'Ladies and Gentlemen, our flight is a bit front-heavy today. We need some of you to volunteer to move to the seats at the back to spread out the weight evenly before we can take off.'

Jassi was still planning his next line, when she got up. 'I'll move down.'

She was gone. Jassi flew all the way to New York alone.

She was just a 7.5, he consoled himself.

Jassi reached New York's JFK airport and got out of the terminal. Priyank had asked him to wait at the pickup area. He wasn't there yet. Jassi called him up and Priyank promised that he would be there in five minutes. 'Almost there, dude.'

He reached an hour later. By now, Jassi had tired of chewing the same piece of gum like a bored cow, but had nothing better to do.

Priyank got out of the car holding a sheet of paper with Jassi's name written on it in bold letters. Jassi located him in the distance and walked up to Priyank.

'How's it going, Perry? I am Jazz.' Jassi introduced himself with a big grin.

Priyank smiled at Jassi and and shook his hand. 'Hi dude, I am Perry.'

The two dudes sized each other up. Jassi saw a short Indian man with spiked hair, ripped low-rise jeans, and a belly showing through his Abercrombie T-shirt. Priyank saw his reflection in Jassi.

Jassi got into Priyank's Toyota Corolla. The door creaked as he closed it.

Priyank cautioned him. 'Easy, dude. That door's a bit messed up, but this car has not had any starting trouble in six months.'

As Jassi settled into his seat, he felt like he would choke. The car smelled of dirty socks. There was a pool of some gooey liquid on the floor beneath his shoes, and Jassi didn't dare guess what it was. This car was putting Suresh's prehistoric masterpiece to shame.

'Ever been to New York before?' Priyank asked as he drove the car from the airport.

'Nopes.'

'Alright, then let me show some sights along the way.'

Soon they approached the Brooklyn Bridge. Jassi held his breath as the famed Manhattan skyline emerged before his eyes.

'Duuuude,' Jassi's voice fell to a whimper. He was spellbound. He was in New York, the greatest city in the world. The city of Ross Geller and Rachel Green. The Big Apple. The city where millions of single women lived. Jassi couldn't wait to be out there and show the ladies of this city what they had been missing all this time.

As they drove through midtown Manhattan, Jassi kept waiting for Priyank to slow down and stop his car in front of his apartment, but he kept driving. Soon they were in a tunnel that never seemed to end. Eventually it did, and behind them Jassi noticed a river that separated them from Manhattan. Priyank drove on for another half an hour and stopped in a dingy road with shabby looking apartments. Jassi felt like he was in one of the poor neighbourhoods of Jalandhar.

'Home,' said Priyank and got off the car.

Jassi mumbled. He had expected the *posh* Perry to live in a better neighbourhood, if not in the heart of New York City. *He sounded so cool on the phone. Surely something good is going to come out of this.*

Turned out Priyank shared the two-bedroom apartment in a run-down part of Jersey City with three other men. Luckily, he had a full room to himself, which Jassi was going to share. It wasn't going to be free. Jassi was going to have to pay 250 dollars per month, plus additional money for groceries and utilities.

Priyank mentioned that he had a part-time job already arranged for Jassi. The Indian storeowner in the neighbourhood was looking for someone to help run the shop for a couple of months while his current help was away in India. The timing was perfect for Jassi. He would be paid 400 dollars per week.

The next morning Jassi was at the store, helping with odd tasks like arranging Maggi packets on the racks or helping old Indian aunties find the packet of spices they were looking for.

Jassi felt humiliated. *This better be worth it.*

✈

Akhil was still asleep, exhausted from his extended trip from Tallahasseee, when Aarti shook him.

'Get up. Some of the neighbours are here, and mom wants you to come and say hi.'

'Yaar, what is this? I am tired. Tell them I am sleeping.'

Mom entered the room. 'Akhil, just come for a minute. Just a minute, beta.'

Akhil got up, rubbed his eyes, and went out. The ladies were all sipping tea and eating the expensive Godiva chocolate truffles Akhil had brought. They had cost some 23 dollars for half a pound, and Akhil hadn't eaten out for a month to compensate the drag on his monthly budget. Most of them melted in the box by the time they got home, and powercuts did the rest. Dad had looked at the chocolates scornfully, tasted one and said, 'What is this? No taste at all. Those Americans can't even put sugar properly,' before spitting it out.

'Oho, there is the foreign-returned boy. He already looks so smart.' Gupta aunty kicked off proceedings.

Akhil looked at his mother. He was being paraded in front of the neighbours as a trophy. Mom beamed at him and informed the group about Akhil's perfect grades. 'He has topped his class. Topped.'

Akhil winced. There was no topper. There were others who also had perfect grades.

A collective sigh emanated from the gathered Punjabi women. Goyal aunty gasped for a second. Even their Priyank had never *topped* his class during his Masters. Akhil returned to his room, covered his face with the bedsheet, and went back to sleep while the aunties outside advised his mother to start looking for a *good* girl for him. Mrs Sharma from A-43 had even brought along the biodata of her niece who 'lived in foreign, but was the sweetest and most cultured girl ever, and apparently made the world's best aloo gobhi'.

Lunch was a sumptuous spread of everything his mom could make in a day. It was like she was trying to feed him a year's worth in a single meal.

Akhil grimaced as mom pushed another puri in his direction. 'No mom. Stop it. I wish I were a camel and could store all of that, but I can't.'

Mom seemed genuinely concerned. 'You don't worry, beta. I'll make sure you return to normal by the end of your holiday.' Aarti giggled.

Akhil called Nandita in the evening from his room. She was going to fly out from Tallahasseee tonight.

Just as they started talking, there was a power cut. The lights went off, and flickered back on again. The air-conditioner stayed shut. Akhil remained silent for a minute, and then started laughing loudly. He had forgotten about load shedding.

They talked for the next one hour. His mother came into the room several times, once with a cup of tea and ten minutes later with a glass of milk. Akhil knew that she was trying to find out who he was talking to, but he didn't mention Nandita yet. *Will tell them when the time is right.*

'So, Akhil beta, how have you been? It has been such a long time since we saw you. Hope America is treating you nicely.'

Akhil eyed Goyalji with suspicion. Goyal uncle never meant any good for him. He surely just wanted to see how he was faring in comparison to his son, Priyank. Akhil wondered if the Goyals had any idea of what their son had turned into, while they went around singing songs in his praise all over town.

'Yes uncle. I am doing well.'

His mom cut him off. 'Goyalji, Akhil is too modest. He has topped the university. Can you believe it? Our Akhil is now a topper.'

Goyalji made some effort of looking happy, but could only manage a constipated smile.

He looked at his watch and made an excuse to leave. 'Achha, Mrs Arora. I'll go now. I just remembered that I need to get milk from Mother Dairy.'

Akhil heaved a sigh of relief as Goyalji left.

'Akhil, how is Priyank? Do you talk to him often? Very sweet boy he is.' Mom asked Akhil. Akhil sniggered. 'Mom, you don't want to know. And you definitely don't want me to follow in his footsteps.'

His mom retreated to the kitchen looking bewildered.

Akhil's two-week vacation was ending. Air India and the flooded Mumbai airport had eaten into two days of his vacation. He had spent the next few days getting over the jet lag, and getting accustomed to the heat and noise. Before he knew it, Akhil had only three more days left for his flight back to the US.

They had decided to go to a nearby shopping mall which had sprung up in the last year. Akhil wanted to buy some new clothes, and he figured they would be cheaper in India. At the mall's entrance, Akhil noticed the security guard frisking everybody entering the place. There was no frisking at American malls, so Akhil felt some surprise. In the last year in the US, he had got used to walking into malls without any security checks.

Akhil left the frisking feeling disgusted. The security guard had given him a full pat down and stopped just short of cupping his crown jewels in his over-zealousness. Even the infamous American airport security agents weren't this thorough. Akhil tried to recall if he had seen this type of frisking at any of the airports he had been to in the US, and couldn't think of anything close. It felt a little absurd. Peace-loving citizens like him didn't carry bombs on them. The people who did would anyway find a way of doing what they wanted. Akhil felt confused. Had America changed him, or was India actually changing for the worse?

Later on, they were at the market to get an ice cream from Baskin-Robbins. As Akhil got out of the car, he noticed a sleek looking Mercedes convertible parked next to them. Akhil marvelled at the car, wondering if he would ever be able to buy such a beauty. Suddenly a window opened, and a female hand wearing a ring adorned by a shiny diamond the size of Rashtrapati Bhavan, dropped a soiled plate of the papri-chaat she had just eaten, barely a few inches from where Akhil was standing. Akhil jumped to avoid assorted chutneys getting spilled on him, and sighed at the irony of the situation. There's some things money just can't buy. For everything else, there's you-know-what.

The triple sundae cost him almost 200 rupees. *Almost five dollars.* Akhil was astonished. This was India, not America, though the price was American. He paid up, smiled at the man at the counter and said 'I appreciate it', more out of habit of saying the American phrase. Back in the car, dad reprimanded him for not even trying to bargain the price. 'You are too innocent, Akhil. If you smile at people, they will overcharge.'

✈

Jassi woke up feeling flustered. He had been in New York for a week now, and all he had managed to do so far was memorize the price of various pickles and snacks at the Indian store. The hard bed in Priyank's room was a constant reminder that he was here not to share a bed with a fat, desi dude. Every day Priyank would return home from work after eight, cook some lousy food, and sit in front of the TV for the next few hours. Jassi hadn't been able to go out as much as he wanted.

As if the evenings weren't annoying enough, Jassi woke up every morning soaked in sweat. Priyank had this habit of turning off the air conditioner in the middle of the night. He said that he felt cold, though Jassi had a feeling he was just trying to save his electricity bill. Things were not turning out the way Jassi had imagined in his head.

It was Friday and Priyank had promised Jassi the night of his life. *Hopefully, this will be a different day.*

His five-hour shift at the store ended at 3 pm. Jassi was already looking forward to some fireworks tonight. They were going to go bar hopping in the trendy *Meatpacking* district. Jassi took out his finest clothes, bathed and shaved, and he was ready for the party by the time Priyank returned from work.

Priyank looked at him and smirked.

'What?' Jassi asked him, surprised.

'Dude, it is 8 pm. Why are you already dressed?'

'Dude, aren't we going to go party tonight?' Jassi was now annoyed with Priyank.

'Boss, the real parties start after midnight. Going now is a waste, especially if you want to get laid. The real players go late, by which time all the girls are drunk, and willing enough to go with anyone. Understood?'

It made perfect sense. Jassi suddenly had a newfound respect for Priyank. *The guy knows what he is talking about.* The week spent learning the prices of frozen chapatis now seemed tolerable.

'Okay. That sounds like a better plan, dude.'

Jassi switched on the TV where a rerun of *Friends* was playing, as Priyank cooked up a sumptuous dinner of Top Ramen noodles. Exhausted from the excitement, Jassi dozed off to sleep.

'Wake up, dude.' Jassi could hear sounds in the distance. Somebody was vigorously shaking him up. He couldn't make much sense of what was happening, until Priyank started making sex sounds. Jassi was out of his slumber. He looked at the clock. It was 12.15 am.

'Dude,' he shouted. 'What happened?'

'Dude, you dozed off. I have been trying to wake you up for the last fifteen minutes.' Priyank seemed dressed for the party. The belly was protruding from under his jacket, but there wasn't much you could do to hide a tummy that looked 3-months pregnant.

Jassi ran to the bathroom and took a quick shower to wake himself up. Ten minutes later, they were out of the house. They were going to drive down to Manhattan.

It was nearly 1 am by the time Priyank parked his car after searching for thirty minutes for an empty free parking slot on the road. The dudes got out of the door and Jassi followed Priyank to an innocuous looking door. The sign read 'Cielo'.

Priyank tried to slip past the burly bouncer, who stopped him. He stared at Priyank and Jassi for a minute, trying to ascertain whether they deserved to be let in.

'Sorry sir, the club's full.'

Priyank sighed. There was going to be no point arguing. Jassi was sure it was potbellied Priyank because of whom he had also been denied entry.

As the dejected duo were walking away, a gleaming BMW rolled up and two girls got out. They were both white, with looks like Jennifer Aniston and Lindsay Lohan, and adorned in barely-there dresses. The bouncer waved them in. Jassi muttered a silent praise to the bouncer's mother.

The next two clubs produced the same result. 'These people are all racist, and get extra choosy on Friday nights,' explained Priyank.

They finally managed entry into the fourth club they tried. It was 2 am. Once inside, Jassi was spellbound. The place was bustling with activity. The music was pulsating, though he found the techno music a bit weird. There was a drink in every hand. The place was swarming with pretty girls wearing short dresses, and in various stages of drunkenness. *Priyank's theory might just work tonight,* Jassi thought.

Jassi and Priyank took a beer each and analysed the scene. Priyank explained that it was important to identify realistic targets and then move for the kill. 'You don't want to try for the really pretty girls; they'll only go with the white boys. Europeans are easy; just act confident. ABCD girls are a no-no. They'll either only go with white boys or they will want you to marry them if they sleep with you.' Jassi found himself trying to absorb each word of the great master. *I would have never known all this theory but for Priyank.*

'Alright dude, now each man to himself. Good luck.' Priyank had identified a target and was about to strike.

Jassi wasn't sure what to do. He looked around for a bit and got himself a second beer. One sip down, a girl came and took the seat beside him.

'Care to buy me a drink?' She was cute, so would have been certainly disqualified by Priyank's criteria.

'Sure.' Jassi always knew the American women would be lining up to bed him. *He was irresistible.*

They got talking. Her name was Jennifer, and she was an artist.

Jennifer turned out to be an alcohol tanker. Soon she was on her fifth vodka, each of which had cost Jassi 10 dollars. With each drink Jennifer gulped down, Jassi's hopes of the night ending in a sexcapade increased. He hoped the 50 dollars were going to be a good investment.

'Are you wanting to dance?' he asked her, slipping back to his Indian-English.

'Nah, I'm alright.' She giggled. Jassi's confidence soared. *She was his for the taking.* Jassi decided to go for the kill. As she stood next to him, her hands resting on the bar counter, Jassi leaned in. Their lips were a few inches apart and Jassi was closing in fast.

She pushed him away at the last second. He was surprised at her reflexes. For a woman who had downed nearly a liter of vodka, she was surprisingly agile. She moved quickly, out of the way of Jassi's eager lips.

'Yo, what's up dude? What are you doing?' She seemed annoyed.

Jassi replied with a baffled, 'Just trying to kiss you, Jen. I think I am in love with you already.'

'Love?' she laughed as the bartender looked on. 'Sorry buddy. Let's just keep it platonic.'

The words hit Jassi like a brick falling on his head. Those 50 dollars had gone down the drain. He was not getting any love tonight. He felt sure she was a lesbian who had tricked him. No straight woman would want to be platonic with *The Jazzminator*. He wondered if he could ask for a refund of his money.

Jennifer stumbled out of the club. Jassi looked around for Priyank, whom he had last seen with a girl whom Jassi likened to a plump cow. Priyank noticed Jassi and came over.

'Look dude, things are going great with this chick. I am going to take her home. Why don't you take the train back to Jersey? The station is a five minute walk from here. I will pick you up from the station early morning.'

Jassi was astounded at Priyank's cheekiness. He was being deserted in the middle of a new city so that Priyank could get it on with a girl.

Priyank left before Jassi could say anything.

There were so many emotions pouring through Jassi, he didn't know which one to feel first. There was disappointment, frustration, annoyance, repentance, and most of all the desire to beat up Priyank. It was 3:30 am. He decided to wait out the night and then leave. He wasn't confident of being able to find the way in his current state, especially in the dark. Besides he didn't want to make it worse by getting mugged in a narrow alley of downtown Manhattan.

The club closed its doors at 5 am. Until then, Jassi just sat in a corner. He didn't feel like approaching any of the increasingly drunk girls anymore. He was too angry. He left the club, managed to find the way to the train station, and took the train back home. From Jersey City, he walked down to Priyank's apartment, which took him half an hour.

Priyank's room was locked. Jassi slept on the couch in the living room, after showing a middle finger to the door of Priyank's room, behind which he was probably still humping the 'cow' from the club.

He woke up as the clock struck noon. Priyank brought a glass of water and a mug of coffee. 'Sorry dude, guess last night was a bit rough on you.'

Jassi clenched his fists. Priyank spoke first. 'I know you are angry, but think about it. What would you have done if you were in my place?'

Despite his annoyed state, it made sense to Jassi. If he had been in Priyank's position, he would have probably done the same thing. *If one of them was getting what they were there for, then what's a little sacrifice from the other person?* His anger subsided somewhat.

'Anyway, dude. I'll make it up to you tonight.' Priyank promised.

Later that night, Jassi and Priyank got off the train at the Queensboro Bridge station in Queens and started walking in the direction of their destination. As per Google Maps, it was about fifteen minutes away. Jassi's heart was pounding.

It was 11 pm. Soon they were in a rather secluded part of the town, with not many people around. Jassi felt nervous. Even though it was America, he had heard stories of people getting mugged and even being stabbed to death in secluded parts of New York.

They were there. The sign read 'Gentleman's Club'. Jassi's heart raced. Priyank took out his wallet and gave Jassi a bunch of dollar bills. Jassi looked at him quizzically. 'You'll need them,' was the cryptic response.

The bouncer seemed friendly and happily ushered the boys in. It was dark, but Jassi could hear loud music. He looked around. The place was big enough for about hundred people, and it seemed like a full house. There were people at the bar talking over beers. There were some guys playing pool on a table next to the bar. Most of the crowd was men, though he spotted a few girls as well.

Then he saw the stage. That was obviously the highlight of the place. A song started and a dancer came on stage. She was very pretty, though her dance wouldn't quite win her any talent show. Two minutes later Jassi's mouth was agape. The woman had gradually taken off most of her clothes, and was dancing very suggestively. Priyank asked Jassi to follow him, and they took front row seats right next to the stage. She noticed them, and came close to their seats. Priyank smiled at her and snuck a dollar bill in her thong.

Jassi was shocked. He headed back to the safety of the bar and ordered a beer. Priyank came over in a little while.

'Dude, what happened? You didn't like her?'

'N...n...n...no, it is not that,' Jassi stammered.

Priyank slapped Jassi's shoulder and laughed loudly. 'Dude, is this the first time you've been to a strip club?'

'Yes,' Jassi said apologetically. He had just chickened out of touching the prettiest woman he had ever seen.

'Hi boys.' A husky voice startled Jassi and Priyank. Jassi turned around to see the girl from the last song standing next to them. There was a new dancer on the stage.

'My name is Angel.' She held out a hand. She was wearing a robe now.

She shook hands with both boys. Jassi noticed Priyank hold on to her hand for far too long. She just smiled on. It was business and they were prospective clients.

'Care for a private dance?' She asked. Jassi hesitated. He didn't even know what a private dance was. *Was it a code word for something more than dance?*

Priyank took her up on the offer. 'Sure, I'll come.' She took Priyank by the hand and led him to the back of the room. Jassi saw them go behind a curtain. Priyank winked at Jassi before disappearing.

Jassi's heart was beating so fast, he thought it would explode. He wondered what Priyank was doing with Angel at this moment.

Ten minutes later Priyank appeared. Jassi had a barrage of questions ready for him. 'Did you have sex with her? Isn't that risky? What if you get bad diseases?'

Priyank replied, 'Shut up dude. You are an idiot. It was just a lap dance. A private strip tease. Do you want to get one?'

Jassi hesitated. 'Umm…maybe next time. Let's go home.'

Priyank asked him if he was sure. 'Take one of the other girls if you don't like Angel. They are all gorgeous.'

'No, really. Let's go home.'

They left. In an hour, Jassi was in bed. That night, he dreamt of Pamelaji doing a private dance for him. Finally, his New York trip was yielding some fruit. The next time he wasn't going to shy away from a pretty stripper.

✈

The next evening, Jassi was back for Angel. Alone. He didn't want Priyank to know. As he entered, the bouncer recognized him and smiled. Jassi smiled back nervously.

A couple of hours later, he walked out of the door, smiling generously at the bouncer. This had been the greatest evening of his life. He had to wait a little while for Angel, but it was worth it.

Angel was the sweetest, prettiest woman Jassi had ever come across. She was a perfect ten. She was a thorough businesswoman though. She charged 20 dollars per song, and refused to give Jassi the 3-for-1 discount offer he asked for. He had ended up spending almost a 100 dollars tonight in repeat lap dance performances from her.

Jassi was in love with her. To his dismay, she said no to going out with him for dinner. She matched all of his criteria. She was smart, intelligent, had good communication skills, was good at dance, and going by her toned body, she clearly ate a healthy diet. Jassi could see himself living a happy life with her. Their children would be pretty like her and smart like him.

Apples and Oranges

'Akhil, get up. There is a call for you.' Mrs Arora came into the room holding his mobile.

'Oh God, who is it mom? I was trying to sleep.' It was 3 pm and Akhil was enjoying his afternoon siesta after his first ever ride on the squeaky-clean Delhi Metro with Aarti and some cousins.

'It's a girl. She says her name is Nandita.'

Akhil jumped out of bed. Mrs Arora was surprised at his speed, and handed him the phone with a puzzled look on her face.

'Okay thanks ma.' Akhil didn't want to talk to his beloved in the presence of his mother.

She gave him a suspicious look and left the room.

'Hi Nandu.'

'Hi Akhil, my Punjabi stud. How many aloo paranthas did you eat today?' Nandita sounded bubbly, like always.

Akhil laughed. 'You know me too well. Only four.'

'Good job, my tiger. If you keep eating at this rate, I think I will get back two Akhils for the price of one. Beware, sometimes fat people are asked to book two tickets on flights these days.'

Nandita broke out into her high-pitched laugh. Akhil lay down on his bed and they talked for the next hour, sharing their experiences so far. Nandita was going through the same India-shock Akhil was experiencing.

Akhil was happy. He wanted to take this relationship to the next level. They could get married in a few years after Akhil was settled in his job and Nandita had completed her PhD. Akhil ended the call with a heavy heart. He didn't know what course the future would take.

His flight back was in two days.

It was time to head to the airport. Akhil's flight was in four hours. The two weeks had gone past in a blur, and it was time to get back to the grind of classes, assignments, and night-outs. His mom was emotional as expected. For now, she was busy in the kitchen preparing aloo paranthas for the flight.

'You take these. Who knows what all they serve on flights these days. Anyway, once you get to Amreeka, you'll only be eating your stupid frozen paranthas,' she said wiping her moist eyes on her apron.

Akhil sighed. His thoughts went back to his initial trip to the US last year. He wondered if there would be tears every time he travelled back to the US from India. Personally, he didn't feel as bad as he did last year. This time he had Nandita to look forward to. He felt for his parents though. They were not in the best of shape. His mom had been cheerful these two weeks, but if it was going to be followed up with a month of sobbing, he wondered if his trip was worth it.

A couple of hours later, Akhil was at the departure gate, waiting for the boarding call. Mrs Arora had cried all the way to the airport. Even his normally impassive dad seemed subdued.

Akhil tried calling Nandita but couldn't get through. *Perhaps she was busy.*

Having nothing else to do, Akhil sat back and reflected on the past two weeks. Things were changing. He was not the same Akhil from last year. America had raised his expectations. India seemed somewhat inefficient after seeing how things could be done better. The powercuts, the irresponsible traffic on the road, the messy airport, the loads of people scampering around for basic existence, it all turned him off now.

Then there were his obnoxious college mates. Last evening he had gone for a reunion with some of his classmates from college who were also back from their respective US universities for their summer breaks.

But the reunion had been disappointing. The group of ten comprised people now studying at prestigious universities like Stanford, Texas, UCLA, and Princeton. Akhil had been excited about meeting his old friends, but wasn't quite prepared for their rude behavior.

It was as if he was an outcast studying in a below par university. They made him feel like he did not belong to the group for studying at a university ranked so far down the charts. Akhil was sure he could spot a few Priyanks and Jassis in the group, which only discussed girls and money in the two hours they were together. Studies seemed secondary to this distinguished group.

Akhil's resolve had only grown stronger. He just had to prove these people wrong. He had to do it. For himself. For his parents. For Nandita. He had to succeed.

He wondered what Nandita was doing at the moment. He shuddered at the thought of spending the next two and a half months without her. It was not going to be easy. He hoped maybe she would change her mind and return to Tallahasseee early.

The airline crew announced start of boarding for the flight, and Akhil joined the long line that formed within minutes.

✈

'Your total will be 23 dollars and 30 cents,' said Jassi handing over the reciept to the next customer in line. Her looks said Indian. Her accent said American. *Must be an ABCD,* Jassi thought.

She looked at the receipt and pointed out a mistake. 'Looks like you charged me for coriander chutney. This one is mint.'

Jassi looked at the bottle of chutney and chuckled. 'Oh well, they all look the same. Why don't you take coriander chutney, now that we have billed it.'

She stared on. 'What do you mean? I'll take what I want.'

'Okay okay, I will make the change.' Jassi muttered an expletive under his breath.

The woman went ballistic. 'What did you just say?' She called out to her friend who was inspecting the fresh fruit on display. 'Listen, come over here, and check out the cheek on this guy.'

Her friend appeared from behind the spice aisle. One look at the Indian behind the counter and she exclaimed, 'Jazz, what are you doing here?'

Jassi gasped. 'Victoria?'

'Jazz, what a pleasant surprise. I remember you mentioning that you were going to spend the summer in New York, but didn't expect to run into you here'

'Yes, same here. Good to see you.' Jassi smiled at his gym partner. Their workouts had continued through the spring semester, and Jassi now had a hint of some abdominal muscles finally making their way out of their hibernation under his stomach fat.

He looked scornfully at Victoria's friend who was now watching the proceedings with a shocked expression. Victoria introduced her. 'Jazz, meet my friend Tapasya. I am staying at her place for the next couple of weeks. She lives just a mile from here.'

Tapasya smiled awkwardly at Jassi. A few minutes ago, she had braced herself to rip the head off this annoying desi guy. Victoria left with a promise to get together for drinks one of the evenings over the next week.

✈

Later that evening, Jassi was on the train into Manhattan. He had now been in New York for a month, with not much luck with the ladies. He was convinced that he was just being unlucky. There was that Dutch girl he had met at a Lower East Side bar who went to the loo in the middle of their conversation and never returned. Jassi wondered if she had been kidnapped, but didn't bother to find out. *No use getting into police trouble in a foreign country.* Then there was the shy NYU med-school student who suddenly got a phone call in the midst of their exciting conversation about the prevalence of STDs in New Yorkers. *Such a shame. She seemed like a nice girl.*

This evening might change all of that. Jassi had set up a profile on a dating site called www.match.com and managed to setup a date with a stunning woman from Belarus called Natalia. Her profile picture on the site reminded Jassi of a particular Hollywood actress whose name he couldn't remember. They had exchanged a couple of messages and Natalia had asked Jassi if he wanted to meet her at her hotel room in midtown Manhattan. Jassi had responded within seconds confirming the date and time.

This is it, he felt. He was about to achieve one of the first targets of his American dream.

The train stopped at the next station and four Latino men entered. They were short, stocky young men wearing similar floral shirts and big hats, called sombreros. One of them had what appeared to Jassi like a harmonium strapped to his chest. They took position in the middle of the compartment and started singing. It was somewhat melodious though Jassi was appalled. *Beggars, in America! Ruining the good name of this great country.* Five minutes later, they finished their song and one of them went around collecting tips. Jassi didn't give him anything. He had no sympathy for American beggars.

An hour later, Jassi knocked on the room of the *W* hotel Natalia had asked him to come to. The door was answered a minute later by a woman Jassi's rating meter judged an 8. She had a pretty face and beautiful blue eyes. She was probably just short of six feet and her waist seemed a little bigger than the 24 inches her profile had claimed.

Natalia seemed charming, but didn't quite look like the woman in her match.com picture. Jassi brushed aside his doubts. He had heard of people using fake pictures on their profiles at dating sites, but 'his' Natalia couldn't possibly be a cheat.

She seemed excited to see Jassi. Jassi's excitement knew no bounds, even though she looked like a giant compared to his 5 feet 6 inches frame. In his mind, her massive body just meant that he had more of her to love. This was going to be special. His mind fast-forwarded to five years in the future. He could see himself getting ready to go to work as Natalia made a breakfast of scrambled eggs for him. They then made passionate love on the dining table (with her lifting him onto the table) in their apartment overlooking New York's Central Park. There were no kids in the picture. *That will have to wait,* thought Jassi.

Jassi came back to his senses as Natalia took his hand in hers and led him inside the room. Her skin was soft like silk. Jassi felt like he was in love. He was ready for some action. He felt in his pocket for the *protection* he had brought along.

Natalia poured a big glass of vodka and handed it to Jassi, who looked at her with surprise. It was neat, with nothing to dilute the alcohol. He looked at her and said, 'This is a lot.'

She spoked in that exotic Russian accent Jassi had only heard in James Bond movies. 'Oh, real men don't worry about alcohol. This will make you warm.' Jassi had to man up and gulp it down in one go.

His throat burnt and he gasped for breath. She smiled

lovingly at him. Jassi thought of this as a welcome drink. He had heard of the Russian obsession with Vodka, and how they consumed it like people in Punjab drank lassi.

Natalia led him to the couch and poured out another glass. Jassi didn't feel this one go down as hard as the first one. There was a slight buzz in his head already.

Natalia was taking off her jacket now. Things were about to get hot. Jassi took off his shirt and threw it on the ground. His head felt heavier with every passing minute. He lied down on the bed for a minute. Natalia appeared to be smiling in the distance.

✈

Somebody was shaking Jassi violently. The hands felt rough.

'Stop it baby,' he told Natalia. The shaking continued. Jassi opened his eyes. A police officer was looking at him. The room was full of people, all of them looking intently in Jassi's direction.

Jassi's hangover was gone in a second. He looked out the window and it seemed like late morning, with the sun shining down brilliantly. He peered down at himself and quickly covered himself with the bedsheet. He was only wearing his underwear.

'Wh...wh...what happened?' he asked the police officer.

'Well son, the woman in this room checked out early morning and later the hotel staff found you passed out and reported the matter to us. You were out cold.'

Jassi couldn't believe what he was hearing. He thought it must be a dream, and blinked vigorously. The police officer was still there. This was not a dream. It was a nightmare.

He looked around for his stuff. He couldn't spot his clothes anywhere. His wallet and mobile weren't where he had left them. He had been cheated by Natalia, the woman who he thought was going to be the mother of his children one day.

The hotel staff offered Jassi a night suit to wear. He quickly put them on. The hotel manager asked him if he was fine. Jassi was perspiring. This had to be the lowest moment of his life. He couldn't understand what happened. *Natalia seemed like an angel. Why would she do that to me?*

His wallet had his state ID, a hundred dollars in cash, and a credit card. The hotel manager advised him to get his card blocked immediately. 'Identity theft is a massive problem, and you don't want that on your hands.' He was more worried about the prospect of Jassi suing the hotel for his troubles. Jassi was too embarrassed to think straight.

The hotel manager offered Jassi a complimentary cab to drop him home, which he thankfully accepted. As Jassi left, he saw the hotel manager wipe the sweat off his forehead.

Jassi didn't know where to look after this embarrassment. He wished there were a way to remove the last day's events from his life. Tears streaked from his swollen eyes all the way back to Priyank's apartment.

✈

Akhil knocked on Dr Narayanan's office door for his daily morning meeting, waited a few seconds for a response, and entered the room on the ground floor of their department building. Dr Narayanan was in, as was a third person. She looked Chinese and seemed to be evaluating some assignments. *Probably a student,* Akhil thought.

'Akhil, meet Wendy, my wife,' said Dr Narayanan introducing him to the person who Akhil had earlier thought was a teaching assistant working for him.

Akhil was astonished. He had started working with Dr Narayanan a few weeks ago. He had offered Akhil a research assistantship and the chance to work on an upcoming project for his thesis. Akhil had happily accepted his offer. Dr Narayanan seemed like a regular guy. He even spoke with an Indian accent despite his years of stay in the US. Akhil had not known any other Tamil-Brahman getting married to Chinese women.

Akhil shook hands with Wendy, and then the professor got down to business. Akhil had a course with him this semester already. The research project was going to be on the same topic. They met for ten minutes every morning to review the plan and track progress.

After the meeting with the professor, Akhil headed to his new research lab setup for Dr Narayanan's project. He had given up his teaching assistant office as he was now on Dr Narayanan's payroll as his research assistant. His research project was with a team of two other students. He already knew Brad, who had started the graduate programme that semester after completing his undergrad requirements. Neil had been on the Advanced UNIX Programming course with Akhil last year, so he knew him as well.

The work was intense, but Akhil was enjoying it. This was high-end research which exercised all the grey cells in his brain that his undergraduate programme had failed to touch.

More importantly, it kept his mind occupied while Nandita was away. Akhil didn't want a second of free time, because that was when he started getting thoughts of taking a flight to Kolkata to be with his love.

As Akhil was getting started with his planned work for the day, Brad walked in to the lab. He had a bottle of beer in his hand, and his girlfriend Aparna by his side, also with a bottle in her hand. He logged on to his computer and started his work. Aparna was sitting next to him, watching intently. It wasn't the first time he was seeing her, but Akhil couldn't help notice that Aparna was gorgeous. A few minutes later, he saw her opening up the Linux kernel code and debugging some of the most complex software code with Brad. This woman was God's answer to people who cribbed about pretty woman not being smart.

Aparna suddenly turned and looked at Akhil staring at her. She smiled at him and laughed as Akhil grinned sheepishly and buried himself in his computer screen. Her laughter was like an orchestra of xylophones and violins. Akhil put on his headphones and turned his diskman on to Manna De's rendition of that epic poem about the life of an alcoholic, *Madhushala*.

July 2005 had arrived. It had now been a month since Akhil got back from his India trip. Life was back to the usual grind of stressful work and coffee-induced late-night sessions. The campus was deserted, with very few students staying on for the summer, but Akhil had his hands full.

Akhil used to wonder what Jassi was upto in New York. Jassi was quirky and outright weird at times, but after living together for almost a year, Akhil thought of Kedar and Jassi as his second family. He was sceptical of Jassi living with Priyank, and hoped for Jassi's sake that he would not get into any mischief.

Meanwhile, things were going great with Nandita. The daily call with her at 6 am was now Akhil's morning alarm, and she wouldn't go to bed until he had called her to wish her good night. They missed each other's physical presence, but mobile phones, calling cards, and Yahoo Messenger had played their part at bridging the distance between them.

Akhil couldn't wait for Nandita to be back. Just about a month and a half to go.

✈

Jassi's phone buzzed. It was a text message from Victoria. 'We're planning to go to the city tonight. Join us for drinks?'

'Sure,' he messaged her back.

The horror of Natalia's deception had taken a week to get over. Jassi had shown Natalia's profile picture to Priyank, who had instantly identified her as a famous Hollywood actress of Russian descent. 'I am absolutely sure, dude. I have about a thousand of her topless pictures on my laptop,' was his confident response to Jassi's incredulous look. Jassi had not stepped out of the house since that fateful day, except to go to the store for his daily shift. The wound had just about healed. He hadn't lost much monetarily, but he felt like a loved one had stabbed him in the back. He had thought of Natalia being better than that.

However, get over it he had, and Jassi was now ready to get back in the action. He couldn't let isolated incidents bog him down. This night might be just the sort of change he needed to get Natalia out of his system for good.

At 5.54 pm, Jassi stepped out of the 34th Street PATH train station. He was to meet Victoria at a lounge nearby. The place was a 20-minute walk, or a five-minute train ride. Jassi had time to kill so he decided to walk.

Jassi recalled his earlier meetings with Victoria. He had got overexcited that night after the dinner when he tried to kiss her, but now he felt that he was a more mature person. They had spent the last month odd bonding over their running sessions at the gym. Victoria was pleasant company to be with, and she laughed at all of his jokes. He felt sure things would work out this time. Victoria was a nice girl, not a crook like Natalia.

He had just passed a homeless man sitting on the pavement with a sign that said in a hastily scribbled proclamation—'The end is near'. The man stank of dried urine and smoke. His life belongings were lying next to him in a stolen shopping cart. Jassi sniggered, reminded of how movies said that New York had all kinds of people. *Must be a bloody drug addict.*

Jassi was almost there. And then he saw *her*.

He felt his heart stop for a second. She was walking on the pavement on the other side of the road, her 8-inch heels clattering on the sidewalk. He felt like Gautam Buddha sitting under that Banyan tree, at the time when he attained Nirvana. This was the moment he had been waiting for all his life.

Jassi's heart leaped. He dodged angry cab drivers as he crossed over to the other side of the road to be with the woman he had always admired. Middle fingers or expletives could not stop him. Not that day.

He was right behind her. In a few seconds, his life would attain its purpose.

But she was walking so fast, despite those heels. Jassi had to run to keep up with her. Eventually he crossed her, and in a quick motion, turned around to face her. She stopped.

Jassi tried to touch her shoulder. She flinched, and before Jassi could know what happened, the beefy man walking with her had his right fist stuck inside Jassi's stomach. Jassi gave her an incredulous stare like the decieved husband of a cheating wife from a Bollywood potboiler, before crumpling to the ground. He could suddenly see two of her in front of him, and from up close neither looked like Pamelaji. It wasn't *her*.

'You fucking idiot!' she gave him a disgusted look and moved on.

The man-gorilla who had punched him pointed his finger at Jassi, who was struggling to get up. 'Next time, watch before you mess with any American woman, you bloody Paki. Now go back to your cave and think about all the innocent people you killed, you little Arab prick.' The nerves on his fat neck were becoming more and more prominent, like they were suddenly going to transform into little serpants. Jassi got distracted. 'Sorry, I missed that. Come again?'

'Screw you.' He ran off to be with the fake Pamela who had caused all the trouble.

The crowd of onlookers dispersed as Jassi picked himself up, brushing the dirt off his clothes. His best shades that he had worn for the meeting with Victoria were shattered. His ripped jeans were a bit more ripped. Jassi was bruised, physically and emotionally. A less resolute person might have crumbled under the pressure, but not the Jazzminator.

Jassi noticed a familiar figure hovering above him. Victoria suddenly looked like an angel from heaven. She was asking him if he was okay. Victoria had noticed Jassi as she was making her way to their agreed venue and ended up witnessing the entire episode. She was aghast at the ugly turn of events.

'That idiot,' she muttered. 'But what exactly were you trying to do there?' she asked Jassi, who closed his eyes in horror.

'Nothing Victoria. Forget about it. I am just stupid.'

'Well, surely a couple of beers should repair the damage.' She held his arm. Jassi felt a hundred amperes of electric current run through his body. He cast a glance at Victoria, who looked gorgeous in a yellow dress that showed off her slender arms and shapely legs.

Victoria had come alone, but she told him some of her friends were going to join her in a little bit. Jassi had some 'private' time with her until then.

They found a table and talked over chicken wings and a pitcher of Budweiser. Victoria had a healthy appetite. Three glasses of beer later, he was feeling the buzz but she seemed like she had just got started. Jassi found himself falling in love. Yet again.

Don't do anything stupid today, he told himself. *Can't mess it up like last time. Must play it cool.*

An hour passed. Another one. Victoria was telling stories of her childhood and college life. She was fascinating. Jassi was listening, though not really registering much. He was just intent watching her speak. He noticed a little smudge of hot sauce on her nose. Jassi reached across and wiped it with his finger. She appeared startled, and then laughed loudly as Jassi held up his sauce-laced finger.

She took his finger and licked the sauce off it playfully. Jassi's heart did a triple somersault. He looked at her. She blinked playfully. Jassi moved his chair to her side of the table. She held his hand. Her silky touch detonated a mini-explosion inside him. He leaned in towards her. Her eyes were closed and her breath slightly heavy.

'Hi guys!' a loud voice appeared at the strategic moment. Jassi looked up in disgust at the sudden interruption.

'Hey Tapasya!' Victoria beamed at her friend.

'Sorry, did I disturb you guys?' She had a naughty smile on, which appeared more like a wicked smirk to Jassi. He had no love for Ms Coriander chutney.

Victoria brushed her off. 'No silly, nothing of that sort. We've been just polishing off some chicken wings and beer. Think I outdrank our friend, the Jazzminator.'

'Jazzminator! Interesting name for Mr Indian store.' Tapasya couldn't stop taunting Jassi, who scowled at her. He wasn't too sure what Victoria meant by 'nothing of that sort'. A few seconds back, she had given him very different vibes.

For the second time in two weeks, Jassi wanted to smash something heavy into Tapasya's ABCD head. Jassi got up. 'You girls carry on. I just remembered I had some work I need to complete urgently. Take care, Victoria.' Tapasya waved him goodbye. Victoria smiled at him and blew a flying kiss.

Jassi returned home feeling frustrated. Priyank was sprawled on the couch watching *American Idol* on the TV. Priyank had been nice to him ever since the Natalia incident and had even let Jassi keep the air conditioner on the entire night for a full week after that fateful day.

'Yo Jassi, what's up bro? You look a bit down?' Priyank took out two bottles of Corona from the fridge and handed one to Jassi who took the bottle, though he already felt like he was full.

Before they knew it, the two had run through the 6-pack case of beer. Jassi went over the Victoria story with Priyank, who listened intently.

'Dude, I am sorry. Sounds like that girl Tapasya ruined your chances tonight.' Priyank placed a comforting arm on Jassi's shoulder. Jassi felt the blast of dried up underarm sweat and grimaced.

Priyank continued. 'Listen buddy, I am sorry. After all my attempts, things just havent worked out for you. I think your stars are messed up. Maybe you just need one opening and then things will fall in place.'

Jassi was all ears, despite being drunk.

'What if we just get it done with, and hopefully that will clear up the opening hurdle for you?'

'What do you mean, dude?' Jassi was confused.

'Get dressed. We are going out.'

Half an hour later, Jassi and Priyank were standing in front of a single floor building in a shabby part of Jersey City.

There were a few people milling around, smoking cigarettes, bottles of beer in their hands.

A neon dashboard in the shape of a woman's curves proclaimed 'Charlie's Angels'.

Separated

'I think my parents are looking for a boy for me.'

Akhil dropped the cup of coffee in his hand as Nandita dropped the bombshell on Yahoo video chat. She had a sleepy look about her and her hair was a greasy, unwashed mess, but to Akhil she had never looked prettier.

The coffee splattered all over his 100 dollars Algorithms book on the study table and scorched his pants 'What!' he exclaimed loudly, out of a combination of shock and his vitals getting burned. This was a disaster. 'I am coming to Kolkata to take you with me.'

'Calm down, my hero. It is okay. Let them look. Nothing will come out of it. I will reject them all and tell them I have already chosen a cute Punjabi boy who cooks great rajma chawal.'

Calming down wasn't proving easy for Akhil. 'No. Tell them now. I cannot take this risk.'

'Okay baba. I will talk to them.'

'Wait. Mom is here. I'll be back in a minute.'

The video crackled and the call went dead.

July was wrapping up. Nandita had been gone for two

months now. Akhil's research work was keeping him very busy. Professor Narayanan was hard to please, never praising his efforts and constantly coming up with questions that shook Akhil's concepts. It was tough work, but Akhil knew the project could be a great success if they could implement all of the ideas proposed by the professor successfully.

Akhil waited patiently for two hours. There was no call back. Nandita had gone offline on Yahoo Messenger.

It was nine in the morning. Jassi was at the departure terminal of New York's JFK airport. His flight back to Tallahasseee was in three hours. He took a cup of Starbucks coffee and sat by the window, watching the planes lined up for takeoff. Tears were still streaking out of his swollen eyes. The shaking had reduced, but he was still far from normal. The last eight hours had been the darkest of his life.

It was all Priyank's idea, he murmured to himself.

Priyank. Where is he? Probably in a police lockup. Jassi shuddered at the thought of what might have been.

They had gone to this strip club last night. Once in, Priyank mentioned the *VIP room* and suggested they try it out. 'It will be fun, dude,' he had said. They paid hundred bucks each and were in the VIP room. The girls were marginally hotter but Jassi realized that this place provided more 'value added services' after Priyank disappeared for half an hour with a girl who seemed to know him.

'Your turn, my tiger,' he told Jassi once he was back. 'Hundred bucks for the deal. Just go and do it.'

'What!' Jassi couldn't believe his ears, or Priyank's brazen suggestion.

'What what? Go for it man. Get it over with. Hopefully this will improve your luck with the ladies.'

Jassi felt sick. He wasn't sure he wanted his first time to be with a hooker. 'I am going to the wash room. Back in five minutes.'

The silence of the washroom was refreshing. Jassi washed his face. The cold water made him feel alive again. He looked at himself in the mirror, and felt a voice asking him if he was sure he wanted to do this. As he prepared to turn the knob of the washroom to return to the club, he heard a loud commotion outside. He opened the door slightly and was shocked to see police officers dragging half-naked men and women out of rooms. Jassi shut the door and hid inside a stall.

He stayed there for a couple of hours before finally daring to peek outside. There was nobody there. Jassi waited another fifteen minutes before daring to walk outside. There were no police officers waiting in ambush there either. Jassi heaved a sigh of relief and noticed his shirt soaked in sweat. He thanked the gods. He had escaped certain arrest by sheer luck, or he would have been dumped in a police car and taken away on prostitution charges.

Jassi ran the five miles back to their apartment. Priyank was not there. Jassi decided he had seen enough of New York and packed his bags. An hour later, he was on a taxi en route to JFK.

✈

Akhil returned home after an exhausting day at work. His sole course for the semester was over. The course had been assessed purely based on assignment grades, and there were no tests. Akhil got an A. From thereon, it was only research work with Dr Narayanan for the rest of the semester. Thanks to the professor who seemed to relish keeping his group of students on their toes, Akhil hadn't been able to manage the time for a decent meal all day. As he entered the apartment, he saw a familiar pair of shoes on the carpet in the living room. There was some noise coming from the kitchen.

Akhil went to the kitchen to find Jassi wearing an apron, busy cooking up a feast. There was stuff simmering on all four stoves. This was most unexpected.

'Jassi! Boss, what a pleasant surprise. I didn't expect to see you back so soon.'

Jassi turned around and hugged Akhil. His voice choked.

'Akhil! I missed you buddy.'

'You're back early. Thought you were going to be in New York for another month, till the start of the fall semester.'

'Forget it yaar. Let's have dinner. I am starving.' Jassi's eyes were swollen and Akhil wondered what was wrong. Jassi hadn't spoken to him once since he left for New York two months ago.

They ate in silence over an episode of *Friends*. Akhil marvelled at how delicious the food was but was confused at Jassi's sudden return.

After dinner, Jassi went out for a walk. As Akhil was settling into his post-dinner work routine, he saw Jassi return with a big bottle of Absolut vodka and a pack of Marlboro cigarettes and head for his room. He frowned. *Something is seriously wrong, unless New York has made him give up beer for Vodka, turned him*

Separated

into a Michelin-starred chef in two months and then bored him enough to make him leave early, thought Akhil.

It was 10 pm, time for Akhil's daily call with Nandita. The call a day ago had been interrupted suddenly. Akhil was worried about what might be happening at her home. He logged into Yahoo Messenger and waited for her to come online. An hour passed. The digital alarm clock he had bought from the Dollar Store read 4 am. Akhil was snoring at his desk, one hand on the mouse, the drool making its way into the crevices of the laptop keyboard.

✈

The next afternoon, as Akhil approached his lab, he heard voices coming from inside. It didn't sound like people talking. Somebody was moaning softly, amidst the sound of the legs of a desk inside creaking with a gradually increasing frequency. It sounded like Brad and his pretty girlfriend indulging in some extra-curricular activities. Akhil felt sick. He gave the door a slight knock and left.

He returned to the room an hour later. The door was now open. Brad was busy working on his computer. Aparna was gone. Brad said a casual 'hi' and continued with his work. His shirt was unbuttoned and hanging out of his jeans.

Akhil didn't really care. He had not been able to talk to Nandita for two days now. She had advised him against calling up directly on her mobile outside of their scheduled times, but in desperation he had tried that as well. Unreachable. He was finding it hard to concentrate on work.

The day somehow passed by.

At 10 pm, Akhil's mobile rang to the tune of 'kuch kuch hota hai', which was his ringtone set for Nandita's calls. Akhil leapt to his feet and picked up the phone before it could go to voicemail.

'Hi Nandu,' he gasped. 'Where have you been?'

'Hi Akhil.' She sounded a little tense.

'I am fine, Nandita. You had me worried. We haven't talked in days.'

'I know, sweetheart. Things have been a bit complicated here.'

'What happened?' Akhil could barely hear his own voice over his loud heartbeat.

'You know I told you about this guy my parents wanted me to marry? It turns out they really like him and have been pushing me to meet him.'

'What! And did you say no? Did you tell them about me?'

'Not yet sweetie. I will talk to them about you, but it is not easy. My dad has something against Punjabis and keeps joking about what might happen if I have a Punjabi boy lined up.'

A shiver ran down Akhil's spine.

'I miss you Nandita. Come back soon, and sort things out with your family. Or I am going to come and get you myself.'

She laughed finally. 'I love you Akhil. You're the sweetest.'

'I have to go now. I'll talk to dad about you today. Wish me luck.'

'Good luck Nandita. You better convince the old man or I'll have to deal with it my way.'

'Shut up, silly. Talk to you later. Bye'

'Bye Nandita.'

Separated

Akhil did not sleep that night, and not because he was busy working on his research.

'What do you mean you did not complete work on your assigned module? You know very well that Brad and Neil depend on your completing it. The entire project is now stalled because of your delays,' the professor thundered.

Akhil stood silently with his head bowed. He didn't even feel like responding. His life was crashing before his eyes, and Professor Narayanan's anger at his performance was the least of his worries.

It had been two weeks since he last spoke with Nandita. In their last phone conversation, she had told him she was going to talk to her family about him. Since then he had not heard from her. The signs were ominous.

There were still three weeks to go before the end of the summer semester and Nandita's return back. Akhil wondered how he would survive these last few weeks if he didn't hear from her.

The professor was furious. Akhil had not done any of his assigned work in the past week and had assured Dr Narayanan that he would have it ready in a day. After waiting patiently for a week, the professor had finally exploded.

'So Akhil, can I expect that you will be able to cover the lost time and have something ready by next week? Brad, maybe you could help him out with a part of the module.'

'Sure, professor,' Brad replied with a sideways glance at Akhil.

'I'll try, Dr Narayanan.' Akhil answered hesitantly.

'*Trying* might not be enough, Akhil. We can't afford to lose more time. This better be done by next Monday before we meet, or…' He left the threat unfinished and slammed the door behind him on his exit.

Aparna entered the lab ten minutes later. As she kissed Brad, Akhil felt miserable. He wondered how to talk to Nandita. He wanted to hear her voice so much right now.

Aparna asked Akhil why he looked so miserable. Akhil gave a wry smile and left the room.

✈

Jassi was working his shift at the gas station when a moustached Indian man came to his counter with a can of milk. He didn't have his Teaching Assistantship job as he had taken the semester off. Doing a part time job would help kill time and provide some supplementary income to cover living expenses. He wondered what his mom would say if she found out. He could totally imagine her go 'Jassi is working at a petrol pump? Spoiling our family name in front of the Amreekan people?'

At first, Sundar didn't recognize Jassi. Then as realization sunk in, he exclaimed loudly.

'Jassi, what are you doing here man?'

Jassi looked at him sheepishly. 'How are you, dude? I just got back last week from New York,' he said trying to evade the question.

'Oh wow. How was it man? You must have had a great time in New York?' Sundar was his usual happy self.

Jassi went silent. He wasn't sure he could share the painful stories from New York with anyone. Those were the darkest two months of his life. He had been robbed, punched in the stomach by a racist white man, and nearly arrested. Two months of fruitless pursuit of girls had taught him that something was not right. He had decided that this was not how he wanted to live his life. He had to change.

✈

The next morning, Akhil returned to the lab to finish some pending work. The professor was mad enough. Any more delays and he might lose his research assistantship.

He logged on to his computer. As he opened up the project source code, he saw Nandita's face flash on his screen. Akhil blinked. *My mind is playing games*, he told himself. He spent the next three hours staring at his screen, oblivious to Brad entering the lab with Neil. The two watched Akhil in his stupefied state and wondered if he had finally discovered the joys of weed.

Brad took the chair next to Akhil. He had always seen Akhil perform brilliantly in classes and assignments. This was not his usual self. 'What's up dude? You look totally pooped out. Don't take professor Narayanan's words to heart. He can be a bit mean at times, but he likes you man. Looks like you just need to mellow out and enjoy life. I don't know what it is, but it will be alright.'

Akhil was touched by the concern. America seemed such a lonely place at times. He had no one to talk to, no one to share his pain with. The one person who would have understood him was missing from the scene. He got up, hugged Brad, and sobbed on his shoulder. Brad looked at Neil, and put a friendly arm around Akhil.

Akhil stayed in the lab all day, but couldn't get any work done, and walked back home in the evening after a fruitless day.

As he opened the apartment door, Akhil could smell the aroma of delicious food. Jassi had prepared tea for his roommates and baked some frozen samosas to go along with it. Akhil felt like hugging Jassi. Something was definitely wrong with him, though Akhil was sure it couldn't be any bigger than the problem troubling him

'So Jassi, how was your experience in New York?' Kedar asked.

Jassi looked around uncomfortably for a few seconds, took a deep sigh, and burst into tears. He couldn't hold it back anymore. He told Kedar and Akhil all about his horrid time in New York, and the reason why he was back early.

'So what happened to Priyank?' Akhil asked when he was done.

'I have no idea, dude. I think he might have got arrested. I haven't even tried calling him ever since I left his apartment. Don't want to get into any more trouble.'

Kedar whistled. 'Wow. This Priyank sounds weird.'

Jassi swore to stay off girls and focus on his studies instead. 'I've been a fool this last year. New York has woken me up. I promise I will never become another Priyank.' He wiped his eyes with the cuff of his shirt.

Akhil patted Jassi's shoulder, returned to his room, and logged on to his computer hoping to find Nandita online. No luck.

Separated

Akhil slept early. He dreamed of the angry professor dragging Nandita away from him, while shouting at him in Bengali for ruining the project.

found and Lost

'Oye Akhil. What are you doing here?'

Jassi came and stood next to Akhil who was sitting on a solitary bench outside the library, watching people go by. The forlorn look on his face told the whole story. He hadn't shaved in a week and the heavy stubble made him look like the homeless man on campus.

'Come, let's go home,' said Jassi pulling up Akhil and walked with him to their apartment.

The Fall-2005 semester was halfway done. The mid-semesters were approaching. After a month of delivering no fruitful output, Akhil had lost his place on Dr Narayanan's research team. Thankfully, the professor had kept him on a teaching assistantship, so he still had the monthly stipend coming in.

Akhil had not talked to Nandita for almost two months now. Every day he got up in time for their morning call and eyed the phone wistfully, wishing for it to ring. It never did. Akhil would cry while taking his shower and eating his breakfast. He was attending his classes, but his mind was elsewhere. His performance was suffering as a result.

With every passing week, his hopes of meeting Nandita were going down. *Maybe they forced her to marry that Bengali boy? Maybe she doesn't love me anymore? Perhaps she realized I wasn't good enough for her? I should have just studied harder for IIT to become worthy of her.* Despair was giving rise to all sorts of negative thoughts in his mind.

Her number didn't seem to work anymore. It was always unreachable. She was never online on Yahoo Messenger. She had not replied to any of the 45 emails Akhil had sent her since their last conversation.

Akhil was turning into a nervous wreck. Luckily, he had Jassi, Kedar, and Sundar keeping a close eye on him at most times, though they were clueless how to get him back to normal again.

No amount of counselling had helped getting Akhil back to his normal self. Venkat had tried going with the classical argument—'Never cry for girls, buses, and trains. One goes and a new one comes along.' It didn't work.

Jassi logged on to Facebook and noticed a friend invite from Victoria. Facebook was a new site that was taking the university by storm. 'Social networking' they called it. You made a profile, added friends, posted on their walls, poked them, and even threw virtual sheep at them. It was fun, though Jassi had just started using it.

In her profile picture, Victoria was sitting at a bar with a pitcher of beer in front of her. Jassi remembered that evening in New York and sighed. He didn't want to be near any girl for now. Victoria had seen him humiliate himself on two occasions already. He didn't want to embarrass himself any more.

Jassi closed the browser window without responding.

His phone rang. It was her.

'Hi there, Mr Jazzminator.'

Jassi hated the name. It brought back painful memories of New York.

'Hi Victoria. How are you?'

'Where did you disappear from Jersey? I never heard back from you after that evening at the lounge. Went to the store a couple of times and you weren't there either. Was it something my friend Tapasya said?'

'Oh no, nothing. Just that I had to return back to Tallahasseee for some work.' Jassi couldn't tell her the truth.

'Not cool, dude. You should have told me. Anyway, we should get together sometime for a drink or something. Or maybe you might need some more English practice. Remember?'

Jassi laughed. Victoria seemed so different from the other girls he had met. Somehow, she seemed genuine in whatever she said.

'Sure,' he smiled as he hung up.

The phone rang again. It was Priyank's number. Jassi hesitated. *What if it is a trap laid by the police to catch him? Nah, I am just overreacting.* He took the call.

Turned out Priyank had not got arrested after all. They had questioned him, but let him off with a warning, as they couldn't prove he was doing anything illegal at the time of the raid. Priyank's tone was different. He sounded cold, though

Jassi could detect a faint desperation behind the tone. Priyank asked him not to utter a word of what happened that night to anyone, ending with a veiled warning. 'We were in it together, remember that.'

✈

Sundar came running to Akhil's apartment and banged loudly on the door. Akhil opened the door with a quizzical expression. 'Sundar, what...'

'Nandita. I saw her. Near the library.' Sundar was panting from running all the way from the campus. He gasped for breath.

Akhil's eyes lit up. He grabbed his hawai chappals and ran out of the apartment, still in his pajamas. Sundar followed him.

They reached the library and Sundar pointed to a bench. 'There, I saw her sitting on that bench there.'

'Where? There's no one there.'

'Maybe she left.'

'Sundar, are you sure it was her? Why would she be here and not tell me?'

'I don't know man. She did seem like Nandita.'

The two searched around for the next hour. Akhil went through all the floors on the library, carefully scanning each desk, much to the annoyance of the students preparing for their upcoming tests.

She was nowhere to be found.

But there was a faint glimmer of hope in Akhil's mind now. *If Nandita is in Tallahasseee, I will find her.*

Later that evening, he called up Rashmi, Nandita's roommate.

'Hi Rashmi, this is Akhil.'

'Oh, Akhil. How are you?' The tone suddenly changed. Akhil wasn't sure if it was sympathy, coldness, or indifference, but it didn't feel normal.

'I'm alright. Listen, I called you up to check if you ever heard back from Nandita from India. I haven't talked to her for two months now and wondering what happened to her. Any idea what she is upto?'

She spoke after what seemed to Akhil like a few minutes.

'No, I have no idea where she is.'

'But she is your roommate? Aren't you worried? Why didn't she come back from India?'

She took another minute before responding. 'I am sure she is okay. Maybe she had her own reasons to stay back.'

Akhil took a deep breath. 'Rashmi, are you sure you're not hiding anything from me? One of my friends thinks he saw Nandita on campus today.'

The line went silent again. She spoke after a good ten seconds. 'I have no clue, Akhil. Your friend probably mistook somebody else.'

Rashmi spoke again, this time her tone definitely sympathetic. 'Akhil, I know you guys had a thing going. Maybe it's time to move on now. Don't torture yourself. I heard you are not doing very well of late.'

'I doubt I can ever move on, Rashmi. Thanks for your help,' replied Akhil and hung up.

Something didn't seem right.

It was 8 pm on a cool October evening. Akhil was waiting on a bench outside Nandita's department building. This had been his routine for a week now. Every day he left home early to scout the campus for Nandita, and again in the evenings he would spend time around her department building hoping to see her.

Elsewhere there was no trace of her. She was not active on the INSAT mailing list, she was not on Facebook, Yahoo Messenger showed her offline at all times, and her phone number didn't work anymore. Akhil didn't know anybody in her department, or he could have found an easy way of determining if Nandita was indeed back.

In his heart, Akhil still wasn't convinced. There was no way Nandita would be back and go two months without even contacting him.

His stomach was rumbling. He hadn't eaten anything all day.

Akhil was about to head for home when he saw a shadow appear out the building gate. It was woman wearing a long black coat, her face was not visible in the dark, but Akhil recognized her in an instant. He could identify Nandita just by the sound of her feet.

Akhil ran towards her. She heard him and turned towards Akhil. Her face turned pale, drained of all blood.

'Hi Nandita.' Akhil's eyes welled up.

'Akhil!' Her sound was a faint whisper. She appeared shocked. Akhil could make out she had lost a lot of weight, her face was pale, her hair dishevelled, and there were dark circles below here eyes. She looked like a ghost. This was not the Nandita he used to know.

'Nandu, what happened? I was dying without you and you were nowhere to be found.'

'Akhil, it is over. Please forget all about me.'

She covered her face with her scarf and prepared to leave. But Akhil blocked her way.

'Over? How? Why? What happened in India? Did you talk to your parents about me?' His head was spinning now. He felt like was going to collapse.

Nandita turned to leave.

'No.' He shouted and blocked her way. 'Answer me first. Why are you doing this to me?'

'Stop it Akhil. Grow up. If you block my way, I will have to call the cops.' She spoke with a stern face and a cold voice.

Akhil looked distraught as Rashmi suddenly came out of the building and Nandita was off with her. He sank to his knees and wept in despair. His world had just come crashing down.

A little past midnight, a campus police car found an Indian student sprawled outside the Geology department building. They had seen drunken students passed out in a pool of vomit before, but this case seemed different. He was not reeking of alcohol. They woke Akhil up, asked him where he lived, and dropped him home with a warning to watch himself in the future.

✈

Akhil woke up the next afternoon to a ringing mobile phone. He let it go to voicemail. It rang again. He didn't move. The phone rang a third time. Akhil got up from the bed and picked up the phone from the bookshelf.

The caller-id read 'Ma'. Akhil picked up the receiver.

'Akhil. How are you beta? It has been so long since I heard your voice. What is going on? Have you become so busy that you forgot your old mother?'

Akhil had not called her for two weeks, and neither answered the phone whenever she called.

He looked at himself in the mirror. He seemed unrecognizable. His hair had grown long and shabby. His stubble represented the foliage of a small equatorial rainforest. His eyes had dark circles below them. Life had taken a sudden turn. Just a couple of months ago, he was the happiest he had ever been. *Why did Nandita do this to me?*

'Akhil, are you there?' His mom sounded worried, and it was not without reason.

'Hello ma,' he answered in a low voice.

'Akhil, is something wrong? What is going on?'

'Nothing ma. Just been busy with work.'

'How come you are so busy that in two weeks you haven't had the time to talk to your mother? Ever since you returned from home, you seem to have changed. Are you alright, son?'

'Yes, ma. I am fine. Just this research work takes up a lot of time.'

'Is it a girl, Akhil?'

Akhil hesitated.

'Tell me Akhil. You have never hidden anything from your mother.'

'No mom. It is nothing. I have to go now,' he said and hung up.

Akhil's thoughts went back to last night's meeting with Nandita. She had changed. She had hidden from him all this time. She had threatened to call the cops on him. And he thought she loved him.

Akhil didn't feel like going for his classes that day. He felt like there was no point in it anymore. In fact, he didn't find any point in anything anymore. He lied on his bed. A shiver ran over his body as he thought about all the pleasant moments Nandita and he had shared together. He had so many plans for them. So many dreams. They would get married in a few years, possibly twice, in separate Punjabi and Bengali ceremonies. There would be two girls. Pratiksha and Khushi. The elder would be like him, calm and patient. The younger one would be like their mother, brash and impulsive. They would go to school holding each other's hands as Akhil and Nandita waved them goodbye. Once the girls were independent, he and Nandita would move to a beach house in Panama City and make love every day of their lives.

It was all gone. Life had lost its meaning. There was nothing to look forward to anymore.

Akhil picked up a shaving blade and headed to the bathroom.

Project Kolkata

'Akhil, you idiot. What the hell were you thinking?' Kedar shouted at his roommate.

Venkat looked at Jassi. 'Forget it Jassi. This dude here thinks he is some modern-age Devdas. Will try to kill himself for a girl, and the world will make a movie for him. Bloody fool.' He was too disgusted to even look at Akhil.

'Man, I just want to slap you so hard Akhil, that it breaks your jaw.' Dilpreet slammed a fist in the wall in disgust.

A nurse asked the guys to keep it low. Sundar took Jassi, Venkat, and Dilpreet out of the hospital room before things got out of hand. The four had gone through the most horrifying experience of their lives and had not slept for the past twenty-four hours.

The afternoon earlier, Jassi had returned home for lunch. Generally, he used to eat on campus. As luck would have it, he chose just the right day to go back to the apartment for food.

As Jassi entered the apartment, he heard the bathroom door shut. Kedar was away for classes, so this had to be Akhil. Jassi was surprised. Akhil had lectures all day. *Why was he home?*

Jassi heard sobbing from the other side of the bathroom door. A few minutes later, it went quiet. Then he heard a different voice. It sounded like someone whimpering in pain.

Fearing the worst, Jassi pounded on the door until it gave way. His worst fears were confirmed. Akhil was sitting in the bathtub, his eyes red and swollen, blood oozing out of his slashed wrists.

Jassi looked at Akhil in despair.

'What have you done, Akhil?'

'I am sorry Jassi. There is no point anymore.'

'Shut up, you idiot,' said Jassi and hurriedly dialled 911.

Half an hour later, they were at the hospital. The doctors confirmed not much damage had been done. Akhil would live.

'You did well, bringing him in on time. Any more delay and God knows what might have happened,' said the doctor patting Jassi on his shoulder as she left.

Akhil's wrists were bandaged heavily. He spent the day under strict medical supervision, treated as a case of attempted suicide. His four desperate friends waited outside, anxious to see the jilted lover get back to his usual self again. They had not informed anyone from his family as they didn't want to worry his family unnecessarily. Plus the doctors assured them that Akhil was in no morbid danger.

Dilpreet had broken down into tears in the waiting room. He had always thought of Akhil as his younger brother, and seeing him in this state had shocked him. He hadn't met Akhil very often this semester, but thought it was because he was busy with work. Jassi and Kedar had filled him in on the real story.

They finally got to see him now, twenty-four hours later. Akhil was conscious, though heartbroken.

Dilpreet hugged him before launching into an angry tirade that ended in a threat to kill him, if he so much as tried anything similar again.

'Stupid kids like you are the biggest reason why people should never have children. Did you even think of what will happen to your parents when they get the call that their son has died in the US and they need to come to collect your body? Next time just ask them to consume poison before killing yourself, because they will be devastated, assuming they survive hearing the news. They give up their lives raising you, and this is how you repay them?'

Akhil was ashamed. He realized he had not been thinking straight and wondered how he let things come to this stage. He told the entire story to the others, who were shocked to find out that Nandita was in town.

Dilpreet advised Akhil to take it easy. 'Never be stupid enough to think a person is your life. And the next time you get suicidal thoughts, think about your family who are waiting for you to return to them.'

Akhil was going to be kept in the hospital for three days. There would be a psychological evaluation to ensure he was not going to try harming himself again before they sent him home.

Rashmi answered the doorbell to find herself standing face to face with two young men outside her apartment. She wondered what Jassi and Kedar were upto. She barely knew them, though she was aware that they were Akhil's roommates.

Jassi spoke first. 'We are here to talk about Akhil.'

Rashmi went silent for a minute. 'I don't think I have anything to help you guys.'

Jassi took out a picture from his pocket and carefully unfolded it. Rashmi looked at it and gasped. 'What did he do?'

'Nothing major. Just tried to kill himself after Nandita broke up with him.'

'Oh my God. This is unbelievable. Come in you two.' Rashmi closed the door behind them.

A week later, Akhil was at the departure lounge of Tallahassee airport. The bandages were off. The doctors at the hospital had cleared him after a psychological evaluation. He was clean-shaven again. The circles around his eyes were gradually disappearing. He looked human again.

Boarding would start in a little bit. His flight would take him to Atlanta and onward to Delhi and Kolkata.

He patted the thick file labelled 'Project Kolkata' in his bag and hoped he would not forget any of the important stuff when it mattered. He felt sleepy. The past few days had been busy and his head felt like it would explode with all that newly-added knowledge, but he felt like his life had a purpose again.

It was all Jassi's initiative. Kedar and he had met Rashmi at her home. She had told them the entire story on seeing a photo of Akhil's bandaged wrists at the hospital.

It seemed straight out of a Bollywood movie. Nandita had talked to her father about Akhil a day before a prospective groom was to pay them a visit. Her father disliked Punjabi people, considering them loud, uncouth, and unprofessional.

The guy he had in mind for her was a PhD from Cornell, had a family that traced its roots back to Rabindranath Tagore, was handsome, cooked great fish, and wrote poems as a hobby. 'He is perfect for you, Nandita. Forget that Punjabi boy,' he had told her.

The ultimatum was strict, and for all her brashness, Nandita could not defy her father. He made her swear to his life that she would never see Akhil again. Nandita was to marry Anirban, her father's choice.

The next day they got Nandita engaged to Anirban in a quick ceremony at home. Nandita had been made to promise that she would never contact Akhil again. She was not to call him, take his calls, send any emails, nothing. No communication.

Nandita had been devastated. Her family was being utterly unreasonable, and there was nothing she could do about it. Her father told her to stay in Kolkata and move to the US only after getting married to Anirban in the winter.

Nandita had cried herself to sleep every night for two weeks after that. Eventually her mom intervened and begged the obstinate dad to let her return to Tallahasseee at least, to continue her studies. He relented after a lot of persuasion, only on the condition that Nandita move to a new apartment on the other side of town, and make sure Akhil or anybody else never finds out. To Akhil and his friends, she must never be visible. Her dad had sent her off with the statement Indian parents have used to emotionally blackmail their children since forever—'If you try to make any contact with that Punjabi boy, just assume that I am dead for you.'

Nandita had returned to Tallahasseee just in time for the last date for registration for courses. She had moved to an apartment far away from the campus and started living the life of a hermit. She didn't go anywhere, didn't meet anyone, didn't have any social life. Her heart cried every day, but she had a promise to keep and her family honour at stake.

She longed for Akhil after receiving each of his emails or voice messages, but she never responded. She had hoped Akhil would get the hint and move on, but she wondered how much time it would take. She had still not been able to move on. Her studies were getting affected. She had returned to Tallahasseee because she couldn't stay in her Kolkata home, waiting to be handed over to that Cornell PhD, but now that she was here, it was proving torturous keeping away from Akhil.

She had taken detours while driving home on several occasions, hoping to just catch a glimpse of Akhil walking home. Then there was that night. She was leaving her department, face covered in a long scarf to avoid getting detected by anyone, when Akhil suddenly sprung upon her. For a second she thought her heart stopped beating. It had taken all of her willpower to not hug him and cry her heart out. But she had to avoid him. He had to move on, for his sake.

✈

Akhil landed at Kolkata airport. The flight had been long and tiring, but he didn't care. He had a plan to execute. He went to the prepaid taxi booth and asked for a taxi.

'Where to?' asked the person at the counter.

'Hotel Seagull. Shyam Bazaar.'

Ten minutes later, Akhil was headed to his destination through North Kolkata's quaint streets, with their old-worldly charm. He had never been to the city before, but it looked exactly like it did in all the movies he had seen in the last few days. There were the ubiquitous yellow taxis and the hand-pulled rickshaws. A tram pulled out of its stop as cars honked all around them. Durga Puja was in two days so the city bore an especially festive look.

Akhil tried to concentrate. He had a detailed plan drawn out, and he needed to execute it to perfection.

The next morning he woke up at 5 am and took a taxi to the Ashu Babur Fish Market. It was a Sunday. The day *he* went for his weekly fish shopping.

As soon as Akhil got off the yellow taxi, the stench choked his throat. It was 6 am, but the place was busy with people milling about. There were rows upon rows of fishmongers with their sharpened curved knifes, cutting up fish of all shape and sizes for their customers. It stank. The place was crowded and very noisy. Akhil was finally realizing what all the teachers back in school meant when they referred to his noisy class as a fishmarket. Akhil was having trouble breathing, when he spotted *him* in the distance. He took out the picture from his pocket. It was definitely *him*.

Akhil checked his appearance, ran his fingers through the freshly oiled hair, and headed in the direction of the man he was pursuing.

He went to the shop next to the one where Dr Amitav Ray was negotiating the price of his Hilsa fish trying to get the seller to bring it down from 700 to 600 rupees per kilo. He had just closed the deal at 645 rupees when Akhil intervened.

'Sir, what do you think of this fish?' Akhil said, holding up a fish he had picked from the pile. His body revolted from holding the dead animal, but he had to do it, that too with a grin on his face.

Dr Ray glanced up at Akhil with a curious look, inspected the fish in his hand, and replied, 'Try the one next to it. Seems much better,' after which he went back to business.

Akhil got the rate down to 650 rupees from the quoted 800 per kilo, making sure the conversation was loud enough for his neighbour to hear. The seller throwing up his hands in despair at this Hindi speaking fish lover provided the icing on the cake. 'Sir, I cannot give the fish for any cheaper. I have a family to feed.'

Dr Ray moved on, done with his shopping. Akhil got his bag and ran after him. He caught up and started walking right behind him. A minute later, he turned around and looked at Akhil quizzically.

'Do I know you?'

'No Dr Amitav Ray, you don't. But I know everything about you.'

'Really? And you are?'

'Akhil Arora, sir. I am currently working on a book on contemporary writers of Indian regional literature, and wanted to do a chapter on you.'

Dr Ray didn't look particularly excited, and walked away. Akhil ran after him.

'Son, I don't think I am too fond of being written about by strangers.'

'Trust me, Dr Ray. I know all about you.'

'Really? What do you know about me?'

Akhil took a deep breath. This was going to be his first test.

'Dr Amitav Ray. Born 1945 at Baharu Village in the 24

Parganas district. Your father, Shakti Ray, was one of the most famous Bengali poets of the first half of the century and served as a lecturer at Vidyasagar College. You did a BA in English Literature from Presidency College in 1965, followed by an MA in the same subject. You went on to become one of the most famous writers of literature from Bengal in the latter half of the 20th century. Your collection of poems *Freedom at Sunrise* is counted as one of the masterpieces of this era and used as a textbook for both the English Literature and Philosophy courses at several colleges in West Bengal. Your unique talent is your expertize in English and Bengali literature, for which some people have drawn comparisons between Gurudev and you. You received a Sahitya Academy award in 1989 for your contribution to Bengali literature...'

Dr Ray raised his arm, asking Akhil to stop. 'Okay, that's impressive. You've done good research. What do you want from me?'

'Just a few minutes of your time, sir.' Akhil was putting on the façade well.

'What did you say your name was?'

'Akhil Arora.'

From Jassi's discussions with Nandita's roommate Rashmi, Akhil knew that Nandita had not got to mentioning his name to her parents.

'Punjabi?'

'Yes, sir.'

Dr Ray paused and mumbled something to himself.

'Sorry, sir?'

'Eh, nothing. How did a Punjabi boy land up in journalism? That too in a place like Kolkata?'

Akhil laughed politely. 'Sir, there are all kinds of Punjabis. Some of us like journalism and literature as well.'

'Very well, then.' He then hesitated for a minute before asking the next question. 'Why would you want to feature me in your book? You do know…'

Akhil cut him off. 'Dr Ray, I am aware of the government's opposition to what it considers your very liberal views on reforms and industrialization. They have tried to curtail your freedom ever since your book *Bengalization* released.'

He added shortly, 'But I agree with your views. The government is being shortsighted. They will eventually need to relent and open up the economy, or risk being left behind in this increasingly open world economy.'

Dr Ray's lips curled in a slight smile. 'You are an interesting young man. I hardly expected today to start with this conversation, especially in this smelly fish market.'

He glanced at his watch. It was just 8 am, but the sun was furious already. The temperature was close to 35 °C.

'I am going to head home now. Do you want to come along for breakfast? My wife makes excellent luchi-torkari. I doubt you get anything that delightful in Delhi.'

Akhil wanted to jump with joy. 'I am sure sir. I would love to come.'

An hour later, he was having breakfast with the man he hoped would one day be his father-in-law, as his future mom-in-law cooked puris for the two men. Pa-in-law was telling stories of his various fights with the state administration. Mom-in-law had beamed at Akhil when Dr Ray introduced him to her. Akhil was reminded of his own mother, and wondered how all mothers were the same—benevolent, smiling, and full of warmth.

'There was this time after the release of *Bengalization* when a huge mob came to my house and asked me to apologize for my comments about the Marxist ideology ruining Kolkata and Bengal. I refused. Things were going to get ugly, when the neighbours gathered in support and drove them away,' he laughed loudly.

Akhil looked around. 'Sir, is it just the two of you here? Anybody else in the family? I believe you had a daughter as well.'

He glared at Akhil suspiciously, who added quickly, 'Sir, I read it somewhere as part of my research.'

Dr Ray laughed loudly. 'I had always thought of Punjabis as the most uncouth, uncivilized, uneducated people in India who only care to show off their gold chains and cars. What did you come here for? Proving me wrong!' He chuckled at the thought. Akhil's heart nearly jumped out of his throat.

'How long will you be in Kolkata?'

'Three days sir. Hopefully that will be enough for my purpose.'

'And where are you staying?'

'Hotel Seagull. It is close by.'

'Why will you live in a hotel? We have this big house and just the two of us old people. You can stay here till your return.'

Akhil wanted to jump up and pump his fist wildly, but resisted the temptation.

'No sir. It will be a lot of trouble for you.'

'Oh no, not at all. We will be happy for you to stay here.'

'Sure sir. If you insist.'

'Excellent.'

Phase 1 of Project Kolkata had gone as per plan. An hour later, Akhil checked out of the hotel and was back to Dr Ray's home with his bags.

They spent the rest of the day discussing Bengali politics. Dr Ray was full of stories around the inefficiencies of the communist regime, and Akhil knew most of them from his research. Dr Ray's eyes lit up as Akhil turned out to be an equal partner in the conversation, and someone who knew what he was talking, backing everything with facts and figures. Akhil noticed Mrs Ray's gaze upon him whenever she was around, and he wondered if she was trying to look inside him to figure out his secrets.

'Young man, you've been quite the revelation.' Dr Ray patted Akhil's back as they were heading out in the evening for the Durga Puja proceedings at the historic Baghbazar pandal. Nandita's mom smiled at him, but Akhil again felt her eyes drilling inside him for information. He felt sure that he had activated the radar that seems to come factory-fitted with most mothers.

Akhil started rattling off the trivia. 'Baghbazar is one of the oldest Durga Puja pandals in Kolkata, having been in existence for over 100 years. It is relatively simple but high on tradition and culture, and people say it has the most beautiful idol of Kali ma.'

Dr Ray laughed. 'Good job, Akhil. Is there anything about Kolkata you don't know?'

Akhil smiled nervously at this man, the father of the woman

he loved. He wondered if he would continue to be so pleased with him once he knew the truth.

Three days later, a creaky white Ambassador car pulled up in front of the Kolkata airport departure terminal.

'You take care, son. Now run quickly, before you miss your flight.'

Nandita's dad loaded up Akhil's bag on a trolley and waved him on. Nandita's mother kissed Akhil's forehead. Akhil touched their feet. She beamed at him.

'I am so happy, beta. You two will be great together.'

'Thanks aunty.' Akhil looked happier than he had been in months. Project Kolkata had been a success.

Everything I Do

The bell rang. She glanced at the wall clock. It was 10.30 pm. A bit late in the day, but she knew who it was. Time was about to stop.

She opened the door and froze. The ground started shaking around her. She was going to fall.

Akhil caught Nandita just in time. He grabbed her by the waist and kissed her, right there at the door. Their lips came together and unleashed a torrent of emotions. Tears ran down their faces like little streams of water making way after the first shower of the season.

Akhil lifted Nandita in his arms and took her inside the apartment. He closed the door behind. The exile was over. The barriers created between them had been broken down. Life was good.

Nandita's mom had called her in the morning. She had been on cloud nine ever since. Just when it all seemed to be over, fate had taken one more turn. Everything was going to be okay. She felt proud of the man she loved more than her life. He had done the impossible. He had turned her father around. Her engagement to that Cornell PhD was going to be called off.

After many months, she had felt like getting dressed up. She took the day off, got a haircut, took a long shower, and got herself cleaned up. She had ignored herself for two months now, and a look in the mirror had shaken her up. She looked like one of those shabby, unkempt cavemen from Discovery channel documentaries. There was no way she could have let Akhil see her in this condition.

'Dinner?' Her first word spoken to him in months.

'Sure. In a bit.' He grabbed her by the waist and took her to the couch. She smiled nervously. Akhil seemed older than he used to be. She noticed the scars on his arms.

'What's this?'

'Nothing. Just a small injury.'

'I am starving. Let's have dinner.' She grabbed Akhil by his hand and led him to the table. She handed him a plate and served supersized quantities of all of his favourite dishes that she had spent the entire evening preparing.

'Whoa! That is a lot of food.'

'Shut up. Look at you. Did you stop eating or what?'

Akhil looked in her eyes. 'Nandu, I think I had stopped living. I thought I was dead without you.'

A tear streaked out of Nandita's kohl-lined eyes. Akhil wiped it with his hand. He was overwhelmed with emotion. Just a few weeks ago, he had tried to kill himself, and now here he was, next to the love of his life. He felt grateful. To his wonderful friends. To God. To his destiny, which had given him a second birth.

The two spent the night in each other's arms. Akhil promised

Nandita that he would never let go of her again. 'I'll kill anyone who tries to take you away from me.'

She laughed, but he was serious.

✈

Akhil woke up the next morning as a pillow landed on top of him.

'Get up mister. Don't you need to go for classes today?' She had another pillow in her hand, aimed at Akhil's head.

Akhil grabbed a pillow and threw it at her. Ten minutes later, they were both on the bed, exhausted, panting for breath. The apartment looked like a tornado had just gone by. Akhil grabbed Nandita by the wrist. She looked at him with a bashful look in her eyes as he pulled her to him and kissed her. They then made sweet love to each other on the couch.

Akhil didn't want to go anywhere, but there was work to be done. He had messed up this semester and lost his research project. It was time to get his life back on track.

Nandita dropped him off to his apartment.

✈

Jassi was at the gym with Nigel. Akhil had returned from Kolkata the night before and gone straight to meet Nandita. Jassi had seen Nandita drop Akhil off at their doorstep, from his room's window. They both seemed happy again.

The mission was a success. He felt happy with the turn of events. Akhil and Nandita had both been in disastrous shape, and he had felt a lump form in his throat seeing Akhil properly dressed up and clean-shaven, heading out to work in the morning.

Jassi had played his part, and done his bit for his roommate. It had taken a few days of intense research with Rashmi and Google search, for inputs.

Rashmi was very close to Nandita and someone with whom Nandita shared all details.

Rashmi and Jassi had spent a week preparing a dossier. If Akhil had to stand a chance, he needed to be well-prepared. There were the Bengali diction lessons, extracts from some of Dr Ray's famous poems, assorted trivia about Kolkata, Bengali people, and Durga Puja. Akhil would travel just in time for the festival. This had great significance. Durga Puja was when Ma Durga returned to her home for a ten-day period, finally returning to her husband with her four children at the end of the festivities. Akhil was going to get his ladylove back. He considered the timing auspicious.

If only he could memorize all the details, and not mess up the plan. Three people had not slept for a week to make it happen. The day after dropping off Akhil to the airport, Jassi had slept for a straight twenty hours, like a tired but happy parent after sending off their newly-married daughter.

Jassi felt a twang of jealousy. He was still alone. New York seeemed like a distant memory. Victoria had called him up yesterday asking if he wanted to go for a movie at the theater on campus. The movies were free for students.

He took out his mobile from his pocket and called Victoria up.

'Akhil, how can I know you will not start slacking again?'

'Professor, it was different the last time. I had some personal issues that affected my work. It's all sorted out now. If I slack for even a day, you can kick me off.'

Professor Narayanan looked at Akhil. He seemed in a much better shape than the last time they had met. He had lost that beard, was wearing clean clothes, and seemed alive. Besides, he had been a good performer before things started going south.

'Okay, Akhil. I will take you back in the research group. You've lost time, but with some extra work, you should be able to get your project back on track. I am putting my faith in you. Don't make me think later that I made a mistake.'

'I promise, sir. I will not let you down this time. I'll kill myself before...' He didn't complete the sentence, realizing the significance of his words.

Dr Narayanan glared at him. 'You dead are no use to me, Akhil. Just work hard, okay?'

'Sure sir.'

Things were getting back to normal.

✈

So what exactly happened in Kolkata?

On the second day of his stay, Nandita's dad had taken Akhil on a trip to Presidency College, where he had taught English Literature to students many years ago. The timing was perfect for Akhil. As they sat on a bench in the college canteen, Akhil had recited an entire poem out of Dr Ray's much-admired collection, *Freedom at Sunrise*.

The tear in Dr Ray's eyes by the time Akhil was done had

been proof enough. Akhil knew that moment that he was getting through the cracks in the tough exterior, and had put an arm around the old man's shoulder. Akhil had felt disgusted seeing that a scholar of such immense intellect had not been allowed to flourish because of his liberal views. Bengal had always been recognized as the land of intellectuals, but things in India had come to such a pass in modern times that you were allowed only one form of expression. The one that suited the establishment. He genuinely felt for the man.

Akhil had asked Dr Ray, 'Sir, how much time has it been since you last wrote?'

'Must be many years, Akhil. I lost all interest once these people started hounding me,' was the response.

Akhil had persisted. 'But sir, whose loss was it? Why not resume writing and be happy doing what you love the most?'

He had sighed and responded with, 'I don't know.'

Akhil had smiled at him, before 'going for the long handle', as a cricket commentator might have called the finishing touch. 'You do, sir. You know this is what you want to do. *Ami aapnar chokhey dekhte pachchi.*'

Dr Ray had seemed pleasantly surprised at the sudden appearance of Bengali. 'Akhil, you are a bag of wonders. Where did you learn Bengali?'

'Oh, it is nothing sir. I just got a little from reading some old literature, and on the Internet.'

Dr Ray's eyes had lit up. Akhil could see the idea forming. 'Okay Akhil. I'll do it,' had been the enthisiastic response.

'Now what other surprises do you have in store for me, young man?' he had asked Akhil.

Akhil had laughed and changed the topic. 'Sir, for the book

maybe you could write about the life of people outside the big cities. The struggles they go through and the reasons for which most of them migrate to the big cities. Gandhiji had said that India's heart is in its villages, but now everybody just wants to move to the cities.'

He had sounded happy with the idea. 'Brilliant idea, my boy.'

He had started pacing around anxiously, and rubbed his hands in glee. A million thoughts were forming in his head at that time. The excitement had got to him and he had sat down. 'We must start immediately. I will start writing when we get home.' Akhil had seen those eyes twinkling with excitement.

There had been a spring in Dr Ray's step as they returned home. Akhil had been barely able to keep up with the professor as they walked towards home that evening.

✈

Akhil picked up his mobile and dialled the India number. The phone rang a few times before it was answered.

'Hello?' Mrs Arora sounded feeble and tired.

'Hello ma'

'Arre, Akhil. How are you son?' The voice suddenly seemed to brighten up.

'It has been two weeks since the last time we talked. What is going on, beta? I've been dying here worried for you.' She was now sobbing.

'No ma, don't say that. Nobody is dying. I am sorry. I have been a bit lost. Sorry for behaving so idiotic.'

Mom's voice crackled over the phone line. 'Akhil, what is going on? It is a girl, isn't it? Tell me, Akhil?'

Akhil took a deep breath. 'Yes mom, it is a girl. But it is okay now.'

'What do you mean it is okay? Who is she? Is she Punjabi?'

Akhil sighed. *Not again.*

They talked for the next hour. Akhil told his mother about Nandita and their story. He did not tell her about his attempted suicide or the trip to Kolkata. He didn't have the heart to tell her. Those details were not important.

'Bengali?' She didn't seem too excited.

'Oh God, ma. Don't go there. I love her and will only marry her.'

'Okay okay, as long as you are happy, why will we object?'

'I love you ma.'

'Love you, Akhil. Take care, beta. I haven't been able to sleep well for a month now.'

'It's all good, ma. I promise.'

The tears streaming down Akhil's face had managed to move that mountain off his chest.

✈

The last day of Durga Puja had ended with the visarjan of the idol in the Hooghly River. Akhil had danced in the procession along with Dr Ray. When they got home tired, mom-in-law had served a sumptuous traditional dinner. Akhil had got up and touched the feet of the couple. They had smiled at the young boy who seemed to have become family in the last two days, and had blessed him with a long, happy life.

'Sir, I have something I want to tell you.' Akhil's legs had threatened to break into a shivering bout any second.

Dr Ray had leaned forward on the table, a curious expression in his eyes. Mrs Ray had looked on, that angelic expression on her face, the drilling machine having resumed digging through Akhil's eyes.

Akhil had barely managed to get out the words. His life hinged on the response to what he was going to say next. 'Sir, I am not really a journalist.'

Dr Ray had smiled knowingly. 'I knew there was more to you than what you told us. So what else? Who are you?'

'My name is Akhil. I am currently pursuing an MS in Computer Science. From Florida State University.'

Two pairs of eyes had suddenly narrowed. Akhil had felt them peering inside him, searching for the truth.

'I...I...I am a friend of your daughter Nandita,' he had continued.

No word from the other side of the table. The air had just turned cold.

'I love Nandita.' Akhil had felt a lump in his throat while saying the three magical words in front of his would-be parents-in-law. The torrent of pent-up emotion he had camouflaged so well had then burst the barrage and come rushing out in a stream of tears. *'Ami aapnar meye ke bhalobashi.'* He had finally confessed his love for their daughter.

He had continued, *Aapnar meye ke ami biye na korle morey jaabo*. I'll die if I don't marry your daughter.

Nandita's mom had come over and sat next to him, keeping a hand on his shoulder to comfort him.

Dr Ray had kept silent for a minute, as Akhil's eyes implored him to speak. *Say something. Shout at me. Curse me. This silence is killing me.*

He had spoken finally. 'Does she also like you?'

'Yes sir, she likes me. We want to get married to each other.'

'Do you know that she is engaged to get married?'

Akhil had bowed his head. 'Yes sir, I do. That is why I came here. I wanted you to meet me, see me for yourself before you make the decision for your daughter. I respect you and will honour your decision, but there's a good chance I won't be able to live a normal life without Nandita.'

Dr Ray had rubbed his chin. 'You kids these days are so brash. Always talking of life and death like it is a joke.'

He had then turned to his wife. 'Get me my phone.'

He had dialled the number. Akhil heard the ringing on the other end as sound leaked from the creaky mobile phone. It was Nandita.

'Baba?'

'Nandita, ki korchho ma?'

Dr Ray had then moved away into his room, and locked it from inside. Akhil's heart was beating faster than the drumbeats of the *dhaks* at the Durga Puja procession a few hours ago. Dr Ray had come out of the room half an hour later.

'How can I be sure you will take good care of my daughter?'

Akhil had taken out a crumpled paper from his pocket. 'Sir, if you'll allow me, I wrote this on the flight while coming here.'

He had then read out the poem written on that sheet of paper.

I had a lonely life
It had no meaning, no purpose
Every day it poked at my heart like a sharp knife.

Along came a whiff of fresh air
There was no negativity, no fear
Suddenly everything about life seemed square and fair.

I now have a reason to live, a hope
I love her like a man possessed
Feels like I am high, without any dope.

My eyes only seek the one I love
Who is not with me any more
I flutter my wings like a wounded dove.

For her is each of my breath
Nowhere can I find my heart or head
Without her, it's like I am living a death.

By the time he had completed reading the poem, there were three pairs of moist eyes in the room. Mrs Ray had come over to Akhil and hugged him, letting loose the pending flood of Akhil's tears.

This poem had not been a part of Jassi's file. It had come straight from Akhil's heart.

✈

'Alright, folks. We've practiced the basic box step. Now let's form pairs and get into the Waltz position.'

Victoria came to Jassi's side. He kept his right hand on her waist and they locked their left hands. The music started. Jassi had not held a woman this close before. Victoria was wearing a black dress that accentuated her slim figure. Her seductive perfume was driving Jassi crazy.

It had all been Victoria's idea. They had watched an old Woody Allen movie at the university theater last week and Victoria had mentioned the University Ballroom Dance club that had classes every Friday. 'Let's go. It will be fun.'

Jassi had agreed to come along, though he wondered how much he would enjoy ballroom dance. It used to appear quite boring in the movies he had seen. Bhangra was way cooler.

'Hey...hey...watch it mister. You're going off beat.' She brought Jassi back to the present. He had stepped on her toe.

'I am so sorry, Victoria. Got distracted.' 'By your beauty,' he added as an afterthought.

'Liar!' She slapped his shoulder playfully, flattered by the compliment.

The song changed. They were supposed to rotate partners. Jassi didn't let go of Victoria until the next one, a skinny Chinese girl, came by. Jassi and Victoria got to dance with each other just one more time all evening, but Jassi could see her giving him teasing glances throughout.

His heart fluttered. He hadn't felt this way ever before.

✈

Nandita took a bite of the paneer tikka and let out a loud whistle. People around them turned to look at table no. 15.

'Stop it Nandu. You're crazy,' said Akhil.

'Man, this is delicious. Eat yours quickly or I'll finish it all off.'

Akhil and Nandita had come to the Indian restaurant in town to celebrate Akhil's research paper being selected for a prestigious IEEE conference. Dr Narayanan had called up Akhil to congratulate him in the morning. 'This is a big, big success, Akhil. You've done a great job on the project, and I am happy to have you back in the team.' Akhil took the repeated usage of 'big' to imply that this must be a pretty major accomplishment. Nandita suggested a candle-lit dinner. They hadn't gone out in weeks, as Akhil had been busy repairing the damage of his *Devdas* phase, like Jassi described it.

The damage had been repaired well. Akhil had been doing well in his coursework, consistently getting top grades on his assignments. The poor scores of the mid terms couldn't be undone, but he had recovered through his performance on assignments. He knew that if he could keep up the momentum over the remaining month and the finals, he would be able to stay on track for his target of perfect grades.

'I have news,' he told Nandita in between mouthfuls of tandoori naan and palak paneer.

'What?'

'I am going to Seattle for an interview with Microsoft.'

There was a loud clang as Nandita fumbled and dropped her fork to the ground. She got up from her chair, came over to Akhil's side and kissed him smack on the lips.

'I am so proud of you, my Punjabi puttar. Well done.' Akhil blushed. 'People are watching, Nandita!'

She prompted him on. 'And? Are you going to keep blushing like a girl or give me more details?'

Akhil turned a deeper shade of red.

'I had sent my CV to Anil who forwarded it on to the HR department at Microsoft. They scheduled a telephonic interview earlier this week. That went well, and the next thing

I know they had booked my tickets to Seattle.'

'Wow, this is so exciting. So now you are going to be a bigshot Microsoft guy!

'Stop it, Nandita. Do you realize what this means?'

'What?'

'I graduate next semester and will be moving out of Tallahasseee. How will I survive then?'

She kept a finger on his lips. 'No. Don't say that. I'll take a transfer to the university nearest to wherever you go. Maybe I'll look at university programmes in Seattle and start applying for a transfer.'

He looked somewhat relieved. 'Maybe you should apply to universities in Seattle, New York, and California. Who knows where I will land up?'

She raised a hand to her forehead in a mock salute. 'Aye aye, sir. Will get it done.'

'Now can we finish our food? My soup has already turned cold.'

He looked on adoringly as she slurped on her soup.

VICTORIOUS

Kedar licked each finger of his hand one by one. 'Jassi, the food is awesome.'

Jassi winced at his uncouth roommate. 'Thanks Kedar. You were supposed to just taste. Don't eat everything; leave something for others also. Remember we are the hosts of this party. Now go wash those fingers. And behave yourself once my guests are here.'

Akhil threw a meaningful glance at Kedar. They knew exactly which 'guests' were being referred to.

Everybody else was already home. Venkat. Sundar. Dilpreet. Rashmi. Nandita.

The year 2005 was drawing to a close. The Fall-semester finals had just ended. Akhil had got his A grades. Jassi had also managed an average performance. Nandita's performance was back on track after the slump at the start of the semester. Jassi had proposed a party for close friends at their apartment in celebration of their results.

The bell rang and Victoria walked in. She was wearing a short pink dress that ended about, what seemed to Jassi to be, a mile above her knees. Jassi covered Kedar's eyes as he gaped at her legs. She came over to Jassi and gave him a tight hug. Venkat whistled, as Jassi blushed. He introduced everybody to Victoria.

An hour later, the group had devoured everything in sight. The rice cooker and bowls of mixed vegetables and chana masala had been wiped clean by the hungry lot.

Dilpreet was the first to burp. Everybody laughed.

Akhil handed out Hajmola tablets to the group. Victoria took one, and then made a wry face as the strong flavour of black salt and tamarind kicked in. Jassi quickly brought her some water.

It was close to midnight. Victoria got up to leave. Jassi offered to walk her to her car, parked a short distance from their apartment.

As she reached her car, Victoria hugged Jassi and whispered in her ear. 'I had a wonderful time today, Jazz. If I had any more appetite, I could eat you right now.' She gave him a light peck on his cheek and got inside the car.

Jassi was barely able to wave her goodbye. His knees suddenly felt weak.

Akhil reached the airport arrival gate and found Nandita waiting for him, looking resplendent in an uncharacteristically short dress. She ran to him and hugged him.

'How was it?'

'I think the interviews went well. They will let me know in some time. Till then, fingers crossed.'

He had returned from Seattle. He felt he had done well,

though they were to get back with their final decision.

It was the last week of December. There was a three weeks break before the spring semester began. Akhil had some more interviews lined up over the break. Luckily, his course work was over so the next semester was only going to be focussed on research work and defending his thesis.

The next interview was a week away—a telephonic round with Ebay, the world's largest online-auction portal with its headquarters in California. There were some others lined up as well, though Akhil was most anxious to hear back from his number one choice—Google.

For now, he was going to take the next few days off before returning to his interview preparation. He had burnt enough midnight oil and drank enough coffee in the last two months to deserve a break.

It was a Friday. The next day Nandita and he were going to drive down to Miami for a relaxed weekend. He could do with some pleasant weather. Tallahasseee was close to freezing.

✈

Jassi was excited for the night's date. It had been a week since Victoria had come over for dinner at their apartment. She had called up in the morning asking if he was doing anything that night. He wasn't, and even if he had, he could drop everything else for time spent with her.

They were going to a diner that served traditional American cuisine. From there, they planned to go club hopping. Jassi put on his favourite blue turtleneck sweater and a pair of Levi's jeans.

At 7 pm, his mobile rang. It was Victoria. He had asked her to give him a missed call when she came to pick him up, but she didn't quite get what he meant.

'Missed call? What is that?'

'Well, never mind. Just give me a call and I'll come down.'

Jassi went downstairs and got in her car. She greeted him with a kiss on the cheek. She was looking radiant, wearing a skirt with a slit long enough to give Jassi a peek at those glorious legs. She was wearing the same perfume she wore at their first ballroom dance class. Jassi muttered a prayer to the Gods and they were off.

At the diner, they took seats at a cozy table by the window. Jassi thought he noticed a strange look from the waiter as he seated them, and wondered if he was surprised to see an Indian chap with a pretty lady like Victoria who was way out of his league.

No, he reassured himself. *That can't be. This is America—the land of justice and equality.*

Victoria urged Jassi to try the steaks. He pondered the suggestion. *I will probably get thrown out of my religion if anyone found out, but what the hell.*

'Sure, I'll have the steak then. Whatever the pretty lady recommends.'

'That's my boy.' She grinned at him. Jassi looked at the shiny red lipstick she was wearing, and wondered what it would be like to kiss those luscious lips. He suddenly remembered his first date with her, and promptly looked away. He didn't want to do anything stupid now.

A minute later, Victoria got up from her seat and came to sit on Jassi's side of the table. Jassi's heart did a pole-vault worthy of a gold medal at the Olympics.

She was sitting right next to him. He could feel the warmth of her body. His heart was beating like an out-of-control drummer at a rock concert.

Their food arrived. Jassi heaved a sigh of relief. The distraction gave him time to breathe.

'Something wrong, Mr Jazzminator? Should I move back to my side of the table?'

'Oh no, not at all.' He held her hand. The drums started banging away again. 'I am just not used to having such pretty ladies sit next to me at dinner.'

She laughed.

The evening was magical. Jassi and Victoria talked until almost midnight, which was when the diner staff started giving them hints to leave. They knew it was time to go when they turned off the lights near their table.

The two headed out of the diner. They were both tipsy, thanks to the two bottles of wines that they had consumed over the last few hours.

Jassi took the passenger side and sat on the seat. Victoria came by his window and knocked, beckoning him to come out. Jassi got out of the car. She was standing facing him, his back to the car.

Victoria took his hand in hers and rested her arms around his neck. She looked into Jassi's eyes and came closer.

'So?' she said, still gazing into Jassi's eyes.

'What so?' Jassi raised his eyebrows in question.

'Are you just going to keep staring? What does a woman need to do to get a kiss around here?'

Jassi's heart was doing cartwheels of happiness. He brought

his lips closer to hers. And then it happened. The first kiss was magical. Jassi felt transported to a wondrous land where there were pretty flowers blooming all over, and people happily doing the waltz in the background.

Jassi was in love. This time for real.

Akhil checked into his hotel. The clock displayed 4 pm, February 20, 2006. He entered his room and saw a bag on the study table. It was in the standard blue colour of Google, and had the logo emblazoned across it. He dumped the contents of the bag on the bed. There was a pair of table-tennis racquets, a couple of wafer packets, energy bars, a Frisbee, and a small envelope.

He opened the envelope to find four fifty dollar bills and a letter that said *Welcome to Google. Here's a small token of appreciation for taking the time out to interview with us.*

Akhil was impressed. These people sure knew how to take care of employees—current and prospective. The company had flown him all the way from Tallahasseee to San Fransisco, put him up at a nice hotel for two days, and now this.

He realized this could just be the culmination of his dream. A job offer from Google would be the icing on the cake. The completion of this glorious first chapter of his American dream. He had his straight A grades and a perfect 4.0 GPA, he had a paper published in one of the top journals in the world, his thesis defense was lined up for next week and, most importantly, he had Nandita. A job with the world's best software company would complete the picture.

It had not been easy. He had been through two gruelling telephonic interviews that had tested his intelligence and knowledge thoroughly. That had been just enough to determine that he was good enough for a proper face-to-face interview. He had the day to rest. The interviews were scheduled for the next day.

Akhil hoped he would get through. He had more interviews lined up with some of the other reputed companies though. The next week was a full house on the calendar, with multiple telephonic interviews scheduled already, besides a trip to New York for a face-to-face interview with a financial company.

Microsoft had not worked out just when he had thought it was almost in the bag. They had called him up two weeks after the interview. 'We are sorry but we will not be able to offer you a position, as our requirements don't match your skills.' Akhil was amazed at the phrasing. They wouldn't even say that you are not good enough for us, though he wondered why it didn't work out.

For the rest of the day, Akhil did some last minute preparation, practiced some coding problems, and prayed to the Gods for success. He slept early, as advised by numerous Internet articles on interview preparation.

The sun dawned on San Jose and Akhil was up, ready to head out for the gruelling test in store.

He returned to his room eight hours later, exhausted. He had done well, but not great. Three interviewers—two Chinese and one Indian—had made him solve some complex coding problems, each taking up an hour. In between, he had been taken on a tour of the famous 'Googleplex' as the office was known, had enjoyed the wonderful food at the Google cafetaria and marvelled at some of the other amenities in the office complex. *No wonder people drool at the opportunity to work here,* he thought.

Masters of America

There was polite applause in the sparsely populated room as Akhil wrapped up his presentation. Somebody hooted. He knew it was Nandita.

Dr Narayanan and Dr Yu came over to Akhil and patted his back.

'Great presentation, Akhil,' said Dr Yu. He was the one who had asked the most questions.

'Thanks professor.' Akhil heaved a sigh of relief. He had completed the final MS requirement of the thesis defense.

Nandita and Jassi came over and congratulated him. 'This calls for a big party, dude.' Jassi gave Akhil a high-five. Akhil was done with his requirements for the Masters of Science degree. The only thing left to do was attend the convocation ceremony in early May, still three weeks away.

'Thanks man. When do we see your defense?'

'I've got some work done already with Dr Singh. I should be able to graduate in the Fall.' Jassi had recovered his grades over the last two semesters, and was expecting to complete his graduation requirements next semester, which was also when

Victoria was graduating. The two were officially a couple now. Akhil had never seen Jassi so content with his life before.

The last member of the thesis committee, Professor Apostolov, came by and shook Akhil's hands. 'Well done, Akhil. "Your people" must be so happy.' Akhil smiled at him thinking the professor was referring to his parents, when he continued. 'Do you guys have some kind of celebration in your kingdom when the prince completes a degree?'

Akhil nearly choked on hearing the words. As the other professors looked in their direction, Akhil noticed the colour of Apostolov's eyes. Green. His head was shiny like a mirror. He suddenly remembered dad's description of a 'tall, very strongly built man with a bald head and green eyes'.

It hit him like a hurricane. David Apostolov was the person dad had befriended last year. The colour faded from Akhil's face and his head began to spin. Apostolov patted him on the shoulder before heading out. 'Say hi to your dad for me, will you?'

Nandita saw the worried lines on Akhil's face and came over. As Akhil started talking about what had just happened, his phone buzzed. He left the room to talk, gesturing to Nandita and Jassi to wait for him.

Five minutes later, he was back, grinning from ear to ear. Google had just made him a job offer.

✈

'So Akhil, can you tell me what a hedge fund is?'

Akhil tried to recall the definition he had seen from his quick search on the Internet. 'Umm... hedge funds are financial firms that invest money using hedging strategies that make them less prone to risk.'

The bald Indian man on the other end of the table laughed loudly. His head was a perfect oval, making him look like a character out of a comic book.

'Actually, that's not quite accurate. It's almost the opposite.'

Akhil looked on nervously. Till twenty-four hours ago, he hadn't ever heard of the term.

The people from GoldRock had made him work on a rushed project with two days' lead-time, flown him to New York in business-class on a one-day notice, and put him up in a five-star hotel. He had already been through four technically challenging interviews. This was the last hurdle. The manager of the group he was going to work with was the last interviewer.

The next question brought him back to the room.

'So what do you want to do in life, Akhil?' he added for good measure. 'Forget all the tips you might have read on the Internet. I need an earnest answer.'

Akhil smiled. The conversation so far had been stimulating. He was already looking forward to working with this incredibly direct man. He sounded like a man from whom Akhil could learn a lot.

'Sir, I am just starting out my career. At this stage, all I want is to learn. I feel the early years are when I have the energy and the willingness to learn more and become very strong technically. I think for the next five to six years I would want to build up my technical capabilities and then possibly move into a bigger role.'

'Excellent. I like that.'

His BlackBerry beeped. 'Oh, didn't realize we've taken over forty-five minutes already.'

'Akhil, I think you have the potential to do well in the team. You have the right skills and aptitude for the job.'

Akhil beamed. This was good.

'Any question you want to ask me?'

'Sir, I have one question if you don't mind my asking.'

'Sure, go for it.'

'If you were me and had an offer from this firm and Google, which would you join?'

For a second, the interviewer looked stumped. Akhil wondered if he had just hit himself in the foot with a giant axe.

He laughed loudly. 'Well, my boy. I admire your courage. Not many people would be able to ask that question. It is a fair question, and I can understand where this is coming from. While I won't comment on other companies, let me tell you something more about our firm, and the financial domain.'

'The financial world employs the best technologies that are out there. To mint money. Quite literally. Technology companies could never pay you as much as you can get in this world. In a way, finance companies are the best, most efficient users of technology out there. Take our company for example. Twenty billion dollars of investment managed by a company of 300 people. If we make a profit of even 5 percent on that amount, can you imagine what it means for employees? No Google or Microsoft can ever match that. And if you think Google is hard to get in, let me tell you we have a much lower selection ratio.'

Akhil smiled. Fate was pushing him in a different direction from the one he had in mind. It was definitely fate that had brought him here. One of his friends in Delhi had mentioned a friend who worked in a finance company in New York, and forwarded Akhil's CV. Akhil had no idea who they were, and took a minute to register the company's name when the recruiter called him up to check his availability for an interview. This happened after he had already got the Google offer and Akhil had half a mind to say no to GoldRock. He was glad he had better sense.

Akhil was to return to Tallahassee the same night. They would get back to him in a few days' time. It was Wednesday. The graduation was on Saturday, three days away. Mom, dad, and Aarti were flying in from India the next day for a two-week trip.

Things had got a bit tight for Akhil with the GoldRock interview being scheduled at the last minute. He had to make sure that his family had a good stay in the US, and all preparations were complete. He had already made reservations for a rental car that they would use to get around.

Akhil would reach home late that night. The next day he would take a cab to go to the rental agency where he and Nandita would pick up the car and go to the airport to pick up his family members. Akhil was nervous about driving though. He had barely got his driving license, but never independantly undertaken a long drive. It was going to be baptism by fire for him.

✈

Victoria pulled the car into the parking at St Augustine's beach after a two-hour drive from Tallahasseee. It was the perfect beach weather. The sun was beating down in full glory. She had packed a picnic lunch of sandwiches and fruit. Jassi had done his part, getting a 6-pack of beer.

Before getting out of the car, Jassi leaned over and gave her a peck on the cheek. The two had been going together for a little over a month, and Jassi had never been happier with his life.

Victoria took off her top and jeans. She was already wearing her swimsuit underneath. Jassi pulled off his shirt, and the two were ready to go. Victoria picked up the food and beer. Jassi grabbed the beach towels and a bottle of suntan lotion.

The beach was gorgeous, and not too crowded. Victoria picked a convenient spot in a corner of the beach and laid out the beach towels.

She handed Jassi the suntan lotion. 'Mr Jazzminator, can you please help?'

Jassi grinned like a silly teenager. He had dreamed of this day numerous times—in classes, in the library, even during final exams. He opened the bottle and started spreading the lotion on Victoria's back. He took his time, generously rubbing Victoria's soft back with the lotion.

'I am done, Vicky,' he announced half an hour later.

'No you are not, sweetheart. You surely don't want ugly tan-lines running across my back, do you?' Victoria replied, and proceeded to untie the back of her bikini top.

Jassi gaped at the sight in front of his eyes. It was happening.

'Come on, tiger, we don't have all day,' came Victoria's voice.

Jassi noticed a group of Indian students standing about a 100-feet away, looking at them. One of them took out a camera. Jassi shouted at them to run away, and they disappeared. Jassi smiled, recalling his early days.

Victoria's back done, it was her turn. She asked Jassi to lie on his back, and gave him a suntan lotion massage.

When she asked him to roll over so she could cover his chest as well, Jassi finally lost all control. He pulled Victoria to him, and they kissed passionately. Victoria spotted a deserted rocky spot in the distance, and asked Jassi to get up.

Half an hour later, Jassi became a man. His American dream had come true, with the unending ocean bearing testimony to his achievement.

✈

Akhil made his way to the graduation ceremony hall at the Tallahasseee, amidst a sea of black gowns and caps. He knew his parents, sister, Nandita, Jassi, and Victoria were watching from the audience galleries above.

This was the culmination of his FSU experience. It was the Spring 2006 convocation ceremony, where he would be awarded his Masters degree. Akhil was graduating with a perfect GPA, and as a member of several honour societies by virtue of his excellent academic performance.

Soon he would move to New York, to join GoldRock LLC, the prestigious multi-strategy hedge fund based in Greenwich, Connecticut. The decision to say no to Google had been a tough one, though the extra 30,000 dollars offered by GoldRock had helped swing the balance in their favour. Besides, of course, there was the advice offered by Sriram, the wise bald man who was to be his manager.

He had also spoken to Anil, who had supported the decision. 'Dude, finance is the way to go. These guys are so elusive that they won't even look at most people, let alone hiring them. Forget Google, this is a much better opportunity.'

The ceremony started. There were a couple of speeches from the University president and the commencement speaker, but Akhil didn't hear any of it. He was lost in his thoughts. There was so much to do. They would leave for Orlando the next morning for their Florida road trip. Akhil had done a lot of research to find the right hotels, and hoped they would live up to their reviews. Luckily the first two days of driving the Towncar the rental company had given him had been uneventful. Akhil had not had any mishaps yet, and was now feeling confident of taking it out for the first real test—the 5-hour drive to Orlando.

After the two-week vacation, he was going to fly out to New York. He had to find accommodation, get a car rental, buy his tickets, pack up his stuff from the apartment, settle his lease with Kedar and Jassi, and say goodbyes to all of the dear friends he was leaving behind, especially the one dearest to him.

Sundar and Venkat were going to be around at FSU for another few years working on their PhDs. Jassi and Priya were close to wrapping up their degrees and expected to graduate in the fall. Kedar had opted out of completing his PhD and planned to graduate with an MS in the next semester. After trying her luck with several men, Pooja was now in a relationship with an Indian Physics PhD candidate who had the highest GPA in his batch and was close to bagging an Assistant Professor position at a prominent university. Dr Narayanan's research group was growing stronger, and he had offered Akhil a fast track PhD if he ever felt like coming back. Brad had been replaced by another student after he was caught having sex in the lab one afternoon. Akhil hadn't met Aparna after that day, but he got a call from Devika who was delighted. Her parents had finally stopped the continuous comparison with her.

Nandita had sent in applications for a transfer to a different university. The results hadn't started coming in, but Akhil prayed to God that she would get through to NYU or Columbia, both based in New York City. He didn't want to live away from her for a day if he could help it. This was the last missing piece in the jigsaw. Everything else was nicely lined up. Akhil had achieved all that he wanted.

He noticed the people in his row start moving towards the stage as their names were called out, and got ready for his turn.

'Akhil Arora,' the announcer called out.

Akhil made his way to the stage. He smiled at the University president as he handed him the degree. Above the din of the hall, Akhil heard three people shout out his name. His dad, Jassi, and Nandita.

The neatly rolled up scroll proclaimed *Masters of Science*. In his heart, Akhil felt like he had completed a *Masters of America*.

Epilogue

'Dr Ray, one smile please, sir?' The photographer shouted to the reclusive author of the groundbreaking book being released. *Sons of the Soil* had been among the most anticipated books of the year in Kolkata, and was nearly sold out just in pre-orders.

Last week Dr Amitav Ray had received an invitation to the Chief Minister's residence to discuss some of his observations around the ever-increasing migration of people to big cities, which he had politely declined, saying *'The government still needs to do a lot of work to prove they are serious about this.'*

A day after his 26th birthday, Priyank got fired from his job for browsing porn sites while at work. Two months later, he is still looking for a job. Goyal uncle and aunty have a shortlist of 30 girls ready for him, whenever he visits India next. They don't know their son doesn't have a job anymore.

All of Akhil's college friends who went to the big universities managed to land jobs in one of the prominent technology companies. They ridiculed Akhil for joining a company whose name no one among them had ever heard of. But then, they agreed unanimously that such a failure was expected from someone who went to a university ranked below 100, and wished him luck.

None of them had an idea of the 20 billion dollars of funds managed by GoldRock LLC, or of Akhil's salary being higher than any of them.

Acknowledgements

My heartfelt thanks to the most important thing that helped bring this book to life—coffee. I couldn't have completed it without my nightly dose of three spoonfuls of it in a glass of milk. Bitter would be a gross understatement. Third-degree torture was more like it.

Thanks mom and dad, for giving birth to this genius, and teaching me all those cool values. Also for reading everything I write and calling it awesome, even when it sucks.

Thanks to Kiran, the missus, for never giving up on me, despite my spending more time with the laptop than her. But then, being the wife of a famous (and deluded) man was never going to be a bed of roses.

Thanks to my crack team of reviewers. Nima, for that first brutal review. Devasmita, for her invaluable inputs (Bengali people, she's the one responsible for the Bangla inputs). My big sister Divya, who eventually gave up after reviewing three versions of the manuscript. Dr B Ramana, for ripping me apart to the point of driving me suicidal. Seema, Sandeep, Amit, Chetna, and Smriti, for basically saying that this is the most

Acknowledgements

wonderful book you've ever read (loosely speaking).

Thanks to fellow writers Sidin and Arnab for their help with the publishing process. Like they say, writing a book is the easy part. Finding a publisher is harder than Titanium.

Thanks to all of my readers, fans, and stalkers. Your support over the years has kept me going, and made me a better writer. You guys are the best.

Thanks to the lovely ladies at Random House India. Milee, for agreeing to publish the book. Rukun, for being the knight-in-shining-armour when I was busy ranting about publishers on Twitter. Gurveen, for giving this book the final, polished state. (More power to my narratttorrr, Gurveen. Please!) Caroline, who is going to ensure that I make my millions in royalty and can retire to Florida (or at least Greater Noida).

Thanks to Florida State University, where I spent a fantastic couple of years during my Masters. This book is set against some real locations on campus, and parts of the story derive from my personal experiences. I made some great friends at FSU, and I will forever stay indebted to them for their love and support. The characters in the book are all fictional though, and are not at all based on anyone I might have met or known. Any resemblances would be a mere coincidence.

Thanks also to America, for being such an awesome, inclusive country. You never made me feel unwanted. Any racist references in the book are merely meant to display the biases people have in their heads.

A big hug for my first born, Adi (this book being the second baby), who is my little bundle of joy. Hopefully my being a published author will help him get through nursery admissions.

A Note on the Author

Atulya Mahajan is the author of amreekandesi.com, a popular Indian satire blog. Born and raised in Delhi, he moved to the US in 2004 for his Masters and stayed on for five years before returning to India, in a *Swades*-inspired moment. During his time in the US, he started his blog to chronicle the lives of Indians living abroad, and this book is the culmination of that vision. He also writes occasional humour columns for the *Times of India*, Crest Edition.

Ever since he returned to India, Atulya has spent thousands of hours shouting at random taxi drivers and motorcyclists who overtake him from the wrong side. If you want to see him convert into the Hulk, just honk at him at a red light.

When not busy writing hilarious pieces, Atulya works at an investment bank as a technologist. He claims to be the first man ever to have 24-pack abs, and has reportedly tried about 485 remedies to stop hairfall, though none of them seem to have worked.

A Note on the Author

Blog: amreekandesi.com
Twitter: twitter.com/amreekandesi
Facebook: www.facebook.com/amreekandesi
Email: contact@amreekandesi.com